U0920123

孙大雨译文集

V

上海译文出版社

英诗选译

致西麗霞

英國 班·絳蓀作

孫大雨譯

將你的明眸代祝酒來眷顧，
　　我自會向你報青恩；
你或在杯中只留下點吻香，
　　我便不想把酒去斟。
從靈魂深處飛昇起的渴慕，
　　要求有神仙底芝飲；
但即令我能飫天帝底瓊漿，
　　也不願換你的明樽。

我新近送你串玫瑰底花環，
　　說不上能給你光彩，
而只會使得它存一个希望，
　　在那裡它不會萎敗；
你若在花上將馨息去噓轉，
　　隨後且將它送回來，
我深信它自會生長、吐芬芳，
　　不為它自己，為你開。

1983,12,20

這首英國十六、七世紀名詩人班·絳蓀底極著名、譜曲而歌唱了約有三百八十年之久的短歌，吟咏的是一見鍾情之戀。原詩兩節，每節八行，單行每行四音步，雙行每行三音步；譯詩以我在本世紀二十年代中期創制的音組來仿彿原來的音步。原詩每節第一、第五行押韻，第二、四、六、八行押韻，第三、七行押韻。譯詩亦率照原詩韻法。

We'll go no more a-roving
by George Gordon Byron

我们将不再去漫游

所以，我们将不再去漫游，
这么晚直到夜未央，
虽然两心还如此地绸缪，
月色还总是这样亮。

因为剑刃比剑鞘要耐久，
灵魂比胸膛要坚实，
心儿得歇下来呼息夷犹，
爱情本身要栖迟。

虽然这夜晚正宜于钟情，
白昼回来得太匆匆，
于是我们将不再去宵行，
在这良夜底月明中。

1980，5，20

夜未央：夜已深而还没有到天明；夜半。
绸缪：即缠绵，情意深厚。
夷犹：即夷由，從容貌。
栖迟：游息。 宵行：夜行。

目录

The Contents

前 言

父亲走完了92年的漫长生活历程，于1997年1月5日永远离开了我们。

进入90年代以后，他的健康每况愈下，已基本上停止了长达70多年的写作生涯。所以，现在呈献于读者面前的他的所有著译都是在此以前完成的作品。

1976年粉碎“四人帮”后，他的作品才有了出版的可能。自80年代起，我们即着手为他的手稿进行整理、誊录、辑编等工作。

1996年1月由上海外语教育出版社出版的《屈原诗选英译》一书的《前言》中，我们曾写道：“他一生中共有11部著译，除8部莎译外，尚有3部著译即《屈原诗选英译》、《古诗文英译集》和《孙大雨诗文集》有待出版。”这篇《前言》写于1994年6月26日，当时我们认为他的全部书稿业已整理完毕，怀着宽慰的心情期待着一部部书稿陆续付梓问世。然而在父亲生命最后一年多的住院治疗期间，我们又发现他还译有英诗名家的诗作百余首，这使我们回忆起多年前他曾说过，他计划在有生之年译英诗366首然后结集成册，他的意思是读者如有兴趣，在闰年可以每天欣赏一首诗。本集的百余首译诗，是该未竟工程中的部分作品，现在我们将其整理出来，献给广大读者。它是父亲一生中第12部作品。

父亲曾说过：“文学作品，特别是诗歌的翻译，要求移植者对于原文和所译文字的造诣都异常高，要能深入理解和摄取原作的形相到奥蕴，又善于挥洒自如地表达出来，导旨而传神，务使他能在他那按着原作的再一次创作的成果里充分体现原作的精神和风貌。”

本诗译作是父亲运用他所创建的新诗格律结构——音组格式移译

的。所谓音组，简要地说来，那是以 2 或 3 个汉字为常态而有相应变化的结构来体现的。试以英国近代诗歌之父赿飏的《康透裒垒故事诗集·序诗》的开首几行为例：

当阳春	四月天	将它的	甘霖	浸淫
三月	干旱里	的花木	根株，	渗沁
万树	千花	每一丝	脉络于	潮润中，
触发了	生机，	使枝头	叶碧	而花红；

这里每行都是 5 个音组。音组理论是在 1925 年夏，他在清华毕业后，赴美留学前，于国内游历期间，盘桓在浙江海上普陀山佛寺圆通庵客舍时，潜心创建的。此后他即运用于新诗创作和译诗的实践中，数十年来他用音组结构创作和翻译了 3 万多行格律诗。

本书得以顺利出版，有赖于上海外语教育出版社的大力支持；父亲的高足吴起仞先生则一如既往尽心尽力给予帮助，在此一并致以谢忱！

孙近仁　孙佳始

1998.10

FOREWORD

On 5 January 1997, Father left us, never to return, having traveled to the end of his 92-year long journey of life.

He had basically stopped his career as a writer and translator that lasted for as long as 70 years, owing to his deteriorating health condition at the turn of the '90s. All the writings and translations now presented to the readers had been done before the last decade of this century.

It was after the smashing of the "Gang of Four" in 1976 that the attempt to publish his writings and translations had become possible. At the beginning of the '80s, we started sorting out, copying (by handwriting) and editing his manuscripts.

In the *Foreword* to *Selected Poems of Chü Yuan* published by Shanghai Foreign Language Education Press in January 1996, we wrote: "In case the publication of Father's life-work could go on without a hitch, altogether eleven books would be introduced to the reading public. Among them, eight are translations of Shakespeare's dramas ... Aside from the above, there are three other books to be published, viz., the English version of *Selected Poems of Chü Yuan, the English version of An Anthology of Ancient Chinese Poetry and Prose* and *Sun Da Yu's Book of Poems and Other Writings*". In fact, the Foreword to *Selected Poems of Chü Yuan* was written in 1994; at that time, we did feel sure that we had made all the manuscripts ready, and, with a sense of relief, were waiting for their publication one after another. During the last year or so of his hospitalization, however, we happened to have found nearly 100 Chinese versions of poems written by well-known English poets; this reminded us of what he had said many years ago of his plan of rendering 366 English poems into Chinese. His intentions had been to let the readers enjoy, in their receptive state of mind, one poem a day in a leap year. So, the approximately 100 poems collected in this book are expected to be part of his unfinished work. This is Father's 12th book.

Once he said: "Literary works, especially versions of poetry, require their translalors to be highly faithful to the original, capable of understanding and reflecting the complexion and hidden sense of the original, so as to fully express the spirit and manner of the original."

The translation in this book was done, using the special rhythmic system, the word-sound group he had created for modern Chinese poetry in his early days. In short, the so-called word-sound group basically consists of 2 or 3 Chinese characters to form a standard unit, and makes its presence in the lines of a poem with certain variations. Take the initial 4 lines of "*The General Prologue of The Canterbury Tales*" by Geoffrey Chaucer, father of the modern English Poetry:

Whan that April with his showers soote
The droughte of March hath perced to the roote,
And bathed every veine in swich licour,
Of which vertu engendred is the flowr;

The Chinese version of which reads:

| 当阳春 | 四月天 | 将它的 | 甘霖 | 浸淫 |
| 三月 | 干旱里 | 的花木 | 根株，| 渗沁 |

|万树|千花|每一丝|脉络于|潮润中，|

|触发了|生机，|使枝头|叶碧|而花红；|

In each line, we have 5 sound groups. The word-sound group theory was created by Father with devoted effort in summer, 1925, upon his graduation at Qing Hua, and during his stay at "Yuan Tong Buddhist Convent" (圆通庵) of the Putuo Mountain in Zhejiang Province that borders the sea. Practising this theory in writing and translating poetry, he had, over the decades, created and translated for more than thirty thousand rhythmical lines.

We are indebted to Shanghai Foreign Language Education Press for their support in the publication of this book, to Mr. Wu Qiren, Father's student, for his persistent and whole-hearted assistance!

Sun Jinren Sun Jiashi

(English Version by Wu Qiren)

Oct. 1998

• 乔弗雷·乔叟 •

Geoffrey Chaucer

(1340?—1400)

康透裒垒[1]故事诗集·序诗

乔弗雷·趏飕[2]（Geoffrey Chaucer，1343?—1400）是英国近代英文诗歌之父。他的父亲约翰·趏飕（John Chaucer，1366 年卒）是当时伦敦城一位酒商。诗人的诞生年大概是 1340 年，17 岁时他是英王蔼特华三世（Edward Ⅲ）第三个公子克拉仑斯（Clarence）公爵赖杭纳尔（Lionel）夫人伊莉莎白·特剖（Elizabeth de Burgh）的侍僮。1359 年英国出师伐法兰西时，他随军前去，在勃列坦尼（Brittany）被俘，次年由英王蔼特华三世赎回。1369 至 1370 年他负英王之命到法国去，1372—1373 年又负命去意大利的杰诺瓦（Genoa）与弗洛伦斯（Florence），遇见知名文士及诗人薄卡邱（Givanni Boccaccio，1313?—1375）与沛屈拉格（Francesco Petrarca，1304—1374）。1388 年 4 月趏飕到康透裒垒朝圣，随后即作此长篇但未完工的叙事诗章，约 1.7 万行。这里所译序诗共 858 行，与原诗行数相等。蓝本为：Walter W. Skeat: *The Complete Works of Geoffrey Chaucer* (Clarendon Press，1931)。1964 年 7 月 24 日开译，同年 9 月 21 日凌晨译毕，9 月 27 日抄录一遍，并稍作修改。

---

① 本书译文中的一些人名、地名和书名非今日之约定俗成译法，如 Edward 今译爱德华；Canterbury 今译坎特伯雷；莎氏的 *Much Ado About Nothing* 今译《无事生非》。编者均不作从今译的改动，为的是为译坛记录一点历史，同时也不失大雨先生的译笔原貌。——编者

② 据译者家人回忆 Geoffrey Chaucer 译为乔弗雷·趏飕大雨先生还有一席趣谈：他认为 Geoffrey Chaucer 年少成名，晚年写就此首堪称英国长篇诗歌之绝唱，“趏”字正可以表示作者轻捷升高的创作历史；而“飕”则可避免“叟”字含义之误解。——编者

The General Prologue

〔1〕 Whan that April with his showres soote
The droughte of March hath perced to the roote,
And bathed every veine in swich licour,
Of which vertu engendred is the flowr;
Whan Zephyrus eek with his sweete breeth
Inspired hath in every holt and heeth
The tendre croppes, and the yonge sonne
Hath in the Ram his halve cours yronne,
And smale fowles maken melodye
That sleepen al the night with open yë —
So priketh hem Nature in hir corages —
Thanne longen folk to goon on pilgrimages,
And palmeres for to seeken straunge strondes
To ferne halwes, couthe in sondry londes;
And specially from every shires ende
Of Engelond to Canterbury they wende,
The holy blisful martyr for to seeke
That hem hath holpen whan that they were seke.
〔2〕 Bifel that in that seson on a day,
In Southwerk at the Tabard as I lay,

康透亰垒故事诗集·序诗

〔1〕 当阳春四月天将它的甘霖浸淫
三月干旱里的花木根株，渗沁
万树千花每一丝脉络于潮润中，
触发了生机，使枝头叶碧而花红；
当熏风也将它那阵甜蜜的嘘息
已经拂过了每一处林丘和原野，
催醒枝丫上纤纤的柔条和嫩叶，
新兴的丽日刚驰过白羊宫半座
宫阙，小鸟们白天里呖呖啭清歌，
夜间在睡梦中通宵睁开了眼睛，
(造化便这般撩拨着它们的心旌)：
这时节人们渴望到远方去朝圣——
行脚游僧们向往赴他邦作远征——
向各地知名的圣迹去晋谒参礼，
尤其在英格兰，从诸州各郡，车骑
一簇簇向康透亰垒去，从容不迫，
去献祭神圣的汤玛斯·亥·白盖德，
那升登极乐九天的殉道的圣徒，
他们在病痛中曾蒙他消灾救苦。
〔2〕 在那季节里有一天，正当我宿夜
进伦敦南市塞寿克的泰巴旅舍，

Redy to wenden on my pilgrimage
To Canterbury with ful devout corage,
At night was come into that hostelrye
Wel nine and twenty in a compaignye
Of sondry folk, by aventure yfalle
In felaweshipe, and pilgrimes were they alle
That toward Canterbury wolden ride.
The chambres and the stables weren wide,
And wel we weren esed at the beste.
And shortly, whan the sonne was to reste,
So hadde I spoken with hem everichoon
That I was of hir felaweshipe anoon,
And made forward erly for to rise,
To take oure way ther as I you devise.

〔3〕 But nathelees, whil I have time and space,
Er that I ferther in this tale pace,
Me thinketh it accordant to resoun
To telle you al the condicioun
Of eech of hem, so as it seemed me,
And whiche they were, and of what degree,
And eek in what array that they were inne：
And at a knight thanne wol I first biginne.

〔4〕 A Knight ther was, and that a worthy man,
That fro the time that he first bigan
To riden out, he loved chivalrye,
Trouthe and honour, freedom and curteisye.

肃志且虔诚，正准备往康透裒垒
去朝圣，却说那晚上来到那旅邸
有足足廿九名诸般各式的行人，
偶然会合在一起，都要去朝觐，
骑着马向康透裒垒趱行；当时
宾馆里卧房舒畅，马厩也宽适，
我们给安排宿歇得都很妥帖，
简单地说来，待红日沉西天光夕，
我已跟他们每个人谈过一阵话，
很快同他们打成了一伙，相约下
天明一清早就起身，互结为伴侣，
赶路前往我适才说过的那里去。

〔3〕　　可是，在我开始讲我的故事前，
还有时间富余和闲白的空篇，
我想和列位谈谈我见到他们
每个人各别的情形，是怎样的人，
属于甚品级，怎么样衣装打扮。
如今且先从一位骑士来开谈：

〔4〕　　有一位骑士，那是个高贵的人物，
自从一开始跨登了鞍马上得路，
他便宝爱那骑士精神：尚忠义，
修令名，豁达恢宏，又彬彬有礼。

Ful worthy was he in his lordes werre,
And therto hadde he riden, no man ferre,
As wel in Cristendom as hethenesse,
And evere honoured for his worthinesse.
〔5〕 At Alisandre he was whan it was wonne;
Ful ofte time he hadde the boord bigonne
Aboven alle nacions in Pruce;
In Lettou had he reised, and in Ruce,
No Cristen man so ofte of his degree;
In Gernade at the sege eek hadde he be
Of Algezir, and riden in Belmarye;
At Lyeis was he, and at Satalye,
Whan they were wonne; and in the Grete See
At many a noble arivee hadde he be.
〔6〕 At mortal batailes hadde he been fifteene,
And foughten for oure faith at Tramissene
In listes thries, and ay slain his fo.
〔7〕 This ilke worthy Knight hadde been also
Somtime with the lord of Palatye
Again another hethen in Turkye;
And everemore he hadde a soverein pris.
And though that he were worthy, he was wis,
And of his port as meeke as is a maide.
He nevere yit no vilainye ne saide
In al his lif unto no manere wight:
He was a verray, parfit, gentil knight.

为爵主服兵役，他作战英勇非凡，
所有基督教世界和异教诸蛮，
他出生入死，都曾去征讨砍斫，
没人赛过他，因军功而威名灼烁。

〔5〕　攻下亚历桑特时，就有他在场；
几次在普鲁士，居别国武士之上，
他位尊首席。前往立陶宛、俄罗斯，
他都曾率领了军兵远征出过师，
和他同等级的教徒再没第二个
转战沙场的次数有他这么多。
攻打阿尔杰齐尔的围城战役里，
他在求那特，他又曾在白尔玛利。
攻克荔晏施、萨塔里埃时，都有他
在场，地中海好多遭登陆的兵马，
其中全有他。

〔6〕　浴血的大战他一生
参加过十五次，三回在屈拉密升
为我们的圣教挥戈，都致果杀敌。

〔7〕　这卓越的骑士，为郡主巴剌底翼，
还在许久前，曾对另一支异教军
在土耳其作战：他誉干青云。
他虽然英武俊杰，却也很智虑
谦和，风采倒像个温柔的处女。
他生平从未对任何人逞威使势，
真是位完美又温文尔雅的骑士。

But for to tellen you of his array,
His hors were goode, but he was nat gay.
Of fustian he wered a gipoun
Al bismotered with his haubergeoun,
For he was late come from his viage,
And wente for to doon his pilgrimage.

〔8〕 With him ther was his sone, a yong Squier,
A lovere and a lusty bacheler,
With lokkes crulle as they were laid in presse.
Of twenty yeer of age he was, I gesse.
Of his stature he was of evene lengthe,
And wonderly delivere, and of greet strengthe.
And he hadde been som time in chivachye
In Flandres, in Artois, and Picardye,
And born him wel as of so litel space,
In hope to stonden in his lady grace.

〔9〕 Embrouded was he as it were a mede,
Al ful of fresshe flowres, white and rede;
Singing he was, or floiting, al the day:
He was as fressh as is the month of May.
Short was his gowne, with sleeves longe and wide.
Wel coude he sitte on hors, and faire ride;
He coude songes make, and wel endite,
Juste and eek daunce, and wel portraye and write.
So hote he loved that by nightertale
He slepte namore than dooth a nightingale.

说到装备和衣衫，他那匹坐骑
是良驹，但他的衣着却并不富丽。
他穿件衲袄用棉麻布料制，全部
被他那锁子铁甲的锈斑所玷污；
不久前结束了长行，从外地归来，
他要去敬觐朝参，谒圣迹，拜灵台。
〔8〕　　陪随他的，他儿子，活跃而健旺，
一名后生的扈从，爱俏的情郎，
是他本人的候补者；他头发卷卷，
仿佛在压榨机里卷过的一般。
他年纪我猜来约莫二十岁；中等
身材，行动很轻捷，身强膂力猛。
有一时他曾加入跨海的远征队，
在弗朗特斯、阿笃阿以及毕伽兑，
在短短时日里表现得成绩斐然，
可指望他那意中人对他垂青盼。
〔9〕　　红白各分明，他衣衫熠熠粲锦绣，
像碧草坪上的鲜花朵朵开蕾秀。
他成天不是唱着歌，便是吹着笛；
真好比阳春五月间，韶华甘如蜜。
他短短的长袍，长袖翩翩大而阔。
他跨上了坐骑，缓急疾徐神出没。
他会编歌词，制曲谱，飞马抡枪，
竞戳刺，又能跳舞、绘画、作文章。
他求爱求得心醉魂飞神颠倒，
夜间睡得像一只夜莺那样少。

Curteis he was, lowely, and servisable,
And carf biforn his fader at the table.
〔10〕 A Yeman hadde he and servants namo
At that time, for him liste ride so;
And he was clad in cote and hood of greene.
A sheef of pecok arwes, bright and keene,
Under his belt he bar ful thriftily;
Wel coude he dresse his takel yemanly:
His arwes drouped nought with fetheres lowe.
And in his hand he bar a mighty bowe.
A not-heed hadde he with a brown visage.
Of wodecraft wel coude he al the usage.
Upon his arm he bar a gay bracer,
And by his side a swerd and a bokeler,
And on that other side a gay daggere,
Harneised wel and sharp as point of spere;
A Cristophre on his brest of silver sheene;
An horn he bar, the baudrik was of greene.
A forster was he soothly, as I gesse.
〔11〕 Ther was also a Nonne, a Prioresse,
That of hir smiling was ful simple and coy.
Hir gretteste ooth was but by sainte Loy!
And she was cleped Madame Eglantine.
Ful wel she soong the service divine,
Entuned in hir nose ful semely;
And Frenssh she spak ful faire and fetisly,

他为人谦逊、殷勤而又礼数足，
餐桌上在他父亲跟前切着肉。
〔10〕　他还带同了一名乡士在身边，
此外再没有其他的仆役供差遣；
他一柄硬弓手上握，上下是一色
鹦鹉绿的头巾和外套，腰间挂得
有一束锋芒锐利的矢镞在闪耀；
像个好乡士，他发射羽箭手段高——
金碧的箭羽，孔雀羽毛插的翅——
它们离了弦，不偏不斜疾飞驰。
脸皮紫棠色，他头发短短剪平头。
森林里边的营生他件件都凑手。
他身旁一边挂着剑和盾，另一边
佩一柄漂亮的短匕首，匣内锋尖
犀利如矛头，刀鞘刀柄俱富丽；
还有件花哨的射韝护着他左臂；
一尊克列斯多弗银像在胸前亮；
翠绿的肩带上，弯弯号角放金光。
当真，他是个山林为家的樵猎户。
〔11〕　还有位女尼，是个修道院女院主，
她嫣然一笑，天真可喜而羞答答，
她最凶的咒誓只凭圣洛埃而发；
她取名唤作野蔷薇夫人。做礼拜，
唱圣诗，她歌声曼妙清幽真可爱，
余音在鼻内低回宛转总相宜；
一口法国话她说来文雅又得体，

After the scole of Stratford at the Bowe —
For Frenssh of Paris was to hire unknowe.
At mete wel ytaught was she withalle:
She leet no morsel from hir lippes falle,
Ne wette hir fingres in hir sauce deepe;
Wel coude she carye a morsel, and wel keepe
That no drope ne fille upon hir brest.
In curteisye was set ful muchel hir lest.
Hir over-lippe wiped she so clene
That in hir coppe ther was no ferthing seene
Of grece, whan she dronken hadde hir draughte;
Ful semely after hir mete she raughte.
And sikerly she was of greet disport,
And ful plesant, and amiable of port,
And pained hire to countrefete cheere
Of court, and to been statlich of manere,
And to been holden digne of reverence.
But, for to speken of hir conscience,
She was so charitable and so pitous
She wolde weepe if that she saw a mous
Caught in a trappe, if it were deed or bledde.
Of smale houndes hadde she that she fedde
With rosted flessh, or milk and wastelbreed;
But sore wepte she if oon of hem were deed,
Or if men smoot it with a yerde smerte;
And al was conscience and tendre herte.

但那是司德拉福那一带的口腔，
巴黎人说的法语她都不会讲。
进餐的一套礼仪她学得很到家：
小块的食物她从不自唇边掉落下，
也不会让手指给汤汁深深地沾湿。
叉起一小块，她放进口里去吃，
那碎块的菜肴不会掉落在胸前。
她爱讲礼仪，煞是细究又精研，
上嘴唇经常抹得这么样干净；
杯中喝过一口酒，她不会有一星
半点的油腻留在杯边或酒上；
她进餐的一切动作文雅复高尚，
她确是个有趣、可喜、和蔼的人物。
她精心去学习宫廷贵妇的礼数，
举止竭力求端庄，言谈显稳重，
总祈人肃然目敬，真华贵又雍容。
可是，说起她的心肠，那却是如此
悲悯而仁慈，只要见一只小耗子
夹上了老鼠机夹，流着血或死掉，
她便会哭泣。她养得有小狗几条，
喂的是烤肉，或牛奶和雪花面包。
但她会痛哭，有一只若忽然死掉，
或有人使棒棍狠狠地将它打击：
她心怀不忍，见苦痛无有不哀惜。

Ful semely hir wimpel pinched was,
Hir nose tretis, hir yën greye as glas,
Hir mouth ful smal, and therto softe and reed,
But sikerly she hadde a fair forheed:
It was almost a spanne brood, I trowe,
For hardily, she was nat undergrowe.
Ful fetis was hir cloke, as I was war;
Of smal coral aboute hir arm she bar
A paire of bedes, gauded al with greene,
And theron heeng a brooch of bold ful sheene,
On which ther was first writen a crowned A,
And after, *Amor vincit omnia*.

〔12〕 Another Nonne with hire hadde she
That was hir chapelaine, and preestes three.

〔13〕 A Monk ther was, a fair for the maistrye,
An outridere that loved venerye,
A manly man, to been an abbot able.
Ful many a daintee hors hadde he in stable,
And whan he rood, men mighte his bridel heere
Ginglen in a whistling wind as clere
And eek as loude as dooth the chapel belle
Ther as this lord was kepere of the celle.
The rule of Saint Maure or of Saint Beneit,
By cause that it was old and somdeel strait —
This ilke Monk leet olde thinges pace,
And heeld after the newe world the space.

她包头的围巾皱襞折得很整齐；
她鼻如小小悬胆；眼珠像玻璃
一般的灰色；软软的红唇樱桃口；
她天庭饱满，宽阔几乎有一叉手；
说实在话，她身材不能算素小。
我还注意到，她穿的斗篷式样好。
臂腕上她套着一串珊瑚小念珠，
其中夹得有绿色的大颗帮点数，
串上挂的是一枚放亮的黄金扣，
扣上先有顶王冠和“爱”字来开头，
接着是“神爱战胜一切”的古箴铭。
〔12〕　　此外还有个姑子和她结同行，
那是她下手，再还有神父另三众。
〔13〕　　又有个修道僧，神完气足威仪隆，
他爱骑马往乡间，四出去射猎，
他体格魁伟，当个住持挺合适。
马厩里养着好几匹良种的龙驹，
他跨上马鞍，一阵风纵辔疾驰驱，
人们能听见他那马勒上的銮铃，
一声声丁零清澈响不绝，那铮鸣
仿如僧院里寺塔的钟声一个样。
那僧院这位大僧正当着位方丈，
因为圣冒勒或者圣佩奈的戒条
有点太严峻，而且总是那老一套，
这僧家尽那陈旧的古董去臭腐，
他走的乃是条通往新世界的路。

He yaf nought of that text a pulled hen
That saith that hunteres been nought holy men,
Ne that a monk, whan he is recchelees,
Is likned til a fissh that is waterlees —
This is to sayn, a monk out of his cloistre;
But thilke text heeld he nat worth an oystre.
And I saide his opinion was good:
What sholde he studye and make himselven wood
Upon a book in cloistre alway to poure,
Or swinke with his handes and laboure,
As Austin bit? How shal the world be served?
Lat Austin have his swink to him reserved!
Therefore he was a prikasour aright.
Grehoundes he hadde as swift as fowl in flight.
Of priking and of hunting for the hare
Was al his lust, for no cost wolde he spare.
I sawgh his sleeves purfiled at the hand
With gris, and that the fineste of a land;
And for to festne his hood under his chin
He hadde of gold wrought a ful curious pin:
A love-knotte in the grettere ende ther was.
His heed was balled, that shoon as any glas,
And eek his face, as he hadde been anoint:
He was a lord ful fat and in good point;
His yën steepe, and rolling in his heed,
That stemed as a furnais of a leed,

规条上说起猎人不神圣那句话，
他认为还不抵一只光毛鸡的价；
或者说僧人双足跨离了寺院门，
便好比出水的鱼儿危机胁命根，
这话他觉得连一只牡蛎都不值；
我得说他这条意见倒卓有见识。
为什么他要在寺院里对着书本
不眨眼地读，读成木头似的笨，
或者胼手又胝足，日夕多勤劳，
如同圣奥司丁的戒条所教导？
尘俗的世务怎能完全不照顾？
让圣奥司丁按着那条律去劳苦。
因此上，他跨登马背，驰骋得飞速，
跟踪着迅捷的灵猩，飞鸟般追逐；
上鞍马急急驰驱，去射猎野兔，
乃是他生平一乐，他挥霍不计数。
我见他袖上沿边所饰的细毛皮
为此邦不常见，寻常百姓所珍奇；
为了在颐下扣住他那顶风兜，
他别着一支金饰针，用精工雕镂：
宽阔的一端，用个情人结镌铸成。
他那秃顶的头皮光亮似明镜，
又如施过了油脂，脸上也放着光。
这位僧官境况好，心广而体胖；
两只眼睛炯炯亮，在额下频转动，
宛如熊熊的炉火在镬下光焰红；

His bootes souple, his hors in greet estat —
Now certainly he was a fair prelat.
He was nat pale as a forpined gost:
A fat swan loved he best of any rost.
His palfrey was as brown as is a berye.
〔14〕 A Frere ther was, a wantoune and a merye,
A limitour, a ful solempne man.
In alle the ordres foure is noon that can
So muche of daliaunce and fair langage:
He hadde maad ful many a mariage
Of yonge wommen at his owene cost;
Unto his ordre he was a noble post.
Ful wel biloved and familier was he
With frankelains over al in his contree,
And with worthy wommen of the town —
For he hadde power of confessioun,
As saide himself, more than a curat,
For of his ordre he was licenciat.
Ful swetely herde he confessioun,
And plesant was his absolucioun.
He was an esy man to yive penaunce
Ther as he wiste to have a good pitaunce;
For unto a poore ordre for to yive
Is signe that a man is wel yshrive;
For if he yaf, he dorste make avaunt
He wiste that a man was repentaunt;

他脚上快靴乃用细软的皮革制，
胯下的马儿腰肥气壮堪驱驰。
当真，他是位人才一表的大长老；
不像个苍白的瘦鬼，七伤又五劳。
肉食里他爱一只肥肥的烤天鹅。
他那匹坐骑颜色深棕如浆果。

〔14〕　　有个在限区之内游乞的托钵僧，
是个放荡不羁、兴冲冲的快乐人。
在全部四个教团里，没人能像他
这么能说又会道，满口的识趣话。
他不惜花费，曾经自己掏腰包，
为好几个年轻娘子合卺成姻好。
他是他自己教团里一根擎天柱。
在他的本乡，当地的员外小地主，
都跟他相熟又相亲，城市里绅士
富商的宅眷也和他相识亦相知：
为的是，他自己声言，比教区神父
便更有权力去听取忏悔颁恩恕，
因为他从他自己教团里领得有
教皇特许的符牒准他去云游。
他听人悔罪的态度和蔼而亲切，
他允准赦罪的神情愉快而可悦；
只要他知道有顿好饭可饱餐，
便任人忏悔，安心去赎罪，不为难。
谁能对一个穷苦的教团作捐献，
便表示他确已获得上天的赦免。

For many a man so hard is of his herte
He may nat weepe though him sore smerte:
Therfore, in stede of weeping and prayeres,
Men mote yive silver to the poore freres.

〔15〕 His tipet was ay farsed ful of knives
And pinnes, for to yiven faire wives;
And certainly he hadde a merye note;
Wel coude he singe and playen on a rote;
Of yeddinges he bar outrely the pris.
His nekke whit was as the flowr-de-lis;
Therto he strong was as a champioun.
He knew the tavernes wel in every town,
And every hostiler and tappestere,
Bet than a lazar or a beggestere.
For unto swich a worthy man as he
Accorded nat, as by his facultee,
To have with sike lazars aquaintaunce:
It is nat honeste, it may nought avaunee,
For to delen with no swich poraile,
But al with riche, and selleres of vitaile;
And over al ther as profit sholde arise,
Curteis he was, and lowely of servise.
Ther was no man nowher so vertuous:
He was the beste beggere in his hous.
And yaf a certain ferme for the graunt:
Noon of his bretheren cam ther in his haunt.

因为他若肯施舍，可大胆地拟揣，
他当已神明内疚，真心有悔改。
因为好些人心肠如此硬，他们
不能流涕泪，即令内心哀痛深。
所以，为了去代替哭泣和祈祷，
人们须付银两与贫僧将罪消。
〔15〕　　他那披肩袋子里装满了小洋刀
与别针，当作礼品去赠送女美姣。
当真，他悦耳的歌喉朗唱复低吟，
讴着歌儿又拉着三弦的小提琴。
歌唱比赛里他总领得有头等奖。
他颈子雪白，白得像百合花那样；
可是他身强力壮，似竞武的冠军。
城镇里的酒家客舍他经常去游巡，
可是癞疯子、女叫花他却不相熟。
因为像他这样一位重要的大人物，
以他的威望和秉性来说，不合适
去跟癞疯人、叫花婆他们相结识。
去跟这样的穷酸滥贱有来往，
未免太难听，也一无好处可指望，
惟有同粮商富户打交道才上算。
但不拘哪里，只要有钱钞可赚，
他便会谦恭多礼，殷勤去奔走。
他是他院里最好的募化僧人；
他付出一笔包揽的定额年金，
别的乞僧便不许侵入他的地界；

For though a widwe hadde nought a sho,
So plesant was his *In principio*
Yit wolde he have a ferthing er he wente;
His purchas was wel bettre than his rente.
And rage he coude as it were right a whelpe;
In love-dayes ther coude he muchel helpe,
For ther he was nat lik a cloisterer,
With a thredbare cope, as is a poore scoler,
But he was lik a maister or a pope.
Of double worstede was his semicope,
And rounded as a belle out of the presse.
Somwhat he lipsed for his wantounesse
To make his Englissh sweete upon his tonge;
And in his harping, whan he hadde songe,
His yën twinkled in his heed aright
As doon the sterres in the frosty night.
This worthy limitour was cleped Huberd.
〔16〕 A Marchant was ther with a forked beerd,
In motelee, and hye on hors he sat,
Upon his heed a Flandrissh bevere hat,
His bootes clasped faire and fetisly.
His resons he spak ful solempnely,
Souning alway th' encrees of his winning.
He wolde the see were kept for any thing
Bitwixen Middelburgh and Orewelle.
Wel coude he in eschaunge sheeldes selle.

因为即使有个穷寡妇连旧鞋
都没有得一只，他的“太初有道”[①]
能讲得那么中听而愉快，不等到
离开，他总会有几文缘金能征集。
他募化所得远超过正常的收益。
他能活像只小狗般，蹦踊又跳跃。
在解怨结缘日，他极忙碌而活泼，
因为在那天，不像个出家的贫僧
好在出言吐语时娃儿似的甜；
一壁厢歌唱，一壁厢手抚着琴弦，
他两只眼睛滴溜溜在眼眶里转，
好比那霜落的夜天星光在闪。
这位托钵的行乞僧名叫胡伯特。

〔16〕　有一个商人，口上下留髭须三抹，
身穿着斑驳颜色的衣服，高高
马上骑，头戴一顶弗兰德海狸帽；
脚上皂靴用漂亮的扣子绾扣起。
他开腔说话，活现出一副自傲气，
说来说去，总不外赢利和赚钱。
他但愿密特尔堡与奥莱威之间，
海疆上无论如何确保着平安。
他经营汇兑，卖出法兰西银元

① 《新约·约翰福音》首数字。

This worthy man ful wel his wit bisette:
Ther wiste no wight that he was in dette,
So statly was he of his governaunce,
With his bargaines, and with his chevissaunce.
Forsoothe he was a worthy man withalle;
But, sooth to sayn, I noot how men him calle.
〔17〕 A Clerk-ther was of Oxenforde also
That unto logik hadde longe ygo.
As lene was his hors as is a rake,
And he was nought right fat, I undertake,
But looked holwe, and therto sobrely.
Ful thredbare was his overeste courtepy,
For he hadde geten him yit no benefice,
Ne was so worldly for to have office.
For him was levere have at his beddes heed
Twenty bookes, clad in blak or reed,
Of Aristotle and his philosophye,
Than robes riche, or fithele, or gay sautrye.
But al be that he was a philosophre
Yit hadde he but litel gold in cofre;
But al that he mighte of his freendes hente,
On bookes and on lerning he it spente,
And bisily gan for the soules praye
Of hem that yaf him wherwith to scoleye.
Of studye took he most cure and most heede.
Nought no word spak he more than was neede,

很得手。这位大商家机灵而干练；
没人知道他，却原来有债务拖欠，
他要价还价，做交易，经纪往来，
竟那么安详无事，一落的气概。
不过说实话，此君仍是个大商家，
但当真，我不知人家怎样称呼他。
〔17〕　　另外还有位牛津来的读书学士，
他随堂听讲逻辑学已有好多时。
他坐下的马匹瘦得像柄草耙，
他自己也不十分胖，我敢说这话；
两颊凹陷，且面容也愀然黯黯。
他上身的短褂显得分外敝烂，
因为他还没领到过什么薪水，
原来他不通世务，怎么会有职位？
他宁愿在他床头高堆着二十卷
亚里斯多德的著作与哲学宝典，
一本本用红皮或者用黑皮装订，
却不要锦袍、提琴或花哨的竖琴。
虽然他是个哲学家，心胸旷达，
但绝少有金银放进他那只宝匣；
他打从亲友处得来的些许钱钞，
全都在书本和学问上面花掉，
他不住为他们的灵魂祈求祝福，
只因他们帮助了他，使他能攻读。
对用功求学，他最是潜心而深虑。
不需要讲的话，他从不多说一句，

And that was said in forme and reverence,
And short and quik, and ful of heigh sentence:
Souning in moral vertu was his speeche,
And gladly wolde he lerne, and gladly teche.

〔18〕 A Sergeant of the Lawe, war and wis,
That often hadde been at the Parvis
Ther was also, ful riche of excellence.
Discreet he was, and of greet reverence —
He seemed swich, his wordes weren so wise.
Justice he was ful often in assise
By patente and by plein commissioun.
For his science and for his heigh renown
Of fees and robes hadde he many oon.
So greet a purchasour was nowher noon;
Al was fee simple to him in effect —
His purchasing mighte nat been infect.
Nowher so bisy a man as he ther nas;
And yit he seemed bisier than he was.
In termes hadde he caas and doomes alle
That from the time of King William were falle.
Therto he coude endite and make a thing,
Ther coude no wight pinchen at his writing;
And every statut coude he plein by rote.

而逢到说的时节总彬彬有礼，
简短敏捷，有深沉卓越的含义。
他言谈出口，涵濡着高风与懋德，
总之，他好学又好教，不渝而不释。
〔18〕　　有一位上等大律师，审慎而聪明，
常到圣保罗前庑去剖析民刑
诉讼案，他是位出众超群之士。
他智虑周详，令人哪个不钦迟。
他神态可敬，语言明智而英断。
他当过多次周期法庭的审判官，
受到皇家委任，有全权去审理
一切民刑案件；因为他博学
际天人，声名冠当世，他领受的公费
和所享的荣衔委实丰裕而奂美。
这样一位代立契据与变更户主
姓名的能手，要算他是人间独步。
只要他捉刀，哪一宗产业都可以
变成没任何条件的绝对世业；
他代订的契据决不会成为无效。
像他这般忙的人你再也找不到，
可是他如今比往常更要冗繁。
从胜王威廉以来的每一件讼案
和判决，他都记得有法律的专词。
他能将它们默记得，书写成卷子，
至于法律条文，他完全能背诵，
没人能找出一星半点的漏洞。

He rood but hoomly in a medlee cote,
Girt with a ceint of silk, with barres smale.
Of his array telle I no lenger tale.
〔19〕 A Frankelain was in his compaignye:
Whit was his beerd as is the dayesye;
Of his complexion he was sanguin.
Wel loved he by the morwe a sop in win.
To liven in delit was evere his wone,
For he was Epicurus owene sone,
That heeld opinion that plein delit
Was verray felicitee parfit.
An housholdere and that a greet was he:
Saint Julian he was in his contree.
His breed, his ale, was always after oon;
A bettre envined man was nevere noon.
Withouten bake mete was nevere his hous,
Of fissh and flessh, and that so plentevous
It snewed in his hous of mete and drinke,
Of alle daintees that men coude thinke.
After the sondry sesons of the yeer
So chaunged he his mete and his soper.
Ful many a fat partrich hadde he in mewe,
And many a breem, and many a luce in stewe.
Wo was his cook but if his sauce were
Poinant and sharp, and redy all his gere.
His table dormant in his halle alway

他骑在马上，衣装平常而朴素，
穿着件外套，料子用的是杂色布，
腰系着丝绸的带子，上面有条纹。
他其余的衣着，恕我不再详细陈。
〔19〕 和他同行的有位小地主员外郎；
白花花胡子，跟草里的雏菊相仿。
他脸色红润，性情开朗而乐天。
一清早他爱吃一块酒浸的糕点。
他惯常过的是逍遥逸乐的生涯，
因为他是晏壁鸠鲁斯的本家，
他素来主张过完全欢快的生活
是人生世上至高无上的极乐。
他是位好客而厚待宾朋的主人；
在他乡间，他简直就是圣裘列恩。
他的酒和肉永远是同样地上挑；
再无人能有他那么多好酒存窖。
他家里从来不会断烧烤的牛肉
和鲜鱼，而且预备得极为富足，
肉和酒在他家里总非常充沛，
一年四季中他每每逐节按时
轮番更换他所进的菜肴和肉食。
笼里他喂养许多只肥肥的鹧鸪，
他家厨司准倒楣，若做的汤汁
不够辛辣而浓烈，或器皿不整饬。
在他餐厅里有只大食桌，一天
到晚铺陈好，可供享客开筵宴。

Stood redy covered all the longe day.
At sessions ther was he lord and sire.
Ful ofte time he was Knight of the Shire.
An anlaas and a gipser al of silk
Heeng at his girdel, whit as morne milk.
A shirreve hadde he been, and countour.
Was nowher swich a worthy vavasour.
〔20〕 An Haberdasshere and a Carpenter,
A Webbe, a Dyere, and a Tapicer —
And they were clothed alle in oo liveree
Of a solempne and greet fraternitee.
Ful fresshe and newe hir gere apiked was;
Hir knives were chaped nought with bras,
But al with silver; wrought ful clene and weel
Hir girdles and hir pouches everydeel.
Wel seemed eech of hem a fair burgeis
To sitten in a yeldehalle on a dais.
Everich, for the wisdom that he can,
Was shaply for to been an alderman.
For catel hadde they ynough and rente,
And eek hir wives wolde it wel assente —
And elles certain were they to blame:
It is ful fair to been ycleped "Madame,"
And goon to vigilies all bifore,
And have a mantel royalliche ybore.

审判官们会聚时，他在那作东道；
他往往是代表本郡的国会议曹。
腰带上挂柄匕首，和一只白缎子
荷包，白得跟早晨的牛奶相似。
他当过郡治奉行官和查账委员；
如此杰出的陪臣乃世上所少见。
〔20〕　　还有个贩帽子客人，一个木匠工，
一个纺织工，一个漂染作坊工，
一个家具商，身穿着同一式服装，
属于同一个重要的行业大联帮。
他们的衣冠收拾得簇崭全新；
他们剑鞘头的帽扣不用黄铜钉，
而是用雪花白银细工铸镂成，
他们的腰带、钱包也色色都齐整。
他们都浑如行帮选出的帮代表，
配在议事厅讲台上据位而凭高。
他们每一个以他智虑的周详，
便足够去当行业帮会的大会长。
因为财产和收入，他们都优裕，
他们的妻子当也会同声加赞许；
否则，有身价人不做，岂不要受埋怨？
给叫声夫人多么开怀称心愿，
圣节前夕超前着众人去守通宵，
斗篷被人显耀地提挈着作前导。

〔21〕 A Cook they hadde with hem for the nones,
To boile the chiknes with the marybones,
And powdre-marchant tart and galingale.
Wel coude he knowe a draughte of London ale.
He coude roste, and seethe, and broile, and frye,
Maken mortreux, and wel bake a pie.
But greet harm was it, as it thoughte me,
That on his shine a mormal hadde he.
For blankmanger, that made he with the beste.

〔22〕 A Shipman was ther, woning fer by weste —
For ought I woot, he was of Dertemouthe.
He rood upon a rouncy as he couthe,
In a gowne of falding to the knee.
A daggere hanging on a laas hadde he
Aboute his nekke, under his arm adown.
The hote somer hadde maad his hewe al brown;
And certainly he was a good felawe.
Ful many a draughte of win hadde he drawe
Fro Burdeuxward, whil that the chapman sleep:
Of nice conscience took he no keep;
If that he faught and hadde the hyer hand,
By water he sente hem hoom to every land.
But of his craft, to rekene wel his tides,

〔21〕 他们带着个厨司务，同路步趋跄，
他将用牛膝骨一起煨煮清鸡汤，
对上些酸香面子和莎根香的料。
呷口伦敦老麦酒，他准知好不好。
他燔炙、烹煮、烧烤、煎炸都来得，
做一个羹汤、烘制糕饼，全出色。
但老大糟糕的事儿，我这么捉摸，
乃是他小腿胫骨上生了处疮毒；
原来他做的白汁鸡丁绝漂亮。

〔22〕 有个船老大，居家远远在西方：
据我所知，他来自窦忒茂塞城，
他跨匹雇来的马儿，勉强踏着镫，
一件毛粗布直裰只覆到膝盖头。
围着他脖子的细绳系着柄匕首，
从头上下垂，挂到他腋下身左侧。
太阳①将他的皮肤晒成了紫棠色；
当真，他是条非同等闲的英雄汉，
船泊在波尔多，他早已酒醉饭饱
好多回，商家货主却还在睡大觉。
良心好歹他觉得不必把神来劳。
跟旁人打架，他若是占得了上风，
便会送人回老家，道经海龙宫。
可是，说起他打量潮水的本领，

① 原文作“炎夏”。赿飔大概忘记了他在篇首所描写的景色是在四月间到五月初，正当艳阳天气；故若说“骄阳”已极勉强，说“炎夏”就太过了。

His stremes and his daungers him bisides,
His herberwe and his moone, his lodemenage,
There was noon swich from Hulle to Cartage.
Hardy he was and wis to undertake;
With many a tempest hadde his beerd been shake;
He knew alle the havenes as they were
Fro Gotlond to the Cape of Finistere,
And every crike in Britaine and in Spaine.
His barge ycleped was the Maudelaine.

〔23〕 With us ther was a Doctour of Physik:
In al this world ne was ther noon him lik
To speken of physik and of surgerye.
For he was grounded in astronomye,
He kepte his pacient a ful greet deel
In houres by his magik naturel.
Wel coude he fortunen the ascendent
Of his images for his pacient.
He knew the cause of every maladye,
Were it of hoot or cold or moiste or drye,
And where engendred and of what humour:
He was a verray parfit praktisour.
The cause yknowe, and of his harm the roote,
Anoon he yaf the sike man his boote.

〔24〕 Ful redy hadde he his apothecaries
To senden him drogges and his letuaries,
For eech of hem made other for to winne:

估计水流以及他近旁的险情，
捉摸港口、月亮的位置与驾驶，
从赫尔到迦太基，没有跟他能相似。
他性情勇猛，做事足智而多谋，
腮边的须髯饱经了雨打又风抽。
东起哥得兰，迤西到非尼斯特角，
他完全熟悉所有的港澳与湾泊，
西班牙、布列丹每条溪流全知道。
他那条出海帆船叫冒特莱纳号。

〔23〕　和我们同道的有一位医药博士，
说到病理与药剂和外科手术，
世间再没有像他这般的第二个；
因为他根基打得稳，深通占星学。
凭他那自然的魔法，他医治病人
总拣有利于治好他们的好时辰。
他善于候他的病家吉星东升时，
替他祛祸而纳福，好好地诊治。
他知道每种疾病的起因与来源，
不管因为气质的热或冷，湿或干，
打哪里引起，是哪种体液的病症；
他是位本领十分高强的好医生。
只待把症候的根子来由诊断出，
他马上配就药物将病家来满足。

〔24〕　他关照药剂师他们充分准备好，
随时送给他需用的药剂和软膏。
他们相互照顾着对方的利益；

Hir frendshipe was nought newe to biginne.
Wel knew he the olde Esculapius,
And Deiscorides and eek Rufus,
Olde Ipocras, Hali, and Galien,
Serapion, Razis, and Avicen,
Averrois, Damascien, and Constantin,
Bernard, and Gatesden, and Gilbertin.
Of his diete mesurable was he,
For it was of no superfluitee,
But of greet norissing and digestible.
His studye was but litel on the Bible.
In sanguin and in pers he clad was al,
Lined with taffata and with sendal;
And yit he was but esy of dispence;
He kepte that he wan in pestilence.
For gold in physik is a cordial,
Therfore he loved gold in special.
〔25〕 A good Wif was ther of biside Bathe,
But she was somdeel deef, and that was scathe.
Of cloth-making she hadde swich an haunt,
She passed hem of Ypres and of Gaunt.
In al the parissh wif ne was ther noon

彼此间的友谊非成于一朝一夕。
他熟知古代的埃斯戈莱比欧斯，
和台斯考列提斯，还有卢孚思，
老伊波革拉底斯，海来，加理恩，
塞拉比盎，拉齐斯，以及阿维森，
阿梵罗珂，达玛沁，与康斯丹丁，
贝娜特，戛载斯滕，与吉尔褒定。
他自己的日常饮食丰俭有节度，
并不太豪奢恣纵，非分地繁芜，
却营养很丰富，且又容易去消化。
他在《圣经》上，功夫并不太多花。
他上下衣装颜色是大红与天蓝，
衬里的料子用的是薄绢和软缎；
可是他平时的用度并不太阔绰，
大瘟疫时期赚的钱他还保存着。
因为在药物里头黄金是强心剂，
所以对黄金无怪他特别要着迷。

〔25〕　从巴斯温泉左近来了个家主妇，
她耳朵有点聋，不免要为她叫苦。
她织布的能耐到得那么样高强，
要比伊不尔、刚忒[1]的来货还漂亮。
整个教区里不许有别家的主母

① Ypres（伊不尔，法文念成只有一个缀音，“不尔”在缀音末被轻轻带过）在今比利时境内西弗兰德省，Gaunt 城（刚，法文“忒”无音）在今比利时之东弗兰德省，当时都以手工纺织闻名，所产布匹行销西欧。

That to the offring bifore hire sholde goon,
And if ther dide, certain so wroth was she
That she was out of alle charitee.
Hir coverchiefs ful fine were of ground —
I dorste swere they weyeden ten pound
That on a Sonday weren upon hir heed.
Hir hosen weren of fin scarlet reed,
Ful straite yteyd, and shoes ful moiste and newe.
Bold was hir face and fair and reed of hewe.
She was a worthy womman al hir live:
Housbondes at chirche dore she hadde five,
Withouten other compaignye in youthe —
But therof needeth nought to speke as nouthe.
And thries hadde she been at Jerusalem;
She hadde passed many a straunge streem;
At Rome she hadde been, and at Boloigne,
In Galice at Saint Jame, and at Coloigne:
She coude muche of wandring by the waye:
Gat-toothed was she, soothly for to saye.
Upon an amblere esily she sat,
Ywimpled wel, and on hir heed an hat
As brood as is a bokeler or a targe,
A foot-mantel aboute hir hipes large,
And on hir feet a paire of spores sharpe.
In felaweshipe wel coude she laughe and carpe:
Of remedies of love she knew parchaunce,

走在她头里，去奉献财物，祈神福；
倘使有的话，她准会大发其雷霆，
把慈悲一股脑丢得一干又二净。
她包头的巾帕质精料细呈华彩；
我敢赌咒，礼拜天她头上的冠戴
和头饰，秤起分量来足有十磅重。
她脚上穿一双长袜火焰般猩红，
吊得紧紧地，她靴鞋皮软极服脚。
她脸皮红白分明，神气有点儿泼。
这一辈子的身世她过得真出色，
教堂门首她有过的丈夫共五客，
年轻时节的同伴还不曾去计算；
不过那个我们此刻且不必谈。
她曾经到过三回耶鲁撒冷城；
异国的河川她曾多次舟横渡；
为了朝圣她到过罗马与波隆，
还有珈列塞的圣约每，加上哥龙。
却说这浪迹各地使她闻见洽：
说实话，她张开口来牙叉又齿豁。
她舒舒服服脚跨着一匹溜蹄马，
头裹巾，颈围帕，戴顶帽儿却蛮大，
宽阔好比那打仗的手牌或圆盾；
一件骑裙围住她的粗腰和厚臀，
脚上马靴扣着副尖尖的踢马刺。
她有说有笑，同大家一块儿去拜寺。
医爱情的诸般妙策她想必都懂，

For she coude of that art the olde daunce.
〔26〕 A good man was ther of religioun,
And was a poore Person of a town,
But riche he was of holy thought and werk.
He was also a lerned man, a clerk,
That Cristes gospel trewely wolde preche;
His parisshens devoutly wolde he teche.
Benigne he was, and wonder diligent,
And in adversitee ful pacient,
And swich he was preved ofte sithes.
Ful loth were him to cursen for his tithes,
But rather wolde he yiven, out of doute,
Unto his poore parisshens aboute
Of his offring and eek of his substaunce:
He coude in litel thing have suffisaunce.
Wid was his parissh, and houses fer asonder,
But he ne lafte nought for rain ne thonder,
In siknesse nor in meschief, to visite
The ferreste in his parissh, muche and lite,
Upon his feet, and in his hand a staf.
This noble ensample to his sheep he yaf
That first he wroughte, and afterward he taughte.
Out of the Gospel he tho wordes caughte,
And this figure he added eek therto:
That if gold ruste, what shal iren do?
For if a preest be foul, on whom we truste,

因为她对于此道曾练过深功。

〔26〕　还有个虔诚好善的宗教信徒，
乃是位乡镇小牧师，生活颇清苦，
但他圣洁的思想和工作却广大
深宏，且是个博学的士子，他总把
基督的福音来真正宣扬播教，
诚心地将他的教区居民来诲导。
他慈祥恺悌，而又勤奋得惊人，
遇到灾祸来临时极耐心隐忍；
事实常证明他确实如此作为。
他极不愿为年金把人逐出教会，
但毫无疑问，却反而会把捐献
或自己私有的些些物资或存钱，
赠与他周围穷苦的教区居民。
他在他稍许所有里能找到丰殷。
他教区辽阔，房栊彼此相远隔，
但不管下雨或打雷，他无时无刻
不亲自去访问区里最远的教民，
不论富贵或贫贱，只要害了病
或遭遇不幸——步行着，拐着根藜杖。
他在牧群中树了这高尚的榜样
首先是以身作则，然后才教导；
这句话他从福音书里边找到；
另外他再加这样个比喻来渲染，
说黄金若生锈，黑铁又将怎么办？
因为若我们信任的牧师不干净，

No wonder is a lewed man to ruste.
And shame it is, if a preest take keep,
A shiten shepherde and a clene sheep.
Wel oughte a preest ensample for to yive
By his clennesse how that his sheep sholde live.
He sette nought his benefice to hire
And leet his sheep encombred in the mire
And ran to London, unto Sainte Poules,
To seeken him a chaunterye for soules,
Or with a bretherhede to been withholde,
But dwelte at hoom and kepte wel his folde,
So that the wolf ne made it nought miscarye:
He was a shepherde and nought a mercenarye.
And though he holy were and vertuous,
He was to sinful men nought despitous,
Ne of his speeche daungerous ne digne,
But in his teching discreet and benigne,
To drawen folk to hevene by fairnesse
By good ensample — this was his bisinesse.
But it were any persone obstinat,
What so he were, of heigh or lowe estat,
Him wolde he snibben sharply for the nones:
A bettre preest I trowe ther nowher noon is.
He waited after no pompe and reverence,
Ne maked him a spiced conscience,
But Cristes lore and his Apostles twelve

无怪一个无知的普通人有毛病；
可耻的是（牧师们要注意这一节），
牧羊人满身腌臜，羊群却纯洁，
一个牧师应当提供出榜样来，
洁身自好，让羊群把他作楷模。
他决不将他的教职出租给旁人，
尽羊群陷在泥潭里不得轻身，
自己却跑到伦敦圣保罗教寺
替施主唱安灵求福的奠祭歌词，
或加入某个教团，去闭门参禅；
他耽在乡里，厮守着他的羊栏，
好叫狼子没法使伎俩，施恶毒；
他是个教师，不是个雇来的佣仆。
虽然他心神圣洁，性行又高超，
对犯下罪孽的人却并不凶暴，
他从不盛气凌人，或侮慢冷酷，
只耐心训诲，亲和地使人信服。
以他芳洁的言行，凭他的表率，
引人入天国，最为他关注而萦怀：
但如果遇见什么人怙恶不悛，
不论他地位的高低，贫富抑卑尊，
他会毫不容情地严辞去斥责。
再比他好的牧师，我深知不可得。
他不事虚荣夸诞，空洞的尊崇，
他也不苛刻吹求，钻头以觅缝，
而只传播基督，以及他十二位

He taughte, but first he folwed it himselve.

〔27〕 With him ther was a Plowman, was his brother,
That hadde ylad of dong ful many a fother.
A trewe swinkere and a good was he,
Living in pees and parfit charitee.
God loved he best with al his hoole herte
At alle times, though him gamed or smerte,
And thanne his neighebor right as himselve.
He wolde thresshe, and therto dike and delve,
For Cristes sake, for every poore wight,
Withouten hire, if it laye in his might.
His tithes payed he ful faire and wel,
Bothe of his propre swink and his catel.
In a tabard he rood upon a mere.

〔28〕 Ther was also a Reeve and a Millere,
A Somnour, and a Pardoner also,
A Manciple, and myself — ther were namo.

〔29〕 The Millere was a stout carl for the nones.
Ful big he was of brawn and eek of bones —
That preved wel, for overal ther he cam
At wrastling he wolde have alway the ram.
He was short-shuldred, brood, a thikke knarre.
Ther was no dore that he nolde heve of harre,
Or breke it at a renning with his heed.
His beerd as any sowe or fox was reed,
And therto brood, as though it were a spade;

使徒的教化，自己先奉行不背。

〔27〕和他一起的有个农夫，他兄弟，
曾经拖载过好多车粪便与污泥，
是个真正的劳动者，上好庄稼手，
活着与世无争，博爱而好友。
他无时不倾注全身心去爱上帝，
顷刻的忧乐不改他恒久的至意，
爱旁人则完全跟爱他自己一般
无二。为基督，他肯替每个穷汉
打麦，挖沟与锄地，不需要工钱，
只要他力所能及，他无不勤勉。
他自己辛劳所得和地上的收入，
他都按价值把什一税好好付足。
他骑匹母马，穿件农夫的短襦。

〔28〕此外还有个都总管和个磨坊主，
一个教会法庭的公差和一个
赦罪僧，一个伙食买办，加上我。

〔29〕说到磨坊主，他是个粗蛮的莽汉，
骨骼生得极壮大，肌肉也饱满；
他时常显本领，因为一到角力场，
他总跟人去竞赛，夺取得奖羊。
他生成短胳膊，阔肩膀，矮胖个子，
没扇门他不能拉掉铰链和螺丝，
或急奔过去用脑袋把它顶破；
他胡须殷红，像猪或狐的那样，
而且宽阔得如田家的铁锹一般。

Upon the cop right of his nose he hade
A werte, and theron stood a tuft of heres,
Rede as the bristles of a sowes eres;
His nosethirles blake were and wide.
A swerd and a bokeler bar he by his side.
His mouth as greet was as a greet furnais.
He was a janglere and a Goliardais,
And that was most of sinne and harlotries.
Wel coude he stelen corn and tollen thries —
And yit he hadde a thombe of gold, pardee.
A whit cote and a blew hood wered he.
A baggepipe wel coude he blowe and soune,
And therwithal he broughte us out of towne.

〔30〕 A gentil Manciple was ther of a temple,
Of which achatours mighte take exemple
For to been wise in bying of vitaile;
For wheither that he paide or took by taile,
Algate he waited so in his achat
That he was ay biforn and in good stat.

〔31〕 Now is nat that of God a ful fair grace
That swich a lewed mannes wit shal pace
The wisdom of an heep of lerned men?
Of maistres hadde he mo than thries ten
That weren of lawe expert and curious,
Of whiche ther were a dozeine in that hous
Worthy to been stiwardes of rente and fond

有个小硬瘤正长在他鼻子尖端，
瘤肿上生出一丛密茸茸的红毛，
乌红黑赤似母猪耳朵上的鬃毛；
他鼻子，两个漆黑的窟窿，很大。
一柄剑，一面圆盾，在他身旁挂；
张开大嘴，犹如火红的炉子口，
满口的淫猥，说废话剌剌不休，
讲的尽是些罪孽案，粗鄙和丑秽。
他惯偷麦子，磨坊抽成要三四倍；
可是他有只金拇指，只有天知道。
头戴蓝风兜，他身上穿件白外套。
他对于吹弄苏格兰袋箫有能耐，
我们便在箫声中被带出城关外。

〔30〕　有个出色的法学院伙食买办，
别的采购员都该学他的好手段，
因为办货时，不论付现或记账，
他采购一应食品，必精明而得当，
善观风色，伺机会，手快而眼捷，
总赶在人家前面，安排得极妥帖。

〔31〕　却说这样个不学无术的相好，
竟智赛一大堆博古通今的俊豪，
岂非上帝给他的秉赋独优厚？
他上面的主人何止三十个出头，
全都是精研法律的硕学弘才；
在那书院里就住得有一打家宰，
他们每一位都能替英格兰不拘

Of any lord that is in Engelond,
To make him live by his propre good
In honour dettelees but if he were wood,
Or live as scarsly as him list desire,
And able for to helpen al a shire
In any caas that mighte falle or happe,
And yit this Manciple sette hir aller cappe!
〔32〕 The Reeve was a sclendre colerik man;
His beerd was shave as neigh as evere he can;
His heer was by his eres ful round yshorn;
His top was dokked lik a preest biforn;
Ful longe were his legges and ful lene,
Ylik a staf, ther was no calf yseene.
Wel coude he keepe a gerner and a binne —
Ther was noon auditour coude on him winne.
Wel wiste he by the droughte and by the rain
The yeelding of his seed and of his grain.
His lordes sheep, his neet, his dayerye,
His swin, his hors, his stoor, and his pultrye
Was hoolly in this Reeves governinge,
And by his covenant yaf the rekeninge,
Sin that his lord was twenty-yeer of age.
There coude no man bringe him in arrerage.
Ther nas baillif, hierde, nor other hine,
That he ne knew his sleighte and his covine —
They were adrad of him as of the deeth.

那一家贵胄管理田庄和岁余，
好让他靠他自己的财富过生涯，
受尊敬，不负债，除非他发疯发傻，
或随他自己的意愿省俭着过活；
假使有什么天灾人祸等不测，
他还能捐资将整个州郡来周济；
可是这买办把他们全蒙在鼓里。

〔32〕　都总管是个瘦削的、有脾气的人，
他满脸髭须刮得一根也不剩。
围着他耳朵，头发剪得特别短；
头顶前方也削平，像神父一般。
一双长长的腿子瘦成两根骨，
细细的棍儿上，小腿腿肚也无肉。
他能好好管理着麦囤和粮仓；
没有查账员能发现他编甚假账。
逢天时干旱或雨水太足，他都能
知道播种的谷子有多少收成。
他主人的牛马猪羊，乳场与酪坊，
所有的牲畜与家禽，都在他执掌
之下，自从他主子二十岁时起，
这桩桩件件便全归他司账登记；
没人见过他缴纳账款有拖延。
没有个管事、牧人或其他长年
夫仆之类，他们的诡计和奸诈
他不是了如指掌、手到即擒拿；
他们害怕他，如遭到瘟疫那样。

His woning was ful faire upon an heeth;
With greene trees shadwed was his place.
He coude bettre than his lord purchace.
Ful riche he was astored prively.
His lord wel coude he plesen subtilly,
To yive and lene him of his owene good,
And have a thank, and yit a cote and hood.
In youthe he hadde lerned a good mister:
He was a wel good wrighte, a carpenter.
This Reeve sat upon a ful good stot
That was a pomely grey and highte Scot.
A long surcote of pers upon he hade,
And by his side he bar a rusty blade.
Of Northfolk was this Reeve of which I telle,
Biside a town men clepen Baldeswelle.
Tukked he was as is a frere aboute,
And evere he rood the hindreste of oure route.

〔33〕 A Somnour was ther with us in that place
That hadde a fir-reed cherubinnes face,
For saucefleem he was, with yën narwe,
And hoot he was, and lecherous as a sparwe,
With scaled browes blake and piled beerd:
Of his visage children were aferd.
Ther nas quiksilver, litarge, ne brimstoon,
Boras, ceruce, ne oile of tartre noon,
Ne oinement that wolde clense and bite,

建在平阳空地上，他住宅极漂亮，
有绿树掩映环抱，茂密而荫浓。
他堆金积玉，本领比主子要灵通。
他秘密窖藏着大大一注财宝；
使他的主子很高兴，他善于弄巧，
所送的、借的，原都是他主子所有，
他却受了谢，还到手大氅和风兜。
年轻时他曾学得一门好手艺，
如今他是个木匠，做上上的活计。
这都管骑着匹胖马有四条矮脚，
毛片斑驳而灰色，马名叫司各脱。
他穿件长长的云破天青色短褂，
左胁下将口铁锈的腰刀来斜挎。
我说的这位总管来自瑙福克郡，
那所在，邻近个叫做包特威的镇。
像个托钵僧，他把他的外褂拴着，
一路上他总在我们行列的最末。
〔33〕　　跟我们一起的、那教会法庭公差，
他的脸像个天使的，火红赤辣，
满脸生痤疮，眼睛夹成两条缝。
麻雀般贪情好色，他性欲常冲动；
眉毛漆黑结满痂，髭须稀邋遢；
孩子们见他这副尊容要害怕。
他那些白头脓疹，颊上的大痤疮，
任凭用红汞、氧化铅、硼砂、硫黄、
白铅、酒石英或任何其他的药膏，

That him mighte helpen of his whelkes white,
Nor of the knobbes sitting on his cheekes.
Wel loved he garlek, oinons, and eek leekes,
And for to drinke strong win reed as blood.
Thanne wolde he speke and crye as he were wood;
And whan that he wel dronken hadde the win,
Thanne wolde he speke no word but Latin:
A fewe termes hadde he, two or three,
That he hadde lerned out of som decree;
No wonder is — he herde it al the day,
And eek ye knowe wel how that a jay
Can clepen "Watte" as wel as can the Pope —
But whoso coude in other thing him grope,
Thanne hadde he spent all his philosophye;
Ay *Questio quid juris* wolde he crye.

〔34〕 He was a gentil harlot and a kinde;
A bettre felawe sholde men nought finde:
He wolde suffre, for a quart of win,
A good felawe to have his concubin
A twelfmonth, and excusen him at the fulle;
Ful prively a finch eek coude he pulle.
And if he foond owher a good felawe
He wolde techen him to have noon awe
In swich caas of the Ercedekenes curs,
But if a mannes soule were in his purs,
For in his purs he sholde ypunisshed be.

都无法洗清或烧净。他最是喜好
吃大蒜、玉葱、青葱；他喝的烈酒
血一般鲜红，酒后便吵闹不休，
与发了疯相似。每逢他纵酒酣饮，
他便不说别的话，只是讲拉丁。
但用词不多，他经常只两语三言，
他学得这些是从罗马教的法典；
那不足为奇，因为他整天听到；
你也该知道，一只听惯了的鲣鸟，
也能和教皇一般，叫一声“喔特”。
不过你若是将他考问个明白，
他嘴上的学问便都会化归乌有。
“问题是，法律怎样说法。”他敞口
嚷着这句拉丁话。
〔34〕 他是个极和易
可亲的混混儿；知交比他更莫逆，
你再也找不到。为着美酒一大壶，
他能让他的好友借用他的情妇
一整年，而毫不在乎；实际却是他，
当真能偷偷地叫人做个大傻瓜。
不论在哪里若遇到这样个相好，
他自会叫他放心，完全用不到
（若真有这事）害怕副主教的诅咒——
被逐出教会，除非在钱包里头
他藏着他那颗灵魂；因为，他将被
处罚，只限于在钱包之内。他将会

"Purs is the Ercedekenes helle," saide he.

〔35〕 But wel I woot he lied right in deede:
Of cursing oughte eech gilty man him drede,
For curs wol slee right as assoiling savith —
And also war him of a *significavit.*

〔36〕 In daunger hadde he at his owene gise
The yonge girles of the diocise,
And knew hir conseil, and was al hir reed.
A gerland hadde he set upon his heed
As greet as it were for an ale-stake;
A bokeler hadde he maad him of a cake.

〔37〕 With him ther rood a gentil Pardoner
Of Rouncival, his freend and his compeer,
That straight was comen fro the Court of Rome.
Ful loude he soong, "Com hider, love, to me."
This Somnour bar to him a stif burdoun:
Was nevere trompe of half so greet a soun.

〔38〕 This Pardoner hadde heer as yelow as wex,
But smoothe it heeng as dooth a strike of flex;
By ounces heenge his lokkes that he hadde,
And therwith he his shuldres overspradde,
But thinne it lay, by colpons, oon by oon;
But hood for jolitee wered he noon,
For it was trussed up in his walet:
Him thoughte he rood al of the newe jet.

声言，“副主教的地狱只是只钱包。”

〔35〕　可是我深知他又在胡说八道；
教会的诅咒，每个犯罪者该悚惧——
因诅咒把灵魂会打入阿鼻地狱，
正如赦罪会使它得救离泉壤——
另外他也得当心被逐出教区。

〔36〕　在他管辖下，他把全管区的年少
男女置在他自己控制下；他知道
各人的秘密，是他们唯一的顾问。
他头戴着花环，陆离五彩斓缤纷，
大得可挂在春酒店杆上作店招；
他手握着个圆盾般大的大面包。

〔37〕　和他在一起骑行的，他的友人
与伙伴，来自朗锡瓦，是个赦罪僧，
刚才从罗马教廷回到僧院里。
他高唱，“这里来，爱啊，跟我在一起”。
那教会法庭的公差拉着大喉咙
伴唱着，再没一半恁响的大号筒。

〔38〕　这僧家的头发拉碴焦黄如黄蜡，
光溜溜挂着，像一束拣好的亚麻；
满头丝丝的垂发一绺绺往下坠，
薄薄的一片披散到肩头撒上背；
为了贪舒适，他不曾将兜巾来戴，
而把它折叠起来装进了头陀袋。
他以为披散着头发不裹带兜巾，
只戴顶便帽骑马，气派最时新。

Dischevelee save his cappe he rood al bare.
Swiche glaring yën hadde he as an hare.
A vernicle hadde he sowed upon his cappe,
His walet biforn him in his lappe,
Bretful of pardon, come from Rome al hoot.
A vois he hadde as smal as hath a goot;
No beerd hadde he, ne nevere sholde have;
As smoothe it was as it were late yshave.
I trowe he were a gelding or a mare.
But of his craft, fro Berwik into Ware,
Ne was ther swich another pardoner;
For in his male he hadde a pilwe-beer
Which that he saide was Oure Lady veil;
He saide he hadde a gobet of the sail
That Sainte Peter hadde whan that he wente
Upon the see, til Jesu Crist him hente.
He hadde a crois of laton, ful of stones,
And in a glas he hadde pigges bones,
But with thise relikes whan that he foond
A poore person dwelling upon lond,
Upon a day he gat him more moneye
Than that the person gat in monthes twaye;
And thus with reined flaterye and japes
He made the person and the peple his apes.

他睁着炯炯的双目，宛如只野兔，
一块圣弗龙尼加的帕儿有基督
圣像在上面，他将它缝在帽儿上。
在他跟前怀里放着的那行囊，
装满从罗马才带来的赦罪符契。
他嗓音如山羊鸣声那么高而细。
他髭髯毫无，将来也不会长得有，
唇边颐上都精光，一似新剃头；
我信他是只去势公驹或牡马儿。
在他行业中，打从贝力克到华尔，
和他同样的赦罪僧再也找不到。
因为，在他那口袋里，他有个枕套，
据他说，是我们圣母用过的头巾：
又有一小片那篷帆——圣彼得曾经
在海上扬帆，随即离船在海上走，
被耶稣基督拉住了，将他来扶救[①]。
他有支黄铜十字架，嵌满假宝石，
还有只玻璃杯，里面装着猪骨髅。
他带了这些个灵宝，只要随时
云游到乡间，找到一个穷牧师，
一天之内他从那牧师处的所敛，
便会超过那个人两个月的薪水钱。
便这样，连哄带骗，弄诡计，耍花腔，
他叫牧师和乡民都上他的当。

---

①《新约·马太福音》第 14 章 24—32 节。

But trewely to tellen at the laste,
He was in chirche a nobl ecclesiaste;
Wel coude he rede a lesson and a storye,
But alderbest he soong an offertorye,
For wel he wiste whan that song was songe,
He moste preche and wel affile his tonge
To winne silver, as he ful wel coude —
Therefore he soong the merierly and loude.

〔39〕 Now have I told you soothly in a clause
Th'estaat, th'array, the nombre, and eek the cause
Why that assembled was this compaignye
In Southwerk at this gentil hostelrye
That highte the Tabard, faste by the Belle;
But now is time to you for to telle
How that we baren us that ilke night
Whan we were in that hostelrye alight;
And after wol I telle of oure viage,
And al the remenant of oure pilgrimage.
But first I praye you of youre curteisye
That ye n'arette it nought my vilainye
Though that I plainly speke in this matere
To telle you hir wordes and hir cheere,
Ne though I speke hir wordes proprely;
For this ye knowen also wel as I:
Who so shal telle a tale after a man
He moot reherce, as neigh as evere he can,

不过，老实说，讲到这临了结末；
他在教会里还是个高贵的角色。
日课和圣徒传，他能诵读得很好，
可是唱奉献曲，他歌声最是圆妙。
因为他知道，那歌儿一经停唱，
他就得去传教，好好将舌头磨光，
尽他的力量设法把银两搜罗来。
因此上，他唱得如此响亮而愉快。

〔39〕　　如今我已简要地告诉了你们，
这群人的地位、衣装、人数，和为甚
要在塞寿克，在贝尔饭店紧隔壁，
这家出色的泰巴客舍里来会集。
现在我想我也该对诸位谈一下，
那晚上我们在那所馆驿里歇马
住店，跟着还有些什么样的行止。
然后我要把我们行程中的事，
与朝圣路上其他的经历来一叙。
但首先我要请诸位对我加宽遇，
莫以为这是我礼数有什么不周，
虽然我言无修饰，朴质不虚浮，
只告诉诸位他们的言谈吐属
和笑貌音容，甚至把他们的陈述，
连一言一语都据实无遗地相告。
因为这一层诸位谁都很知道，
不论谁要把别人的故事来重讲，
他便得重复（尽量照原来的式样）

Everich a word, if it be in his charge,
Al speke he nevere so rudeliche and large,
Or elles he moot telle his tale untrewe,
Or feine thing, or finde wordes newe;
He may nought spare although he were his brother:
He moot as wel save oo word as another.
Crist spak himself ful brode in Holy Writ,
And wel ye woot no vilainye is it;
Eek Plato saith, who so can him rede,
The wordes mote be cosin to the deede.

〔40〕 Also I praye you to foryive it me
Al have I nat set folk in hir degree
Here in this tale as that they sholde stonde:
My wit is short, ye may wel understonde.

〔41〕 Greet cheere made oure Host us everichoon,
And to the soper sette he us anoon.
He served us with vitaile at the beste.
Strong was the win, and wel to drinke us leste.
A semely man oure Hoste was withalle
For to been a marchal in an halle;
A large man he was, with yën steepe,
A fairer burgeis was ther noon in Chepe —
Bold of his speeche, and wis, and wel ytaught,
And of manhood him lakkede right naught.
Eek therto he was right a merye man,
And after soper playen he bigan,

原讲者的每个字，假使记得的话，
不去管原来怎么样粗鄙与不雅；
否则他就会把故事叙述得失真，
或矫揉杜撰，等于唱北调，用南音。
他含糊不得，即令讲兄弟的故事，
务必要逐字讲来，求始终都一致。
基督自己在圣书里说得极坦白，
你们很知道，那对他可并不辱没。
柏拉图也曾说过（谁若能读懂他），
一个人的行为必须符合他的话。

〔40〕　我也要请诸位对我屈加原谅，
在这故事里我没把各人安置上
他应有的地位，如他理有所应得；
你们很了解，我智虑欠少判断仄。

〔41〕　我们的店主人对我们每人表示
很大的欢迎，当即把晚餐开来吃；
供应上来的尽是些最好的肴馔。
酒是芳烈的，我们很乐于把盏。
我们的官人眉宇轩昂风姿爽，
堪在宴会厅上任一位司仪郎。
他体态魁梧，神采奕奕目光明，
找遍奇泊市，再没这般的好市民：
他言谈豪放，聪明，且又很温雅，
一派的男儿气概，堂皇而正大。
此外，他为人开朗愉快风趣多，
等我们用毕了晚餐，饭账已付过，

And spak of mirthe amonges othere thinges —
Whan that we hadde maad oure rekeninges —
And saide thus, "Now, lordinges, trewely,
Ye been to me right welcome, hertely.
For by my trouthe, if that I shal nat lie,
I sawgh nat this yeer so merye a compaignye
At ones in this herberwe as is now.
Fain wolde I doon you mirthe, wiste I how.
And of a mirthe I am right now bithought,
To doon you ese, and it shal coste nought.

〔42〕 "Ye goon to Canterbury — God you speede;
The blisful martyr quite you youre meede.
And wel I woot as ye goon by the waye
Ye shapen you to talen and to playe,
For trewely, confort ne mirthe is noon
To ride by the waye domb as stoon;
And therefore wol I maken you disport
As I saide erst, and doon you som confort;
And if you liketh alle, by oon assent,
For to stonden at my juggement,
And for to werken as I shall you saye,
Tomorwe whan ye riden by the waye —
Now by my fader soule thai is deed,
But ye be merye I wol yive you myn heed!
Holde up youre handes withouten more speeche."

他随即开始对大家谈笑风生，
说些赏心的乐事，探幽奇，访佳胜；
他说道，“哎也，众位公孙，委实的，
对大驾光临小店，俺欢迎至极，
因为，说实话，这年头还从未见过
济济跄跄的高宾贵客如此多，
像如今这般，一齐下降到小店里。
俺很想寻些娱乐叫列位都欢喜。
小可此刻正想起一桩欢娱事，
能使诸君尽开颜，却不用把钱使。
〔42〕　　列位去康透裒垒，祝一路福星；
愿极乐的圣徒覆蔽你们以神灵。
在下很知道，诸君走在路上时，
兀自会找到机缘相谈笑，讲故事；
因为，说实话，一路骑跨着马背
石头般不则声，无精打采没安慰；
所以，正如俺才对列位曾说过，
想提供些笑乐，借供你们岑寂破。
若是诸君能大家彼此都同意，
采纳了小子如今所提的这建议，
按着俺此刻就要来说的去行事，
明天（俺凭俺先父的亡魂起个誓）
列位在路上骑行时，如果不兴高
而采烈，俺准把脑袋向你们来抛。
请诸君将手举起来，不必再多谈。”

〔43〕 Oure counseil was nat longe for to seeche;
Us thought it was not worth to make it wis,
And graunted him withouten more avis,
And bade him saye his voirdit as him leste.
〔44〕 "Lordinges," quod he, "now herkneth for the beste;
But taketh it nought, I praye you, in desdain.
This is the point, to speken short and plain,
That eech of you, to shorte with oure waye
In this viage, shal tellen tales twaye —
To Canterburyward, I mene it so,
And hoomward he shal tellen othere two,
Of aventures that whilom have bifalle;
And which of you that bereth him best of alle —
That is to sayn, that telleth in this cas
Tales of best sentence and most solas —
Shal have a soper at oure aller cost,
Here in this place, sitting by this post,
Whan that we come again fro Canterbury.
And for to make you the more mury
I wol myself goodly with you ride —
Right at myn owene cost — and be youre gide.
And who so wol my juggement withsaye
Shal paye al that we spende by the waye.
And if ye vouche sauf that it be so,
Telle me anoon, withouten wordes mo,
And I wol erly shape me therefore"

〔43〕　我们要打定主意毫不感为难；
大家认为不值得去多作犹豫，
当即同意他，不曾再踌躇考虑，
请他把他所乐意的决定讲出来。

〔44〕　“列位公孙，”他道，“请听俺来交代；
可是请你们，莫把这事太小觑；
说得直截了当些，要点乃在于：
为使诸君得排遣，好缩短这行程，
俺意思要列位在这旅途中，每人
在前往康透裒垒参礼回来时，
他将高坐这厅上，挨近这柱子，
大家来作东，请他作客用晚餐。
而为了更使诸君沿途胸襟欢，
小可愿意乘马追随在列位后，
费用由俺自己负，为你们作导游。
谁如果违反了俺这令官的话，
要请他负担俺们全部的所花。
诸位若是同意按照俺说的去办，
那便不必说别的，请就告诉俺，
好让俺赶早来为旅途作打点。”

〔45〕 This thing was graunted and oure othes swore
With ful glad herte, and prayden him also
That he wolde vouche saul for to do so,
And that he wolde been oure governour,
And of oure tales juge and reportour,
And sette a soper at a certain pris,
And we wol ruled been at his devis,
In heigh and lowe; and thus by oon assent
We been accorded to his juggement.
And therupon the win was fet anoon;
We dronken and to reste wente eechoon
Withouten any lenger taryinge.
〔46〕 Amorwe whan that day bigan to springe
Up roos oure Host and was oure aller cok,
And gadred us togidres in a flok,
And forth we riden, a litel more than pas,
Unto the watering of Saint Thomas;
And ther oure Host bigan his hors arreste,
And saide, "Lordes, herkneth if you leste:
〔47〕 Ye woot youre forward and it you recorde:
If evensong and morwesong accorde,
Lat see now who shal telle the firste tale.
As evere mote I drinken win or ale,
Who so be rebel to my juggement
Shal paye for al that by the way is spent.
Now draweth cut er that we ferrer twinne:

〔45〕　　这件事我们全赞成，而且都开颜
起誓说要把他的话做到，且请他
也要保证按着他自已的说法
去照办，一致请他当大家的领袖，
记住及评判我们故事的好丑
和名次，且规定那顿晚餐价多少；
我们又对他说，不论事情多大小，
大家都听他去指挥；便这般，全场
一致，跟他的决定融洽得没两样。
于是，临睡的酒儿立即斟满杯；
我们空了樽，每人各自去安睡，
再没有什么其他的耽搁或迁延。
〔46〕　　次日凌晨还只是朦胧的破晓天，
我们的舍主东便起身，充当公鸡
为大家报晓，将我们召集在一起
成一群；我们骑上了鞍马比行步
略快些，去到圣汤玛斯饮马处。
那里，我们的店主人开始勒住马，
说道，“众位公孙，请听俺说句话。
〔47〕　　你们都知道跟俺的约言，请记起。
若是晚祷和早祷彼此相投契，
现在且来看谁开讲第一个故事。
正如俺喝麦酒，喝甜酒，软硬兼嗜，
不论谁他若对俺的决定有违抗，
就得将大家的路费一律去承当。
此刻，俺们散骑前，请大家抽个签；

He which that hath the shorteste shal biginne.
〔48〕 "Sire knight," quod he, "my maister and my lord,
Now draweth cut, for that is myn accord.
Cometh neer," quod he, "my lady Prioresse,
And ye, sire Clerk, lat be youre shamefastnesse —
Ne studieth nought. Lay hand to, every man!"
〔49〕 Anoon to drawen every wight bigan,
And shortly for to tellen as it was
Were it by aventure, or sort, or cas,
The soothe is this, the cut fil to the Knight;
Of which ful blithe and glad was every wight,
And telle he moste his tale, as was resoun,
By forward and by composicioun,
As ye han herd. What needeth wordes mo?
And whan this goode man sawgh that it was so,
As he that wis was and obedient
To keepe his forward by his free assent,
He saide, "Sin I shal biginne the game,
What, welcome be the cut, in Goddes name!
Now lat us ride, and herkneth what I saye."
And with that word we riden forth oure waye,
And he bigan with right a merye cheere
His tale anoon, and saide as ye may heere.

谁抽了最短的，讲故事由他领先。
〔48〕　　“骑士老人家，”他说道，“俺的长官
和爵主，请你来抽签，照俺的话办。
骑得略近些，”他说，“修道院女住持；
也莫再读书了；大家来，都来抽吧。”
〔49〕　　只顷刻之间每人都来抽一下，
简单说来，事情的结果是这样，
出于偶然，或者说，机会，或无常，
那根短签终于被骑士所抽到，
大家对此没有人不欢呼叫好；
于是，你已经听说过，根据约言
和彼此间的同意，按理他应当首先
把故事来讲，那何用再说别的话？
当这位好人儿见到在这情势下，
理应由他来开场，而且他为人
端敏，对自愿的前约谨守而恪遵，
当说道，“既然由我来击节开弦，
那么，以上帝的名义，欢迎这支签！
如今且向前骑行，听我来诉叙。”
听了那句话，我们都骑向前边去；
他随即开始讲他的故事，欢欢
乐乐、娓娓动听地如此来详谈。

• 威廉 · 莎士比亚 •

William Shakespeare

（1564—1616）

Who is Silvia

〔1〕 Who is Silvia? What is she,
That all our swains commend her?
Holy, fair and wise is she;
The heaven such grace did lend her,
That she might admired be.
〔2〕 Is she kind as she is fair, —
For beauty lives with kindness?
Love doth to her eyes repair,
To help him of his blindness;
And, being help'd, inhabits there.
〔3〕 Then to Silvia let us sing,
That Silvia is excelling;
She excels each mortal thing
Upon the dull earth dwelling:
To her let us garlands bring.

The Two Gentlemen of Verona, Ⅳ, Ⅱ, 39–53

谁是秀薇雅

〔1〕　谁是秀薇雅？她品性怎么样，
　　招得大伙儿妙龄郎尽夸她？
清纯又姣好，她再加心眼亮；
　　上天赋予她的光彩如此大，
直叫她给众人这般来赞赏。
〔2〕　她可真温顺跟姣好两相仿，
　　为的是美妙同温良相偎依？
小丘璧飞进她眼睑来借光，
　　好使她无明的两眼瞅千里，
他借到灵明耽下来不彷徨。
〔3〕　那么，让我们来讴歌秀薇雅，
　　歌唱她委实出色且高超；
她超越这个沉闷的尘寰界，——
　　这世上凡庸的浮生十百兆：
都来啊，大家来对她花鬘加。

——《梵罗那两士子》中之歌。

Spring

〔1〕 When daisies pied and violets blue,
And lady-smocks all silver-white,
And cuckoo-buds of yellow hue
Do paint the meadows with delight,
The cuckoo then on every tree
Mocks married men; for thus sings he,
Cuckoo;
Cuckoo, cuckoo: O word of fear,
Unpleasing to a married ear!

〔2〕 When shepherds pipe on oaten straws
And merry larks are ploughmen's clocks,
When turtles tread, and rooks, and daws,
And maidens bleach their summer smocks,
The cuckoo then on every tree,
Mocks married men; for thus sings he,
Cuckoo;
Cuckoo, cuckoo: O word of fear,
Unpleasing to a married ear!

Love's Labour's Lost V, II, 878–899

阳 春

〔1〕 当斑斓的雏菊、青莲的紫罗兰，
　　当苦碎米荠花发一片银白，
布谷鸟剪秋罗放金黄的灿烂，
　　点缀得芳草地满目呈绮罗，
这时节杜鹃在每一棵树上，
　　嘲笑着已娶的汉子；因它唱，
　　　　克珂！

〔2〕 克珂，克珂！——啊，恼死人，
　　娶过妻的汉子都落魄丧魂！
牧羊子吹起了燕麦的管哨，
　　欢乐的百灵是农夫的时计，
斑鸠踩步走，白嘴鸦、穴乌鸟，
　　小姑娘漂洗她们的夏衬衣，
这时节杜鹃在每一棵树上，
　　嘲笑着已娶的汉子，因它唱，
　　　　克珂！
克珂，克珂！——啊，恼死人，
已娶的汉子都落魄丧魂！

——《爱情的徒劳》中之歌

1980.3.10 译

Winter

〔1〕 When icicles hang by the wall,
And Dick the shepherd blows his nail,
And Tom bears logs into the hall,
And milk comes frozen home in pail,
When blood is nipt and ways be foul,
Then nightly sings the staring owl,
Tu-whit;
Tu-who, a merry note,
While greasy Joan doth keel the pot.

〔2〕 When all aloud the wind doth blow,
And coughing drowns the parson's saw,
And birds sit brooding in the snow,
And Marian's nose looks red and raw,
When roasted crabs hiss in the bowl,
Then nightly sings the staring owl,
Tu-whit;
Tu-who, a merry note,
While greasy Joan doth keel the pot.

Love's Labour's Lost, V, II, 904–939

隆 冬

〔1〕 当冰凌高挂在后院墙顶上，
牧羊子狄克把指头暖气哈，
汤摩背驮着柴火进客堂，
牛奶冰冻在桶里拎回家，
当手脚生冻疮，路上泥污脏，
这时节猫头鹰瞪着眼夜夜唱，
“吐嗯咀，吐呼！”欢乐的鸣啼，
当油污的乔安把锅边泡沫撇。

〔2〕 当北风呜啸得呼呼尽哗响，
牧师讲不清，满堂尽咳呛，
鸟儿像孵卵，在雪压的枝丫上，
曼玲的鼻子红得像破皮伤，
当糖炙的山楂在碗里咝咝响，
这时节猫头鹰瞪着眼夜夜唱，
“吐嗯咀，吐呼！”欢乐的鸣啼，
当油污的乔安把锅边泡沫撇。

——《爱情的徒劳》中之歌

1980.3.4 译

Over Hill, Over Dale

1

Over hill, over dale,
    Thorough bush, thorough brier,
Over park, over pale,
    Thorough flood, thorough fire,
I do wander every where,
Swifter than the moon's sphere;
And I serve the fairy queen,
To dew her orbs upon the green.
The cowslips tall her pensioners be:
In their gold coats spots you see;
Those be rubies, fairy favours,
In those freckles live their savours:
I must go seek some dewdrops here,
And hang a pearl in every cowslip's ear,
Farewell, thou lob of spirits; I'll be gone:
Our queen and all her elves come here anon.

A Midsummer Night's Dream, Ⅱ, Ⅰ, 1–16

仙 境

1

过冈峦，过山谷，

　　穿蔓荆，穿灌木，

过猎苑，过栏栅，

　　穿波涛，穿火焰，

我到处去逍遥，

比月轮还快到；

我侍候蓬莱世界的仙后，

替她去露滋草地上的花球。

高高立金花是她的卫士，

它们金氅上耀星星的点子；

那些是红玉，仙家的恩宠，

那些斑点里冒它们的香浓；

我得在这里寻几颗珠露，

在每朵立金花耳垂上挂一颗。

［最后两行译者未译。——编者］

2

〔1〕 You spotted snakes with double tongue,
Thorny hedgehogs, be not seen;
Newts and blind-worms, do no wrong,
Come not near our fairy queen.
〔2〕 Philomel, with melody
Sing in our sweet lullaby;
Lulla, lulla, lullaby; lulla, lulla, lullaby:
Never harm,
Nor spell nor charm,
Come our lovely lady nigh;
So, good night, with lullaby.

〔3〕 Weaving spiders, come not here;
Hence, you long-legg'd spinners, hence!
Beetles black, approach not near;
Worm nor snail, do no offence,
〔4〕 Philomel, with melody
Sing in our sweet lullaby;
Lulla, lulla, lullaby; lulla, lulla, lullaby:
Never harm,
Nor spell nor charm,
Come our lovely lady nigh;
So, good night, with lullaby.

A Midsummer Night's Dream, Ⅱ, Ⅱ, 10–31

2

〔1〕 吐双叉红舌的花点儿青蛇，
　　锋芒的刺猬，别到这儿来；
水蜥和蛇蜴，莫来此作恶，
　　不许靠我们的仙后身边挨。

〔2〕 夜莺喂，用轻歌曼妙，
　　同我们唱催眠曲调；
嘞啦，嘞啦，嘞嘞吧；嘞啦，嘞啦，嘞嘞吧！
　　决不许灾祸，
　　也莫叫邪魔，
　　挨近到我们的仙后身边跑，
　　所以，夜别了，唱着嘞啦吧。

〔3〕 织网的蜘蛛，别到这儿来；
　　走开，长脚的蜘蛛，走开！
黑甲虫，别挨近我们在一块；
　　蜒蚰和蜗牛，都莫来作歹。

〔4〕 夜莺喂，用轻歌曼妙，
　　同我们唱催眠曲调；
嘞啦，嘞啦，嘞嘞吧；嘞啦，嘞啦，嘞嘞吧！
　　决不许灾祸，
　　也莫叫邪魔，
　　挨近到我们的仙后身边跑，
　　所以，夜别了，唱着嘞啦吧。

——《仲夏夜之梦》中之歌

Tell Me Where Is Fancy Bred

Tell me where is fancy bred,
Or in the heart or in the head?
How begot, how nourished?
    Reply, reply.
It is engender'd in the eyes,
With gazing fed; and fancy dies
In the cradle where it lies.
    Let us all ring fancy's knell;
    I'll begin it, — Ding, dong, bell.
    Ding, dong, bell.

The Merchant of Venice, Ⅲ, Ⅱ, 62–72

告诉我爱情产生在何方

告诉我爱情产生在何方，
出自头脑里，或出自心房，
它怎样产生，又怎样养育？
　　回答我，回答我。
爱情的光焰在眼中点亮，
用凝视喂饲；但迅速消亡，
它的摇篮便是它的灵床。
让他们把爱情的丧钟敲响；
我来开始敲，——丁当、丁当。
　　丁当，丁当。

——《威尼斯商人》中之歌

Sigh No More, Ladies, Sigh No More

〔1〕 Sigh no more, ladies, sigh no more,
Men were deceivers ever;
One foot in sea and one on shore;
To one thing constant never:
Then sigh not so,
But let them go,
And be you blithe and bonny;
Converting all your sounds of woe
Into Hey nonny, nonny.

〔2〕 Sing no more ditties, sing no moe
Of dumps so dull and heavy;
The fraud of men was ever so,
Since summer first was leavy.
Then sigh, not so,
But let them go,
And be you blithe and bonny;
Converting all your sounds of woe
Into Hey nonny, nonny.

Much Ado About Nothing, Ⅱ, Ⅲ, 64–79

别再叹息，娘子们，别叹息

〔1〕　别再叹息了，娘子们，别叹息，
　　汉子们永远只是玩欺骗，
一只脚在水里，一只脚岸上立，
　　凡事从来不忠诚一片：
故而莫叹息，让他们去吧，
　　你们要欢乐加上愉快，
将你们一切悲苦的挥发，
　　化成嗨哟，诺尼诺乃。

〔2〕　别再唱小曲了，别再去呜唱，
　　别再唱忧郁、沉痛的曲调！
汉子们的欺诈从来就这样，
　　自从夏天里树木变荣茂：
故而莫叹息，让他们去吧，
　　你们要欢乐加上愉快，
将你们一切悲苦的挥发，
　　化成嗨哟，诺尼诺乃。

——《无风起白浪》中之歌

1980.3.7 夜译

Fie on Sinful Fantasy

Fie on sinful fantasy!
Fie on lust and luxury!
Lust is but a bloody fire,
Kindled with unchaste desire,
Fed in heart; whose flames aspire,
As thoughts do blow them, higher and higher.
Pinch him, fairies, mutually;
Pinch him for his villainy;
Pinch him, and burn him, and turn him about,
Till candles and starlight and moonshine be out.

The Merry Wives of Windsor, V, V, 96–105

去它的，邪恶的狂幻

去它的，邪恶的狂幻！
滚开去，放恣和欲念！
淫欲只是团可恶的火焰。
是用浪荡的性感所点燃。
喂养在心头，用意念燔燎，
那火焰升高了又复升高。
用手指捻他，小仙们，交互捻；
捏他，捻他，惩罚他的奸邪；
拧他，火烧他，团团旋转他，
到蜡烛、星星、月亮都熄灭。

——《温莎的风流妇人》中之歌

Under the Greenwood Tree

〔1〕 Under the greenwood tree
Who loves to lie with me,
And turn his merry note
Unto the sweet bird's throat,
Come hither, come hither, come hither:
Here shall he see
No enemy
But winter and rough weather.

〔2〕 Who doth ambition shun
And loves to live i'th'sun,
Seeking the food he eats
And pleased with what he gets,
Come hither, come hither, come hither:
Here shall he see
No enemy
But winter and rough weather.

As You Like It, Ⅱ, Ⅴ, 1–16

有绿树浓荫高头罩

〔1〕 有绿树浓荫高头罩，
谁爱来同我横卧倒，
唱他欢乐的好调门，
协同鸟儿的俏歌声，
嗨哟，这里来，这里来，这里来：
　　这儿我敢保
　　不得有仇家到，
在隆冬只有寒天的大风籁。

〔2〕 谁要将野心回避开，
爱耽在阳光里曝晒，
寻找他爱吃的东西，
过日子求安舒和熙，
嗨哟，这里来，这里来，这里来：
　　这儿我敢保
　　不得有仇家到，
在隆冬只有寒天的大风籁。

——《如君所好》中之歌

1980.2.26 译

Blow, Blow, Thou Winter Wind

〔1〕 Blow, blow, thou winter wind,
Thou art not so unkind
As man's ingratitude;
Thy tooth is not so keen,
Because thou art not seen,
Although thy breath be rude.
Heigh-ho! sing, heigh-ho! unto the green holly:
Most friendship is feigning, most loving mere folly:
Then, heigh-ho, the holly!
This life is most jolly.

〔2〕 Freeze, freeze, thou bitter sky,
That dost not bite so nigh
As benefits forgot:
Though thou the waters warp,
Thy sting is not so sharp
As friend remember'd not.
Heigh-ho! sing, heigh-ho! unto the green holly:
Most friendship is feigning, most loving mere folly:
Then, heigh-ho, the holly!
This life is most jolly.

As You Like It, Ⅱ, Ⅴ 11, 174–193

刮啊，凛冽的寒飙

〔1〕 刮啊，凛冽的寒飙
你并不那么凶暴，
　　如像人忘恩而负义，
你牙齿并不那么尖，
因你的形相瞧不见，
　　虽你的嘘息很凌厉。
嗨哟！唱嗨嗬！对那碧绿的刺冬青：
大多的友情是装假，大多的爱好——蠢事情：
　　那么，嗨嗬！刺冬青！
　　这辈子才过得挺开心。

〔2〕 冰冻啊，冰冻，苦寒天，
你咬人并不恁凶险，
　　如有人把恩情一片丢：
你虽然把水冻坚硬，
你的刺可不恁刺人疼，
　　如像人把友情一笔勾。
嗨嗬！唱嗨嗬！对那碧绿的刺冬青：
大多的友情是装假，大多的爱好——蠢事情：
　　那么，嗨嗬！刺冬青！
　　这辈子才过得挺开心。

——《如君所好》中之歌

1980.2.24 译

It Was a Lover and His Lass

〔1〕 It was a lover and his lass,
With a hey, and a ho, and a hey nonino,
That o'er the green corn-field did pass
In the spring-time, the only pretty ring-time,
When birds do sing, hey ding a ding, ding.
Sweet lovers love the spring.

〔2〕 Between the acres of the rye,
With a hey, and a ho, and a hey nonino,
These pretty country-folks would lie
In spring-time, the only pretty ring-time,
When birds do sing, hey ding a ding, ding:
Sweet lovers love the spring.

这是个情郎和他的小姑娘

〔1〕 这是个情郎和他的小姑娘，
哼着嗨，哼着嘀，哼着嗨，诺尼诺，
穿过那青青的田垄稞麦场，
在阳春时节，换指环，调恩情，
小鸟儿歌唱，嗨亭啊亭亭；
甜蜜的郎妹喜春心。

〔2〕 多少亩稞麦田间垄头上，
哼着嗨，哼着嘀，哼着嗨，诺尼诺，
这两个俏丽的人儿田头躺，
在阳春时节，换指环，调恩情，
小鸟儿歌唱，嗨亭啊亭亭；
甜蜜的郎妹喜春心。

〔3〕 This carol they began that hour,
With a hey, and a ho, and a hey nonino,
How that a life was but a flower
In spring-time, the only prety ring-time,
When brids do sing, hey ding a ding, ding:
Sweet lovers love the spring.

〔4〕 And therefore take the present time,
With a hey, and a ho, and a hey nonino;
For love is crowned with the prime
In spring-time, the only pretty ring-time,
When birds do sing, hey ding a ding, ding:
Sweat lovers love the spring.

As You Like It, Ⅴ, Ⅲ, 17–40

〔3〕 这欢乐的颂歌他们开头唱，
哼着嗨，哼着嘀，哼着嗨，诺尼诺，
唱一枝花儿开人生活一场，
在阳春时节，换指环，调恩情，
小鸟儿歌唱，嗨亭啊亭亭，
甜蜜的郎妹喜春心。

〔4〕 所以要今天花开今天笑，
哼着嗨，哼着嘀，哼着嗨，诺尼诺，
因为爱情要开花春天好，
在阳春时节，换指环，调恩情，
小鸟儿歌唱，嗨亭啊亭亭，
甜蜜的郎妹喜春心。

——《如君所好》中之歌

1980.2.27 译

O Mistress Mine,
Where Are You Roaming

〔1〕 O mistress mine, where are you roaming?
O, stay and hear; your true-love's coming,
    That can sing both high and low:
Trip no further, pretty sweeting;
Journeys end in lovers' meeting,
    Every wise man's son doth know.

〔2〕 What is love?'tis not hereafter;
Present mirth hath present laughter;
    What's to come is still unsure:
In delay there lies no plenty;
Then come kiss me, sweet-and-twenty,
    Youth's a stuff will not endure.

Twelfth Night, Ⅱ, Ⅲ, 42–53

甜蜜的二十来

〔1〕 我的姣娃喂，你往哪里去漫游？
耽下听我说，你情哥到来请你留，
　　他善于高歌，他又会低声吟唱；
别再去跋涉辛劳，美妙的甜心，
一对情人聚了首，旅游就得停，
　　每个聪明人的儿子都会这样想。

〔2〕 爱情是什么？它不是期待明朝；
眼下的欢乐就在于眼下的哗笑。
　　未来的东西如今还待去追求：
迟延里边找不到什么华彩；
那么来同我亲吻，甜蜜的二十来，
　　韶华这东西容易老，它不能长久。

——《第十二夜》中之歌

1980.2.28 深夜译

Come Away, Come Away, Death

〔1〕 Come away, come away, death,
And in sad cypress let me be laid;
Fly away, fly away, breath;
I am slain by a fair cruel maid.
My shroud of white, stuck all with yew,
O, prepare it!
My part of death, no one so true
Did share it.

〔2〕 Not a flower, not a flower sweet,
On my black coffin let there be strown;
Not a friend, not a friend greet
My poor corpse, where my bone shall be thrown:
A thousand thousand sighs to save,
Lay me, O, where
Sad true lover never find my grave,
To weep there!

Twelfth Night, Ⅱ, Ⅳ, 52–67

悲 歌

〔1〕　到我这儿来，到我这儿来，死亡，
让我用哀痛的绉绸[①]来包扎装殓；
　飞走，飞走，我这口气息，好痛创；
我给个娇媚狠心的姑娘所摧残。
我的尸衾用白布，要戳满紫杉枝，
　　嗳呀，准备好！
我丧生绝命的份儿，没有人如此
　　真情同过道。
〔2〕　莫要有朵花，莫要有朵香的花，
朝我的黑漆棺材上头去撒布；
　不要有朋友，不要有友好亲家，
来迎接我的尸首，到我的埋骨处：
免掉成千，成千声的叹息呜咽，
　　把我埋葬进
悲伤的真正钟情人找不到的墓穴，
　　去哭我的亡灵！

——《第十二夜》中之歌

1980.3.21 深夜译

---

① 原文 cypress 有人解作柏木，用来做棺材，或解作放在棺材里的柏树枝，作为哀悼的标识。但 Francis T. Palgrave 在他的《金藏》（*Golden Treasury*）诗选的注释里说，此词应作 crape（绉绸）解，谓系来自法文 crespe，或者是从 Cyprus 岛输出的绉绸，故可作 cyprus，用来包裹尸体。

Take, O, Take Those Lips Away

Take, O, take those lips away,
    That so sweetly were forsworn;
And those eyes, the break of day,
    Lights that do mislead the morn:
But my kisses bring again, bring again;
Seals of love, but seal'd in vain, seal'd in vain.

Measure for Measure, Ⅳ, Ⅰ

去掉啊，去掉那两片嘴唇

去掉啊，去掉那两片嘴唇，
　　它们那么甜蜜地赌假咒，
也去掉那双秀眼，如凌晨，
　　它们的光芒把朝晖诳诱：
可是要把我的亲吻招回，
　　　　　　　要招回；
恋爱的印章，但打印得功亏，
　　　　　　　　太功亏。

——《果报相因》中之歌

1980.3.3 译

Hark, Hark! the Lark at Heaven's Gate Sings

Hark, hark! the lark at heaven's gate sings,
    And Phoebus gins arise,
His steeds to water at those springs
    On chaliced flowers that lies;
And winking Mary-buds begin
    To ope their golden eyes:
With every thing that pretty is,
    My lady sweet, arise;
      Arise, arise!

Cymbeline, Ⅱ, Ⅲ

晨 歌

听啊！云雀鸣唱在天门前，
　　阳君开始在升空，
驱他的神骏去饮吸清泉，
　　自芳樽千千万万中；
闪眼的金盏花开始在睁启
　　它们耀金光的眼睛；
和一切俏丽的东西在一起，
　　我的美娇娘，趁晨兴，
　　　　起来，起来。

——《辛白琳》中之歌

1980.3.4 译

Fear No More the Heat O'the Sun

〔1〕 Fear no more the heat o'the sun,
Nor the furious winter's rages;
Thou thy worldly task hast done,
Home art gone, and ta'en thy wages:
Golden lads and girls all must,
As chimney-sweepers, come to dust.

〔2〕 Fear no more the frown o'the great,
Thou art past the tyrant's stroke;
Care no more to clothe and eat;
To thee the reed is as the oak:
The sceptre, learning, physic, must
All follow this, and come to dust.

再不用害怕太阳的猛烈

〔1〕 再不用害怕太阳的猛烈，
　　也不用恐惧隆冬的狂暴；
你已完成了这世上的事业，
　　回到家，收得了你的酬报：
绝妙的小子和姑娘终于会，
如通扫烟囱的工人，变成灰。

〔2〕 再不用害怕权贵的挥斥，
　　你已不可能给暴君所打击；
再不用耽心衣着和饮食，
　　对于你，芦草和橡树二而一：
王威同博学，武艺同医术，
一切都同途，终于变灰土。

〔3〕 Fear no more the lightning-flash,

Nor th'all-dreaded thunder-stone;

Fear not slander, censure rash;

Thou hast finish'd joy and moan:

All lovers young, all lovers must,

Consign to thee, and come to dust.

〔4〕 No exorciser harm thee!

Nor no witchcraft charm thee!

Ghost unlaid forbear thee!

Nothing ill come near thee!

Quiet consummation have;

And renowned be thy grave!

Cymbeline, Ⅳ, Ⅱ, 257–280

〔3〕　再不用害怕电光的闪烁，

　　也莫再恐惧惊雷的霹雳；

不要怕诽谤和躁动的煎迫：

　　你已经结束了欢乐和哀泣：

一切年轻的爱侣都向你

给交托，都会要化作灰泥。

〔4〕　莫要让巫师将你伤害！

也莫叫魔法使你迷挨！

　　解脱的鬼魂莫对你作祟！

莫叫不祥近到你身边来！

让你安享着宁静的完美；

　　你的墓披着荣誉的光辉！

——《辛白琳》中之歌

1980.3.8 深夜译

Come Unto These Yellow Sands

Come unto these yellow sands,

    And then take hands:

Court'sied when you have and kist, —

    The wild waves whist, —

Foot it featly here and there;

And, sweet sprites, the burden bear.

    Hark, hark!

            Bow, wow.

    The watch-dogs bark:

            Bow, wow.

    Hark, hark! I hear

    The strain of strutting chanticleer.

    Cry: Cock-a-diddle-dow.

The Tempest, Ⅰ, Ⅱ, 374–386

来到这一片黄沙滩

来到这一片黄沙滩，
然后手挽手互相搀：
你们彼此都屈过膝，
接了吻，叫海浪，“静寂！”
要步子跳踊得挺轻灵；
小妖们，这合唱要齐鸣。
　　听啊，听啊！
　　　　　　汪，汪。
　　狗儿们在叫：
　　　　　　汪，汪。
　　听啊，听啊！我听见
　　昂头阔步的大公鸡
在叫，喔喔啼特儿啼。

——《暴风雨》中之歌

Where the Bee Sucks, There Suck I

Where the bee sucks, there suck I:
In a cowslip's bell I lie;
There I couch when owls do cry.
On the bat's back I do fly
After summer merrily.
Merrily, merrily shall I live now
Under the blossom that hangs on the bough.

The Tempest, V, I, 88–94

蜜蜂吸蜜处，我也在吮蜜

蜜蜂吸蜜处，我也在吮蜜；
我在立金花铃铛里歇息；
我躺在那里听猫头鹰啼，
看星月消隐，日上耀晨曦。
在蝙蝠背上我骑着南飞，
去欢欢乐乐把良夏追随，
兴匆匆我将把生源安度，
在挂在枝头的花朵下漫步。

——《暴风雨》中之歌

Full Fathom Five Thy Father Lies

Full fathom five thy father lies;
    Of his bones are coral made;
Those are pearls that were his eyes;
    Nothing of him that doth fade
But doth suffer a sea-change
Into something rich and strange.
Sea-nymphs hourly ring his knell:
                    Ding-dong.
Hark! now I hear them, — Ding-dong, bell.

The Tempest, Ⅰ, Ⅱ, 396–405

你父亲躺得足有五哼深

你父亲躺得足有五哼深；
　　他的骨头是几撮红珊瑚；
　　他的眼睛已变成了珍珠；
他身上并无皮肉毁了形，
不过经受了一场海变异，
变化得又是富丽又惊奇。
海仙女每小时敲响他的丧钟：
　　　　　　　　　丁当。
听啊！我此刻正听到——
　　　　　　　　　丁当。

——《暴风雨》中之歌

1980.3.6 夜深译

12

When I do count the clock that tells the time,
And see the brave day sunk in hideous night;
When I behold the violet past prime,
And sable curls all silver'd o'er with white;

12①

当我在报时的钟上计数时间，
看到辉煌的白日丑化的暗夜；
当我眼见到紫罗兰香散花残，
鬓黑的华鬘丝丝夹杂着霜雪；

① 莎士比亚的《商乃诗集》共有诗 154 首，初次印行于 1609 年，为一小四开本，与邵泊（Thomas Thorpe）的《情人的愁叹》（*Lover's Complaint*）印在一起，大概是出于邵泊的盗印。1598 年弥欧斯（Meres）隐约提起过莎氏的“甜蜜的商乃诗”（sugared sonnets）在莎氏朋友间流传。写作时间延续有几年。印本上写的是献给一位“W.H.”的人，有一个说法认为这人可能就是潘勃洛克侯爵威廉·赫伯忒（William Herbert, Earl of Pebroke），莎氏死后他的两个环球剧院（Globe Theatre）的伶人同事好友在替他出版的第一对折本（First Folio）上就将全集献给侯爵和他的兄弟。另一个说法是：“W.H.”只是介绍这些商乃诗给印书人的一个朋友，与莎氏无关，还有个说法是：这“W.H.”是指第三邵山泼登侯爵亨利·列奥塞司莱（Henry Wriothesly, third Earl of Southampton），只不过将“H.W.”两个字母颠倒过来了。集子起初 126 首是写给一位年纪比莎氏轻好几岁的年轻人的，这是一个美男子，莎氏深深爱念他。从 127 首起，除最后两首，是写给一个女子的，是他的情妇，一个不是白面金发碧眼的美人，而是个黑牡丹，她对他的恩主也卖俏耍风情，有点瓜葛。集子里有两首说起作者对他自己作为一个伶人的社会地位深怀不满，这是因为当时的公众瞧不起伶人这一职业，虽然他自己多年从事于此，很早可以离开却并不舍弃它。
——摘译自伊凡契玲·屋康诺（Evangeline M. O'Connor）的《莎士比亚作品中谁是谁，什么是什么》（*Who's Who and What's What in Shakespeare*），1887。

When lofty trees I see barren of leaves,
Which erst from heat did canopy the herd,
And summer's green, all girded up in sheaves,
Borne on the bier with white and bristly beard;
Then of thy beauty do I question make,
That thou among the wastes of time must go,
Since sweets and beauties do themselves forsake,
And die as fast as they see others grow;
    And nothing 'gainst Time's scythe can make defence,
    Save breed, to brave him when he takes thee hence.

当枝丫大树卸脱了绿叶青枝，
不久前还替牛羊掩蔽着炎天，
夏日田间的翠碧被捆束堆置，
叠放在架上凝思着刚毛苍髯：
那时节我便疑问到你的存在，
只恐你要同时光的逝波同去，
因为芳香郁丽的人物要离开，
速速殒谢，眼见后起者来代序；
　　没有东西能对抗时光这镰刀，
　　只除了生育，当它会将你划掉。

1979.7.27 译

18

Shall I compare thee to a Summer's day?
Thou art more lovely and more temperate:
Rough winds do shake the darling buds of May,
And Summer's lease hath all too short a date:
Sometime too hot the eye of heaven shines,
And often is his gold complexion dimm'd;
And every fair from fair sometime declines,
By chance, or nature's changing course, untrimm'd;
But thy eternal Summer shall not fade,
Nor lose possession of that fair thou ow'st;
Nor shall Death brag thou wander'st in his shade,
When in eternal lines to time thou grow'st:
    So long as men can breathe, or eyes can see,
    So long lives this, and this gives life to thee.

18

可要我将你比作初夏的晴晖？
你却焕耀得更可爱，也更温婉：
狂风震撼五月天眷宠的嫩蕊，
孟夏的良时便会变得太短暂：
晴空里赤日有时光照得过亮，
它那赫奕的金容会转成阴晦；
被机运或被造化变迁所跌宕，
任何美妙的形象会显得不美；
但你这丰华的永夏不会衰颓，
你不会丧失你这无比的修好；
死亡不会夸你在它影下低回，
有这些诗行将你的韶光永葆：
　　只要人们还活着，眼睛还能看，
　　这首诗便能栩栩赋予你霞丹。

1979.5.12 译

29

When, in disgrace with fortune and men's eyes,
I all alone beweep my outcast state,
And trouble deaf heaven with my bootless cries,
And look upon myself, and curse my fate,
Wishing me like to one more rich in hope,
Featured like him, like him with friends possest,
Desiring this man's art and that man's scope,
With what I most enjoy contented least;
Yet in these thoughts myself almost despising,
Haply I think on thee, — and then my state,
Like to the Lark at break of day arising
From sullen earth, sings hymns at heaven's gate;
    For thy sweet love remember'd such wealth brings,
    That then I scorn to change my state with kings.

29

当我遭到命运和人们的白眼，
独自为我的弃逐伤心而哀哭，
徒然用怆呼干扰聋聩的昊天，
对我的际遇，诅咒自己恁命舛，
但愿跟某人一样，也富于希望，
容貌亦相似，像他济济多朋好，
想有此人的才艺，那人的宽广，
对自己最怀喜爱的却最懊恼；
当我这般萦思，要轻蔑自己时，——
偶然忽地想起你：我的这心神
便仿如破晓时刻百灵奋双翅，
从沉沉大地飞唱圣歌薄天门；
　　因为我，记起你深情如此宏富，
　　不屑同熠熠君王们易地相处。

1979.5.24 译

30

When to the sessions of sweet silent thought
I summon up remembrance of things past,
I sigh the lack of many a thing I sought,
And with old woes new wail my dear time's waste:
Then can I drown an eye, unused to flow,
For precious friends hid in death's dateless night,
And weep afresh love's long-since-cancell'd woe,
And moan the expense of many a vanisht sight:
Then can I grieve at grievances foregone,
And heavily from woe to woe tell o'er
The sad account of fore-bemoaned moan,
Which I new pay as if not paid before.
　　But if the while I think on thee, dear friend,
　　All losses are restored, and sorrows end.

30

当我唤起对往昔情事的回忆，
甜蜜、悄静的思念会集上来，
我为曾追求、未得的东西叹息，
重新因旧恸对蹉跎兴起新哀：
于是我不惯泪流的眼睛泫然
为在永夜中长眠的亲友恸哭，
又复饮泣恋爱所久捐的悲感，
悼伤好些消亡者形影的颠仆：
于是我便对旧愁再含殷衔苦，
沉重地将多年宿怨屈指重温，
反复早已呜咽过的陈怆夙诉，
再次去排遣二度勾起的遗恨。
　　但此时我倘若想起了你，挚友，
　　一切丧痛都苏复，愁苦全乌有。

1979.6.20 译

31

Thy bosom is endeared with all hearts,
Which I by lacking have supposed dead;
And there reigns love, and all love's loving parts,
And all those friends which I thought buried.
How many a holy and obsequious tear
Hath dear religious love stol'n from mine eye,
As interest of the dead, which now appear
But things removed, that hidden in thee lie!
Thou art the grave where buried love doth live,
Hung with the trophies of my lovers gone,
Who all their parts of me to thee did give;
That due of many now is thine alone:
　　Their images I loved I view in thee,
　　And thou, all they, hast all the all of me.

31

你胸中，众心荟萃得热烈而殷亲
(我因没有得它们，故猜想已经死)，
有真情主宰，有它心爱的各部分，
还有我许多好友，我以为已殒逝。
我流过多少圣洁和哀怜的泪珠，
亲爱和诚敬的挚情曾从我眼底
被吸引去悼伤死者，如今显见都
已消疏，却隐藏在你的胸中心里！
在你这座埋着情爱的墓里它们
活着，那里悬挂着他们的留念品，
他们都把我那份心向你作献赠；
总共许多份如今都归了你一人。
　　在你这身上我闻见他们的音容，
　　而你，既有了他们，就有我的拢总。

1979.11.9 译

32

If thou survive my well-contented day,
When that churl Death my bones with dust shall cover,
And shalt by fortune once more re-survey
These poor rude lines of thy deceased lover:
Compare them with the bettering of the time,
And though they be outstripped by every pen,
Reserve them for my love, not for their rhyme,
Exceeded by the height of happier men.
O, then vouchsafe me but this loving thought:
"Had my friend's Muse grown with this growing age,
A dearer birth than this his love had brought,
To march in ranks of better equipage:
    But since he died and poets better prove,
    Theirs for their style I'll read, his for his love."

32

你倘然活过了我这惬意的天年，
当死亡那伧夫已尘掩我的尸骸，
你若偶然有机会再一次能眼见
你这已死眷慕者的粗陋的咏怀，
将它跟当代最秀美的华辞相比，
虽然我这些篇什远逊于其他人，
请留着它们为恩情，不是为绮丽，
我这枝拙笔原不能跟它们等伦。
啊，请惠赐给予我这么样个眷念：
“假使我友人的诗才与时日俱长，
他对我的情辞会更加华滋清婉，
能同最英秀的诗篇齐飞和雁行。
　　但他已作古，诗人们却日进无疆，
　　我吟哦他们的丽句，吟他为绵想。”

1979.8.16 译

33

Full many a glorious morning have I seen
Flatter the mountain-tops with sovereign eye,
Kissing with golden face the meadows green,
Gilding pale streams with heavenly alchemy;
Anon permit the basest clouds to ride
With ugly rack on his celestial face,
And from the forlorn world his visage hide,
Stealing unseen to west with this disgrace:
Even so my sun one early morn did shine
With all-triumphant splendour on my brow;
But, out, alack! he was but one hour mine;
The region cloud hath masked him from me now.
    Yet him for this my love no whit disdaineth;
    Suns of the world may stain when heaven's sun staineth.

33

好多个瑰丽的晴朝我曾见到，
以至尊的照瞰夸赞群山之巅，
用灿烂的金颜俯吻遍地芳草，
将铅灰的江河变作金川漫点；
忽然有弥天晦暗的飞云驰来，
乌黝一片盖满了澄净的青苍，
将它的空灵向人寰苦境隔开，
晨分便向西悄逝，丧失掉荣光：
就这样我的太阳有一天清晨，
把宏盛的光华耀上我的眉宇；
但是，唉！他只一时间对我情深，
如今有层云掩蔽了他的炳煜。
　　可是我对他的爱不因此稍减；
　　天上的太阳还暧昧，何况人间？

1979.7.18 译

54

O, how much more doth beauty beauteous seem
By that sweet ornament which truth doth give!
The rose looks fair, but fairer we it deem
For that sweet odour which doth in it live.
The canker-blooms have full as deep a dye
As the perfumed tincture of the roses,
Hang on such thorns, and play as wantonly
When summer's breath their masked buds discloses:
But, for their virtue only is their show;
They live unwoo'd, and unrespected fade;
Die to themselves. Sweet roses do not so;
Of their sweet deaths are sweetest odours made:
    And so of you, beauteous and lovely youth,
    When that shall fade, my verse distils your truth.

54

啊，美好会显得多么琦玮呀，
由于它有真实去为它作华饰！
玫瑰花看来美，可是我们大家
觉得它含的芳菲使它更出色。
野蔷薇的色泽同样殷红俏丽，
比得上甘馨馥郁的真种玫瑰，
也挂在枝头，摇曳得娇娆出奇，
当初夏熏风展放欲吐的蓓蕾：
但因它们的艳质只在于相貌，
开时无人爱，谢落时也无人怜，
悄然死去。浓香的玫瑰却奇妙；
它们临终前发散浓重的香甜：
　　所以将来你，俊美可爱的萧郎，
　　萎谢时，这诗会将你永远揄扬。

1979.8.1 译

55

Not marble, nor the gilded monuments
Of princes, shall outlive this powerful rhyme;
But you shall shine more bright in these contents
Than unswept stone, besmear'd with sluttish time.
When wasteful war shall statues overturn,
And broils root out the work of masonry,
Nor Mars his sword nor war's quick fire shall burn
The living record of your memory.
'Gainst death and all-oblivious enmity
Shall you pace forth; your praise shall still find room
Even in the eyes of all posterity
That wears this world out to the ending doom.
    So, till the judgement that yourself arise,
    You live in this, and dwell in lovers' eyes.

55

云母石或者王公们镀金的碑碣，
都不会比这诗句留存得更悠久；
但你将在此，比曾被腌臜的岁月
所玷污的石碑，辉耀得更加灵秀。
当消耗的战火将会把雕像颠覆，
鏖战将把砖石工的砌座掏空掉，
战神的长剑、战祸的急火摧不枯
纪念你赫赫英名的风范和高标。
背着死亡和湮没掉一切的敌对，
你将会跨大步前迈；对你的赞扬
将在后世人心目中长存而永在，
直到这尘寰的末日最后来临场。
　　所以，直等到最后审判时你升起，
　　你在这诗中，将活在多情人眼里。

1979.8.20 译

57

Being your slave, what should I do but tend
Upon the hours and times of your desire?
I have no precious time at all to spend,
Nor services to do, till you require.
Nor dare I chide the world-without-end hour
Whilst I, my sovereign, watch the clock for you,
Nor think the bitterness of absence sour
When you have bid your servant once adieu;
Nor dare I question with my jealous thought
Where you may be, or your affairs suppose,
But, like a sad slave, stay and think of nought
Save, where you are how happy you make those.
　　So true a fool is love, that in your Will,
　　Though you do any thing, he thinks no ill.

57

由于是您的奴才，我除了侍候您
愿望的时辰晷刻外，还该做什么？
我没有任何可浪费的宝贵光阴，
也无事可做，除了应对您的謦欬。
我也不敢呵斥那没穷尽的钟点，
当我，我的君王啊，守着您的时钟，
也不敢认为离别您多凄苦烦厌，
当您一声告别后，我人去而楼空；
也不敢以我忌妒的疑虑来思量
您在哪里，或对您做的事下猜测，
而像个可怜的奴才，什么也不想，
只除您所在的那里，大家都欢乐。
　　痴情叫人这样傻，使您的这威廉，
　　不论您做什么事，他总是满心欢。

1979.11.12 译

60

Like as the waves make towards the pebbled shore,
So do our minutes hasten to their end;
Each changing place with that which goes before,
In sequent toil all forwards do contend.
Nativity, once in the main of light,
Crawls to maturity, wherewith being crown'd,
Crooked eclipses 'gainst his glory fight,
And Time that gave doth now his gift confound.
Time doth transfix the flourish set on youth,
And delves the parallels in beauty's brow;
Feeds on the rarities of Nature's truth,
And nothing stands but for his scythe to mow:
    And yet, to times in hope my verse shall stand,
    Praising thy worth, despite his cruel hand.

60

犹如波浪涌向多卵石的岸滩，
我们的分阴都急忙赶到尽头，
前推和后拥，不断地更迭变迁，
连续又绵延，奋勇挣扎个无休。
诞生，一度出现在荧荧光海里，
爬登了精壮，戴上显耀的王冠，
阴邪的晦蚀对他的辉煌施戾，
时光曾赋予，如今把所赠搅乱。
岁时戳穿了加给青春的荣茂，
在华颜额上掘出平行的沟渠，
造化的菁琼佳妙尽被它填楞，
再没东西能对它的镰刀抗拒。
　　可是我的诗有希望抵御时间，
　　赞扬你的品德，不管它多凶险。

1979.11.16 译

64

When I have seen by Time's fell hand defaced
The rich proud cost of outworn buried age;
When sometime lofty towers I see down-razed
And brass eternal slave to mortal rage;
When I have seen the hungry ocean gain
Advantage on the kingdom of the shore,
And the firm soil win of the watery main,
Increasing store with loss and loss with store;
When I have seen such interchange of state,
Or state itself confounded to decay;
Ruin hath taught me thus to ruminate, —
That Time will come and take my love away.
  This thought is as a death, which cannot choose
  But weep to have that which it fears to lose.

64

当我见凋零埋葬的前代光华，
被时间的毒手抹煞它的芳颜，
当我有时见崇楼高堡全倒塌，
不坏的黄铜摧折，给销融毁殄；
当我眼见到饿号咆哮的汪洋，
吞噬掉荡荡原野沿岸的汪畿，
又目睹坚实的地土克胜苍茫，
化损耗为丰盈，沧海凝成旱地；
当我看到这样的变迁和荣朽，
或者事态本身就堕化为销歇，
衰蚀和沉沦使我不禁要含愁，
时间会到来迫使我的恋人殒灭。
　　这忧愁仿如死亡，我不能闪避
　　迫切要追求生怕失去的东西。

1979.6.10 译

65

Since brass, nor stone, nor earth, nor boundless sea,
But sad mortality o'er-sways their power,
How with this rage shall beauty hold a plea,
Whose action is no stronger than a flower?
O, how shall summer's honey breath hold out
Against the wreckful siege of battering days,
When rocks impregnable are not so stout,
Nor gates of steel so strong, but Time decays?
O fearful meditation! where, alack,
Shall Time's best jewel from Time's chest lie hid?
Or what strong hand can hold his swift foot back?
Or who his spoil of beauty can forbid?
    O, none, unless this miracle have might,
    That in black ink my love may still shine bright.

65

既然黄铜、磐石、平陆和大海洋，
全被无常所挥运，都不免消乏，
姣丽怎能跟这股威棱相匹伉，
她的行动温存得好似一朵花？
啊，良夏蜜一般的嘘息怎么能
抵拒朝朝轰击的破灭性围攻，
当崇隆的磐石尚且不够强劲，
钢门也不牢，会被时间所穿通？
啊，可怕的沉思！在哪里，真可悲，
时间的最好瑰宝能逃避劫数？
什么壮腕能制止它疾足如飞？
谁能禁阻它掠得俊美的猎捕？
　　啊，不可能，除非这奇迹能发生，
　　我爱能在这诗中永久凝菁瑛。

1979.6.12 译

66

Tired with all these, for restful death I cry, —
As, to behold desert a beggar born,
And needy nothing trimmed in jollity,
And purest faith unhappily forsworn,
And gilded honour shamefully misplaced,
And maiden virtue rudely strumpeted,
And right perfection wrongfully disgraced,
And strength by limping sway disabled,
And art made tongue-tied by authority,
And folly, doctor like, controlling skill,
And simple truth miscalled simplicity,
And captive good attending captain ill:
    Tired with all these, from these would I be gone,
    Save that, to die, I leave my love alone.

66

厌倦了这种种，我求死亡来给我
安息，如眼见才能被命定做乞丐，
不学无术者欢乐得竟意兴疯魔，
精纯的忠信被摈弃而遭受祸害，
金冠高耸在猥琐庸碌辈的头上，
闺女的清贞被强暴的荒淫玷辱，
宏正的完美蒙受到不白的肮脏，
刚直的力量给跛子当权所荼毒，
美艺被权威镇压得箝口而结舌，
愚顽乔装得博士般控制着灵妙，
淳朴的真理竟受人诬妄为笨贼，
被俘的善良侍候着那首长宵小：
　　厌倦了这些，我但愿跟它们告别，
　　只是我若死，将离她独自，堪痛惜。

1979.8.21 译

71

No longer mourn for me when I am dead
Than you shall hear the surly sullen bell
Give warning to the world that I am fled
From this vile world, with vilest worms to dwell:
Nay, if you read this line, remember not
The hand that writ it;for I love you so,
That I in your sweet thoughts would be forgot,
If thinking on me then should make you woe.
O, if, I say, you look upon this verse
When I perhaps compounded am with clay,
Do not so much as my poor name rehearse;
But let your love even with my life decay;
    Lest the wise world should look into your moan,
    And mock you with me after I am gone.

71

我死后别为悼念我感觉哀伤，
当你听到那阴沉悲痛的钟声
告知人们说我已离浊世出亡，
去和鄙陋不堪的蛆虫共墓茔：
假使你读到这诗行，请莫记起
是谁的手写它的；因为我的爱
对你这般深，我愿你将我忘记，
若是想起了我时，会使你悲哀。
啊，我说呀，如果你看到这首诗，
当我也许和泥土已混成一片，
甚至请莫提起我可怜的名字，
让你对我的爱与我生同朽烂，
　　否则人们会看透你那声悲叹，
　　在我死后把我嘲弄你作笑谈。

1979.8.26 译

73

That time of year thou mayst in me behold
When yellow leaves, or none, or few, do hang
Upon those boughs which shake against the cold,
Bare ruin'd choirs, where late the sweet birds sang.
In me thou see'st the twilight of such day
As after sunset fadeth in the west;
Which by and by black night doth take away,
Death's second self, that seals up all in rest.
In me thou see'st the glowing of such fire,
That on the ashes of his youth doth lie,
As the death-bed whereon it must expire,
Consumed with that which it was nourish'd by,
    This thou perceivest, which makes thy love more strong,
    To love that well which thou must leave ere long.

73

那样的时节你在我身上可见到，
当黄叶，无叶，或只是枯叶两三张，
挂在树梢头，摇曳着，对寒风紧峭——
残破的歌厢，啼鸟们曾在上边唱。
在我的胸头你见到这样的暮曛
晚照的光芒已经在西天消逝掉，
这些时，黑夜，死寂的化身，它掩隐
一切于静止中，会来把余昏尽扫。
在我这心里你见到烧剩的烈焰，
在它那英华的灰烬上面作残燎，
凭着它临终快命绝时分的床毡，
耗尽了它当初丰盈炽盛的恋胶。
　　这情景你如今眼见，当能使你对
　　不久将诀别的人儿加爱而含悲。

1979.6.22

87

Farewell! thou art too dear for my possessing,
And like enough thou know'st thy estimate:
The charter of thy worth gives thee releasing;
My bonds in thee are all determinate.
For how do I hold thee but by thy granting?
And for that riches where is my deserving?
The cause of this fair gift in me is wanting,
And so my patent back again is swerving.
Thyself thou gavest, thy own worth then not knowing,
Or me, to whom thou gavest it, else mistaking;
So thy great gift, upon misprision growing,
Comes home again, on better judgement making.
    Thus have I had thee, as a dream doth flatter,
    In sleep a king, but waking no such matter.

87

告别了！你太珍贵，我不配占有你，
颇有可能你知道你自己的评价：
你人品的权状使你释去了依倚，
我对你的羁绊已变得完全解化。
不经你同意，我怎能将你来拥有？
我哪有福分来消受这一份宏富？
我自忖我欠佳这份盛礼的因由，
故而这特许就回头转归了原处。
你将你给了我，因不知你的价值，
或则对我这受惠者全没有了解；
所以这一份盛礼，你发现了错失，
经考虑，作出抉择后，回归到本界。
　　便这样，我有你正好比春宵一梦，
　　熟睡中是个君王，醒来时一场空。

1979.8.29 译

90

Then hate me when thou wilt; if ever, now;
Now, while the world is bent my deeds to cross,
Join with the spite of fortune, make me bow,
And do not drop in for an after-loss:
Ah, do not, when my heart hath scaped this sorrow,
Come in the rearward of a conquered woe;
Give not a windy night a rainy morrow,
To linger out a purposed overthrow.
If thou wilt leave me, do not leave me last,
When other petty griefs have done their spite,
But in the onset come: so shall I taste
At first the very worst of fortune's might;
  And other strains of woe, which now seem woe,
  Compared with loss of thee will not seem so.

90

那么，你要恨我就恨吧，趁如今；
现在，当世人蓄意要跟我为难，
和命运的怨毒携手，使我伛身，
别在我饱受打击后再叫难堪：
啊，别在我的心逃过了这苦恼，
跟在已被克制的悲哀后边来；
莫在风吹了一夜再来个雨朝，
延长一个存心对我的磨难灾。
如果你要离开我，别最后相弃，
当其他小悲伤都已沓来纷至，
请来个迎头突击：好叫我立即
开头就尝到命运的无比威势，
　　和哀愁的其他腔，它们眼下
　　显得凄惨，可比失掉你差得大。

1979.9.19 译

94

They that have power to hurt and will do none,
That do not do the thing they most do show,
Who, moving others, are themselves as stone,
Unmoved, cold, and to temptation slow;
They rightly do inherit heaven's graces,
And husband Nature's riches from expense;
They are the lords and owners of their faces,
Others but stewards of their excellence.
The summer's flower is to the summer sweet,
Though to itself it only live and die;
But if that flower with base infection meet,
The basest weed outbraves his dignity:
    For sweetest things turn sourest by their deeds;
    Lilies that fester smell far worse than weeds.

94

那些力能害人而不害人的人，
他们显得最能做的事不去做，
能掀动别人，自己却石头般稳，
不动摇，冷静，对引诱安定、沉着，
他们恰当地秉有上天的仁德，
善于省俭地使用造化的财富：
他们是自己面貌的主人、标格，
旁人只司理他们美质的总务。
夏日的花朵对于夏日显芳香，
对于它自己只活着以及死掉，
但假使有颗花遭到病毒摧残，
最贱的野草会使它相形不妙：
　　因为最好的东西受摧残会毁；
　　百合花腐烂远比野草更臭秽。

1979.11.20 译

97

How like a winter hath my absence been
From thee, the pleasure of the fleeting year!
What freezings have I felt, what dark days seen!
What old December's bareness everywhere!
And yet this time removed was summer's time;
The teeming autumn, big with rich increase,
Bearing the wanton burden of the prime,
Like widow'd wombs after their lords' decease:
Yet this abundant issue seem'd to me
But hope of orphans and unfather'd fruit;
For summer and his pleasures wait on thee,
And, thou away, the very birds are mute;
    Or, if they sing, 'tis with so dull a cheer,
    That leaves look pale, dreading the winter's near.

97

我跟你离别多么像隆冬的季节，
你乃是飞逝的岁华的欣荣欢乐！
我深感暗阍时日的峭寒加冰雪，
处处是残年腊月的空乏和严苛！
可是这消逝的良时乃是那盛夏，
丰裕的高秋的朗日，累累且殷殷，
满怀着荣旺季度的繁茂的结纳，
像夫君死后新寡的嫠妇怀孺婴：
可是这丰盛的收获，在我这眼中，
只能是孤儿和无父果实的希望；
因为华夏和欢乐要有你来伴同，
你不在，嘤鸣的佳禽便噤声不唱；
　　或者，它们若是鸣，会唱得恹喑哑，
　　使绿叶苍白，生怕寒冬近，行杀伐。

1979.10.6 译

98

From you have I been absent in the spring,
When proud-pied April, dressed in all his trim,
Hath put a spirit of youth in every thing,
That heavy Saturn laught and leapt with him.
Yet nor the lays of birds, nor the sweet smell
Of different flowers in odour and in hue,
Could make me any summer's story tell,
Or from their proud lap pluck them where they grew:
Nor did I wonder at the lily's white,
Nor praise the deep vermillion in the rose;
They were but sweet, but figures of delight,
Drawn after you, — you pattern of all those.
    Yet seem'd it winter still, and, you away,
    As with your shadow I with these did play.

98

在春季时节我和你不耽在一起，
当斑斓的四月装饰得锦簇花团，
将俊俏的精神充塞每一件东西，
迟钝的农神也同它跳踊和交欢。
可是鸟儿们的歌喉呖呖又嘤嘤，
和繁花的异彩奇香，都不能使我
将良夏的故事一桩桩诉叙歌吟，
也不能叫我把它们从地上采掇；
我对百合花的洁白不表示惊奇，
也不对玫瑰花的殷红称颂赞赏；
它们只是香，只是欢快的形体，
它们仿效你，你乃是模拟的榜样。
　　可是这还像是冬天，当你人不在，
　　我同这些像跟你的影儿共徘徊。

1979.10.9 译

99

The froward violet thus did I chide:
Sweet thief, whence didst thou steal thy sweet that smells,
If not from my love's breath? The purple pride
Which on thy soft cheek for complexion dwells
In my love's veins thou hast too grossly dyed.
The lily I condemned for thy hand;
And buds of marjoram had stol'n thy hair:
The roses fearfully on thorns did stand,
One blushing shame, another white despair;
A third, nor red nor white, had stol'n of both,
And to his robbery had annex'd thy breath;
But, for his theft, in pride of all his growth
A vengeful canker eat him up to death.
    More flowers I noted, yet I none could see
    But sweet or colour it had stol'n from thee.

99[1]

我对任性的紫罗兰这样斥责：
偷看贼，你从哪里偷来这温馨，
若不从我爱呼息里？这般紫色，
原在我姣人静脉中显露深缥，
染到你颊上呈艳。我怪百合花
偷你手上的凝脂，玛娇兰嫩蕊
偷你的金发：玫瑰颤巍巍含葩
在枝头，一朵羞红，一朵白悲摧；
又一朵不红不白，红白都偷窃，
再加窃取了你呼息里的芳香；
可是，为了这窃案，它傲然挺立；
一条尺蠖虫，为惩罚，把它咬伤
　　以致死。还有许多花，芬芳、光彩，
　　这些香和美都从你身上偷来。

1979.11.21 译

① 这首诗原文 15 行，现紧缩为 14 行。

102

My love is strengthen'd, though more weak in seeming;
I love not less, though less the show appear;
That love is merchandized whose rich esteeming
The owner's tongue doth publish everywhere.
Our love was new, and then but in the spring,
When I was wont to greet it with my lays;
As Philomel in summer's front doth sing,
And stops her pipe in growth of riper days:
Not that the summer is less pleasant now
Than when her mournful hymns did bush the night,
But that wild music burthens every bough,
And sweets grown common lose their dear delight.
    Therefore, like her, I sometime hold my tongue,
    Because I would not dull you with my song.

102

我的爱已经加强，虽看来似减弱；
我爱你是多了，虽然显得好像少；
那个嘴上尽宣扬的怎么样优渥，
乃是把亲爱当作做买卖的虚标。
当我们的亲爱还在开始的春天，
那时候我惯于轻讴曼唱不知休，
如夜莺在初夏的良宵酣啭连绵，
待夏深的时日便停止它的歌喉；
并不是如今夏天比初夏不可爱，
当它凄楚的悲鸣使众声都悄静，
乃是因每一枝枝头都喧聒再再，
而甜蜜太庸滥，便不能蕴蓄深情。
　　故而好像它，我有时停止了歌唱，
　　因为我不愿厌烦你，使你感心慌。

1979.10.10 译

104

To me, fair friend, you never can be old,
For as you were when first your eye I eyed,
Such seems your beauty still. Three winters' cold
Have from the forests shook three summers' pride;
Three beauteous springs to yellow autumn turn'd
In process of the seasons have I seen,
Three April perfumes in three hot Junes burn'd,
Since first I saw you fresh, which yet are green.
Ah, yet doth beauty, like a dial-hand,
Steal from his figure, and no pace perceived;
So your sweet hue, which methinks still doth stand,
Hath motion, and mine eye may be deceived:
    For fear of which, hear this, thou age unbred, —
    Ere you were born was beauty's summer dead.

104

对于我，俊友，你永远不会衰老；
好似当初我双睛凝对你双睛，
你如今还是那么风光无限好。
隆冬三度从林间摇落了青荫，
三次艳阳春色在时序更新中
我眼见尽都变成黄萎的凛秋，
四月的芳菲三回被六月焚红，
你依旧如我初见时那样英秀。
唉！美容颜，像一支日晷的时针，
悄悄在移动，不见它跨步前趋；
你这妙风姿，我信它总能站稳，
却还在轻移，我的眼光受了欺：
　　为怕那必然，听着，未至的衰年：
　　华颜的盛夏已死，在你出生前。

1979.10.16 译

106

When in the chronicle of wasted time
I see descriptions of the fairest wights,
And beauty making beautiful old rhyme
In praise of ladies dead and lovely knights,
Then, in the blazon of sweet beauty's best,
Of hand, of foot, of lip, of eye, of brow,
I see their antique pen would have exprest
Even such a beauty as you master now.
So all their praises are but prophecies
Of this our time, all you prefiguring;
And, for they looked but with divining eyes,
They had not skill enough your worth to sing:
　For we, which now behold these present days,
　Have eyes to wonder, but lack tongues to praise.

106

当我在杳远颓年的史乘记载中，
见描叙风华绝代的菁英人物时，
古艳的佳辞将天仙美女和骁勇
超伦的骑士称颂得翩翩来再世，
在那些揄扬美质的琼篇丽什里，
咏赞起手和足、眼波、眉额和朱唇，
我读到如许的生辉彩笔正把你
赋有的这各色音容笑貌来歌吟。
故而那诸般的叹赏无非在预言
我们这时代，都不过将你来影兆；
可是那夸诩运巧思，凌空驰灵感，
却欠少妙艺把你的品德来观照：
　　而我们，如今亲眼目睹着这奇观，
　　只知道惊异，可没有文采来言宣。

1979.10.21 译

107

Not mine own fears, nor the prophetic soul
Of the wide world dreaming on things to come,
Can yet the lease of my true love control,
Supposed as forfeit to a confined doom.
The mortal moon hath her eclipse endured,
And the sad augurs mock their own presage;
Incertainties now crown themselves assured,
And peace proclaims olives of endless age.
Now with the drops of this most balmy time
My love looks fresh, and Death to me subscribes,
Since, spite of him, I'll live in this poor rhyme,
While he insults o'er dull and speechless tribes:
  And thou in this shalt find thy monument,
  When tyrants' crests and tombs of brass are spent.

107

不论我衷心的忧虑，或则是梦见
这广大世界的未来万物的警敏，
都不能控制我真诚爱慕的期限，
作为一个命定的劫数的抵偿品。
人间的月亮已熬过它晦蚀之灾，
凶眚的占卜嘲讽其本身的征兆；
犹疑不能决如今已得到了安泰，
平安宣告了橄榄枝的永世高翘。
如今在这温馨的时日的安抚下，
我的爱显得新鲜，死神会承认我，
因为，不管它，我会在这里英发，
而它将会把庸滥的群氓都泯没；
　可是你就会在这里有你的旌铭，
　当暴君的钢盔和铜的墓碑消泯。

1979.10.26 译

109

O, never say that I was false of heart,
Though absence seem'd my flame to qualify.
As easy might I from myself depart
As from my soul, which in thy breast doth lie:
That is my home of love. if I have ranged,
Like him that travels I return again,
Just to the time, not with the time exchanged,
So that myself bring water for my stain.
Never believe, though in my nature reign'd
All frailties that besiege all kinds of blood,
That it could so preposterously be stain'd,
To leave for nothing all thy sum of good;
For nothing this wide universe I call,
Save thou, my Rose; in it thou art my all.

109

啊，切莫责备我曾对你负过心，
虽然别离像使我减少了炽热！
我离开自己好像向我的魂灵
告别，它原来在你的胸中耽着：
那是我的爱之家：我若漫游过，
像个旅游人，我终于回到家中，
准时按刻，没有把光阴空蹉跎，
而且带回洗污点的清水一桶。
切莫相信，虽然我性情里含有
能围攻各式血种的诸般弱点，
我能那么荒唐地沾上了污垢，
去为乌有舍弃你整个的华年；
　　因为这个大宇宙我当作虚空，
　　只有你，我的玫瑰，是我的汇总。

1979.11.21 译

111

O, for my sake do you with Fortune chide,
The guilty goddess of my harmful deeds,
That did not better for my life provide
Than public means which public manners breeds.
Thence comes it that my name receives a brand;
And almost thence my nature is subdued
To what it works in, like the dyer's hand:
Pity me, then, and wish I were renew'd;
Whilst, like a willing patient, I will drink
Potions of eisel 'gainst my strong infection;
No bitterness that I will bitter think,
Nor double penance, to correct correction.
  Pity me, then, dear friend, and I assure ye
  Even that your pity is enough to cure me.

111

啊，为了我，请斥责那命运的女神，
她是我有害行止的纵祸的老姥，
她对我的生活别无较好的温存，
只提供公众所产生的公众习俗。[①]
我不幸的名声遭受到一层玷辱，
因而使我的生性蒙上了我职业[②]
给予的委屈，像染工手上的皮肉：
可怜我请你祝愿我能得到洗雪；
像一个甘心的病人，我愿饮几服
醋汁[③]，来医治我缠身难治的沉疴；
任多么酸涩，我也决不会示畏缩，
正好比赎重罪，忏悔必须要深彻。
　　那么，可怜我，至友，我向你作保证，
　　你的怜悯已足够治愈我的重病。

1979.10.30 译

① “公众所产生的公众习俗”，指伦敦市民喜欢看戏。
② “职业”指当伶人的职业。
③ 当时人以为醋能治愈瘟疫。

116

Let me not to the marriage of true minds
Admit impediments. Love is not love
Which alters when it alteration finds,
Or bends with the remover to remove:
O, no! it is an ever-fixed mark,
That looks on tempests, and is never Shaken,
It is the star to every wandering bark,
Whose worth's unknown, although his height be taken
Love's not Time's fool, though rosy lips and cheeks
Within his bending sickle's compass come;
Love alters not with his brief hours and weeks,
But bears it out even to the edge of doom.
    If this be error and upon me proved,
    I never writ, nor no man ever loved.

116

我确认真心诚意的两心相投契
不会有故障。那感情不是真感情，
如果它遇到可以变易时会变易，
或者会随迁流移动者摇摆不定：
啊，决不会！它是个不变的定标志，
面对着狂风暴雨决不会稍摇晃；
是颗北极星，对每条飘流的船只，
它的价值无限度，尽管它高可望。
挚情并不是时间的优孟，虽朱唇
和芳容都会被它的镰刀所割断；
真情尽管只有它暂忽的短时辰，
但能坚持到命运的边缘不涣散。
　　假使我不对，且确实证明我有错，
　　我便没有写过诗，也没人真爱过。

1979.11.2 译

129

The expense of spirit in a waste of shame
Is lust in action; and till action, lust
Is perjured, murd'rous, bloody, full of blame,
Savage, extreme, rude, cruel, not to trust;
Enjoy'd no sooner but despised straight;
Past reason hunted; and no sooner had,
Past reason hated, as a swallow'd bait,
On purpose laid to make the taker mad:
Mad in pursuit, and in possession so;
Had, having, and in quest to have, extreme;
A bliss in proof, and proved, a very woe;
Before, a joy proposed; behind, a dream.
    All this the world well knows; yet none knows well
    To shun the heaven that leads men to this hell.

129

把精神耗在一片耻辱的荒原里，
乃是情欲在进行中；而在进行前，
欲情便破誓，罪辜，要凶杀，血腥气，
蛮横，趋极端，粗暴而残忍，没信践，
到美处还不久，就立即鄙弃不遑；
没情没理地追逐，但一等到了手，
便没情没理地憎恶，像钓饵进腔，
故意叫吞吃，使鱼儿发疯上了钩；
追求时疯狂，到了手还疯狂如故，
在已有，正有，追求过程中走极端；
证实时极乐，待到证实好，便愁苦；
事前，志在求欢乐；梦破时，空喜欢。
　　这一切人们都知道；可是无人知，
　　须避免那上天的生，会入地去死。

1979.11.4 译

130

My mistress' eyes are nothing like the sun;
Coral is far more red than her lips' red:
If snow be white, why then her breasts are dun;
If hairs be wires, black wires grow on her head.
I have seen roses damaskt, red and white,
But no such roses see I in her cheeks;
And in some perfumes is there more delight
Than in the breath that from my mistress reeks.
I love to hear her speak, yet well I know
That music hath a far more pleasing sound:
I grant I never saw a goddess go;
My mistress, when she walks, treads on the ground.
    And yet, by heaven, I think my love as rare
    As any she belied with false compare.

130

我情妇，她一双眼睛不像太阳，
珊瑚远远胜过她那红唇两片：
雪若算白，那她的胸膛起乌光，
假使头发是，她头上长满铁线。
我看到玫瑰花开得又白又红，
可是在她脸颊上我不见花开；
有些芳香里馥郁又好闻又浓，
远比我相好的鼻息爽心开怀。
我喜欢听她说话，可是我知道，
音乐的声音远比她语音好听；
我承认我未见女神临风飘飖，
我的相好走动时在地上跳跐行。
　　可是我起誓，我想我这个亲亲，
　　堪比哪个她歹说坏话的精灵。

1979.11.7 译

146

Poor soul, the center of my sinful earth,
Thrall to those rebel powers that thee array,
Why dost thou pine within and suffer dearth,
Painting thy outward walls so costly gay?
Why so large cost, having so short a lease,
Dost thou upon thy fading mansion spend?
Shall worms, inheritors of this excess,
Eat up thy charge? Is this thy body's end?
Then, soul, live thou upon thy servant's loss,
And let that pine to aggravate thy store;
Buy terms divine in selling hours of dross;
Within be fed, without be rich no more:
    So shalt thou feed on Death, that feeds on men,
    And Death once dead, there's no more dying then.

146

可怜的灵魂，我重戾身躯的中心，
这些盛装你的叛逆势力的奴隶，
为什么你在里边愁苦而受艰辛，
将你的外表华饰得这么样富丽？
你赁期恁短暂，为何你如此豪奢，
在你这颓谢的庄院上耗费华装？
蛆蚁，承袭这宏富余剩的继承者，
可要吞噬你的付托？你这样收场？
灵魂，你须得消耗你仆人来富裕
你自己，使它衰竭，你自己要充实，
付出渣滓的时辰，买神明的期许，
内里要饱饫，外表却毋须呈显赫：
　　你得要这样吞噬那噬人的死亡，
　　而死亡死后，便不会再出现殒丧。

1979.11.8 译

• 班·绛荪 •

Ben Jonson

(1572—1637)

Song: To Celia

〔1〕 Drink to me only with thine eyes,
And I will pledge with mine;
Or leave a kiss but in the cup,
And I'll not look for wine.
The thirst that from the soul doth rise
Doth ask a drink divine:
But might I of Jove's nectar sup,
I would not change for thine.

〔2〕 I sent thee late a rosy wreath,
Not so much honouring thee,
As giving it a hope that there
It could not withered be;
But thou thereon did'st only breathe,
And sent'st it back to me;
Since when it grows and smells, I swear,
Not of itself but thee.

致西丽霞 ①

〔1〕 将你的明眸代祝酒来眷顾，
我自会向你报青恩；
你或在杯中只留下点吻香，
我便不想把酒去斟。
从灵魂深处飞升起的渴慕，
要求有神仙的芝饮；
但即令我能饫天帝的琼浆，
也不愿换你的明樽。

〔2〕 我新近送你串玫瑰的花环，
说不上能给你光彩，
而只会使得它存一个希望，
在那里它不会萎败；
你若在花上将馨息去嘘唏，
随后且将它送回来，
我深信它自会生长吐芬芳，
不为它自己，为你开。

1983.12.20 译

① 这首英国十六七世纪名诗人班·绛荪的极著名、谱曲而歌唱了约有 380 年之久的短歌，吟咏的是一见钟情之恋。原诗两节，每节 8 行，单行每行四音步，双行每行三音步；译诗以我在本世纪 20 年代中期创制的音组来仿佛原来的音步。原诗每节第一、第五行押韵，第二、四、六、八行押韵，第三、七行押韵。译诗亦率照原诗韵法。

• 约翰·弥尔顿 •

John Milton

（1608—1674）

L'Allegro

〔1〕 Hence loathèd Melancholy,
Of Cerberus and blackest midnight born,
In Stygian cave forlorn
'Mongst horrid shapes, and shrieks, and sights unholy,
Find out some uncouth cell,
Where brooding Darkness spreads his jealous wings,
And the night-raven sings;
There under ebon shades and low-browed rocks,
As ragged as thy locks,
In dark Cimmerian desert ever dwell.

〔2〕 But come thou goddess fair and free,
In heaven yclept Euphrosyne,
And by men, heart-easing Mirth,
Whom lovely Venus at a birth
With two sister Graces more
To ivy-crownèd Bacchus bore;
Or whether (as some sager sing)
The frolic wind that breathes the spring,
Zephyr with Aurora playing,
As he met her once a-Maying,

欢 欣

〔1〕 去你的，可憎的惆怅，善恨而多愁，
那守护冥府洞口的三头的狗怪
和沉沉漆黑的午夜乃是你爹娘；
你出生的岩穴偎傍着阴河之流，
那里人迹所不至，常妖惊而鬼骇，
尽是些现形的魅魑，叫嚣的魍魉。
离我而去吧，找一个荒凉的洞窟
有黑暗在上方展放着遮天大翼，
永夜无声里只偶闻鸮鸟的悲啼，
洞中间要磊磊的顽石，狰狞可怕，
围在你周遭，历乱得像你的乱发：
到那片阴影无边下去永远蛰伏。

〔2〕 但你啊，女神，自由而佳丽，
天上称呼你优弗露西妮，
在人间以舒心的欣喜闻名，
我请你，啊，我请你来降临。
相传维纳斯一胎生你们，
(你们的父亲是疯魔的醉酒神，)
光彩和芳华，连同你自己，
三位曼妙天成的女仙姬。
另一说更新颖奇巧，据说是

There on beds of violets blue,
And fresh-blown roses washed in dew,
Filled her with thee a daughter fair,
So buxom, blithe, and debonair.

〔3〕 Haste thee nymph, and bring with thee
Jest and youthful Jollity,
Quips and Cranks, and wanton Wiles,
Nods, and Becks, and wreathèd Smiles,
Such as hang on Hebe's cheek,
And love to live in dimple sleek;
Sport that wrinkled Care derides,
And Laughter holding both his sides.

〔4〕 Come, and trip it as ye go
On the light fantastic toe,
And in thy right hand lead with thee
The mountain nymph, sweet Liberty;
And if I give thee honor due,

爱好玩耍的春飔翟飞使，
有一回艳阳天气五月——
那年青男女的美景良辰节，
恰巧在郊头遇到了小朝暾，
她正也出外觅情侣，遣欢兴，
他们俩彼此一目就成双，
青青的紫罗兰，露滴的乍放
新苞红玫瑰，铺地成锦褥，
春郊权作床，上有蓝天覆——
她一下便怀孕有了你，生成
你这般姣好，愉快，又轻盈。
〔3〕 快些来，女神仙，带领着调笑
一同来，还有那年轻的欢闹，
俏皮的打趣，和妙语双关，
点头跟招手，淘气的小麻烦，
细盼含欣的圆庞的微哂，
(他啊，天上司琼酒的女神
喜琵她脸上时常挂着有，
又总在少女［润滑的］笑涡边上浮，)
嬉戏——他调侃愁苦的忧劳，
和哗笑——他伛背，捧腹，又弯腰。
〔4〕 来吧，你来时踮起了脚尖
轻轻儿跳的舞步要新鲜；
甜蜜的自由，洒脱的女山神，
你来时要手牵手儿将她引，
并且，欣喜，我对你很敬爱，

Mirth, admit me of thy crew
To live with her and live with thee,
In unreprovèd pleasures free;
To hear the lark begin his flight,
And, singing, startle the dull night,
From his watch-tower in the skies,
Till the dappled dawn doth rise;
Then to come in spite of sorrow,
And at my window bid good morrow,
Through the sweetbriar or the vine,
Or the twisted eglantine.
〔5〕 While the cock with lively din
Scatters the rear of darkness thin,
And to the stack or the barn door,
Stoutly struts his dames before;
Oft listening how the hounds and horn
Cheerly rouse the slumbering morn,
From the side of some hoar hill,
Through the high wood echoing shrill.
Sometime walking not unseen
By hedgerow elms, on hillocks green,
Right against the eastern gate,
Where the great sun begins his state,
Robed in flames and amber light,
The clouds in thousand liveries dight;
While the plowman near at hand

所以也让我跟着在一块，
跟你也跟她，同过着欢乐
无邪的日子，悠闲而自得。
还让我，欣喜，听云雀的起飞
响彻天，把暗夜从守天的堡垒
之中震惊得仓皇逃走开，
直等到片片的朝霞升上来。
再让我，欣喜，谢绝了悲伤
稳步到窗前，对坦荡的晨光
世界，隔着荼蘼架，木香栏
或缭绕的蔷薇幔，道一声晨安。
〔5〕 这时候，鸡公在高声唱晓，
顷刻把暗夜的后卫全赶跑；
他雄视阔步，在粥粥群雌前，
走向草堆旁或谷仓的门边。
也常闻远处猎哨鸣，猎狗吠，
在霜华白遍的山前，从小睡
蒙眬里，把清晨尖声地唤醒，
一声声回响透过那寒林，
也有沿着篱树和荆圈，
我登上碧绿的平冈或山峦，
遥望着天庭把东门大敞，
门开处旭日正升朝坐帐；
他身披琥珀光辉的赤焰袍，
满朝的冠盖是彩云千万条。
这时候农夫已离了茅庐，

Whistles o'er the furrowed land,
And the milkmaid singeth blithe,
And the mower whets his scythe,
And every shepherd tells his tale
Under the hawthorn in the dale.

〔6〕 Straight mine eye hath caught new pleasures
Whilst the landscape round it measures,
Russet lawns, and fallows gray,
Where the nibbling flocks do stray;
Mountains, on whose barren breast
The labouring clouds do often rest;
Meadows trim with daisies pied,
Shallow brooks, and rivers wide;
Towers and battlements it sees
Bosom'd high in tufted trees,
Where perhaps some Beauty lies,
The cynosure of neighbouring eyes.

〔7〕 Hard by, a cottage chimney smokes
From betwixt two aged oaks,
Where Corydon and Thyrsis met
Are at their savoury dinner set
Of herbs and other country messes,
Which the neat-handed Phillis dresses;
And then in haste her bower she leaves,
With Thestylis to bind the sheaves;
Or if the earlier season lead

吹着哨，在犁过的畴头行步；
挤奶的牛娃欢声在歌唱；
刈草的樵夫磨刀于涧水旁；
牧童计数着羊儿缺少否，
在山楂树下，山南谷里头。

〔6〕 我任意纵眼向四方观看时，
随即见悦目赏心的新景致，
锈红的牧地，灰色的闲田，
羊群聚散得团团又点点；
高岩胸臆间荒芜无所有，
只常见孕雨的云雾在停留；
草坪如碧茵，成片的黄花草，
浅浅的溪流和阔阔的江涛。
更望见碉楼和雉堞，高耸
在蓬茸一碧的丛树怀抱中；
那第宅许有个绝色佳人住，
四近的芳邻都眸凝而目注。

〔7〕 左旁那小屋的烟囱在抽烟，
介在两株杈丫的古橡间，
屋里相会着两个牧羊人，
名松山，叫宝马，同进着乡村
美味——那野菜山禽真可口，
而烹调又出自金凤的手。
她匆匆关上屋门向外行，
去帮同小青把麦草扎成捆；
或者看天色睛明秋光好，

To the tann'd haycock in the mead.
〔8〕 Sometimes with secure delight
The upland hamlets will invite,
When the merry bells ring round
And the jocund rebecks sound
To many a youth and many a maid,
Dancing in the chequer'd shade;
And young and old come forth to play
On a sunshine holiday,
Till the live-long daylight fail;
Then to the spicy nut-brown ale,
With stories told of many a feat,
How fairy Mab the junkets eat;
She was pinch'd, and pull'd, she said,
And he, by friar's lantern led,
Tells how the drudging goblin sweat
To earn his cream-bowl duly set,
When in one night, are glimpse of morn,
His shadowy flail hath thresh'd the corn
That ten day-labourers could not end;
Then lies him down the lubber fiend,
And stretch'd out all the chimney's length,
Basks at the fire his hairy strength;
And crop-full out of doors he flings,

向陇上的草墩那方走一遭。

〔8〕 有时原头的村镇闹哗哗，
逗得我意兴飞腾心花放，
听欢乐的钟声不住在悠扬，
多少把弦琴一齐都响亮，
看郎领小妹，小妹跟定郎，
穿梭着树影秋阳舞蹈忙；
还有满村的孩童和老年，
也趁这佳节晴明玩一天；
直等到长日的天光已逝去，
新月出，晚风静，星斗满天宇，
便呼朋聚友同进杏花村；
各人一杯喷香的栗壳春；
跟着就谈仙说鬼讲故事，
女的说蛮宝那女仙贪糖食，
又把她拧得这里青，那里痛；
男的说他夜行迷了鬼灯笼，
又道泼克那小妖不怕累，
为求得人家备好那奶油杯，
有一回整夜使着影连枷，
死劲儿加工把谷子去打，
待赶完十多工长年的活，
那家伙才躺倒身子歇一刻，
他横着一身只烟囱那么宽，
遍体的长毛，烤火取着暖，
随后装饱了肚子慌忙跑，

Ere the first cock his matin rings.
Thus done the tales, to bed they creep
By whispering winds soon lull'd asleep.
〔9〕 Tower'd cities please us then,
And the busy hum of men,
Where throngs of knights and barons bold
In weeds of peace high triumphs hold,
With store of ladies, whose bright eyes
Rain influence, and judge the prize
Of wit or arms, while both contend
To win her grace, whom all commend.
There let Hymen oft appear
In saffron robe, with taper clear,
And pomp and feast and revelry,
With masque and antique pageantry;
Such sights as youthful poets dream
On summer eves by haunted stream.
〔10〕 Then to the well-trod stage anon,
If Jonson's learned sock be on,
Or sweetest Shakespeare, Fancy's child,
Warble his native wood-notes wild.
And ever against eating cares

当时第一声鸡鸣还未报。
这般把故事讲完去安眠，
夜风轻轻吹，一觉真甜香。

〔9〕 然后是楼台堡邸满城厢，
我们也心爱那人声热闹场，
但见得公侯郎尉聚高堂，
照眼的升平优晏锦衣裳，
神仙宝眷们善笑的明眸
微微盼，好比是数中的星斗
命定着文才武略谁中彩，
而双方又都对琼林争赛
厅上的美后——将她的青宠
当作这良宵第一等殊荣。
广开的金殿内，灯烛正辉煌，
有身穿绛袍的婚祇来登堂；
筵张着玳瑁，长乐未央夜，
化装的歌舞起，绣鞋珠履谐；
鹧鸪襦，银红褂，簪带细钗
交相映，袖里的奇香习习来：
那景象只有诗人们在春阳
五月暮暖的溪边去遐想。

〔10〕 跟着就去到粉墨场中看，
绛荪的喜剧当已在台上扮，
更或许神思飞逸的莎士比［亚］，
正演唱幽林一曲会佳期。
还有为永远不叫忧袭心，

Lap me in soft Lydian airs,
Married to immortal verse
Such as the meeting soul may pierce
In notes with many a winding bout
Of linkéd sweetness long drawn out,
With wanton heed and giddy cunning,
The melting voice through mazes running;
Untwisting all the chains that tie
The hidden soul of harmony;
That Orpheus' self may heave his head
From golden slumber on a bed.
Of heap'd Elysian flowers, and hear
Such strains as would have won the ear
Of Pluto, to have quite set free
His half-regain'd Eurydice.
These delights if thou canst give,
Mirth, with thee I mean to live.

请吹弹那钧天绝奏醉仙音，
名辞匹配着妙谱呈宫商，
纷纷的丝管，会心人自来赏，
再加连绵曲折的脆歌喉
高歌接朗唱，流啭复低讴，
声声的促迫间一阵舒徐，
直叫人听得乐极神驰去，
而桎梏和谐之灵的锁链
也早已消成了灰烬化成烟；
乐神奥斐斯，他原在仙宫
深处堆花的床上做金梦，
听到了如此妙乐也抬头，
因为这曲调，他当年若能奏，
准能使地府的冥神泊吕陀，
放他的爱妻出幽冥，渡阴河。
这样的欢愉你若能给我有，
就让我，欣喜啊，跟你作好友。

译于重庆南泉

1944.10

· 威廉·勃莱克 ·

William Blake

（1757—1827）

A Poison Tree

〔1〕 I was angry with my friend:
I told my wrath, my wrath did end.
I was angry with my foe:
I told it not, my wrath did grow.
〔2〕 And I waterd it in fears,
Night and morning with my tears;
And I sunned it with smiles,
And with soft deceitful wiles.
〔3〕 And it grew both day and night,
Till it bore an apple bright.
And my foe beheld it shine,
And he knew that it was mine,
〔4〕 And into my garden stole,
When the night had veiled the pole;
In the morning glad I see
My foe outstretchd beneath the tree.

一棵毒树

〔1〕 我跟我朋友动怒：
只敞口一表，便心气平和。
我对我敌人怀恨：
却不声不响，恨愈结愈深。

〔2〕 栽培这仇恨用惧怕，
朝晚我又把眼泪去浇它，
再用些巧笑，加上
柔媚和狡诈的伎俩作阳光。

〔3〕 仇恨尽朝生暮长，
结成了一个果子放着亮；
我那敌人一见到，
就以为是我园中的至宝。

〔4〕 等黑夜幕住了天空，
他轻轻蹑足偷进我园中：
早上我一天的大喜，
敌人在树下已倒地不起。

Introduction
from *Songs of Innocence*

〔1〕 Piping down the valleys wild,
Piping songs of pleasant glee,
On a cloud I saw a child,
And he, laughing, said to me:
"Pipe a song about a Lamb!"
So I piped with merry cheer.
"Piper, pipe that song again;"
So I piped: he wept to hear.
〔2〕 "Drop thy pipe, thy happy pipe;
Sing thy songs of happy cheer!"
So I sang the same again,
While he wept with joy to hear.
〔3〕 "Piper, sit thee down and write
In a book, that all may read."
So he vanish'd from my sight;
And I plucked a hollow reed,
〔4〕 And I made a rural pen,
And I stain'd the water clear,
And I wrote my happy songs
Every child may joy to hear.

《天真的歌》序诗

〔1〕　我吹箫漫步沿荒溪野谷间，
吹几曲飘拂心旌的小山歌；
有一个孩子在一片白云边，
一边说着话，一边笑呵呵：
“吹一曲歌唱那‘羔羊’的调儿！”
我心花怒放，把调儿吹一遍。
“吹箫的，再把那调儿来吹。”
我吹着，他听得眼泪流满了面。

〔2〕　“放下你的箫，那快乐的箫儿，
再把那快乐的歌儿唱一遍。”
于是我再把那歌儿来唱，
他听着，快乐得眼泪流满面。

〔3〕　“吹箫的，坐下来，你就把歌儿
记下来，好让大家都能念。”
那孩子说完这话就不见，
我顺手撷了一支空芦管。

〔4〕　我把芦管裁了支土制的笔，
蘸一点溪间流着的清水泉，
我把快乐的歌儿记下来。
个个孩子听了都喜欢。

初载于《新诗》第三期
1936年12月出版

• 威廉 · 华兹活斯 •

William Wordsworth

（1770—1850）

Lines

Composed a Few Miles Above Tintern Abbey, on Revisiting the Banks of the Wye during a Tour, July 13, 1798

〔1〕 Five years have past; five summers, with the length
Of five long winters! and again I hear
These waters, rolling from their mountain-springs
With a soft inland murmur. — Once again
Do I behold these steep and lofty cliffs,
That on a wild secluded scene impress
Thoughts of more deep seclusion;and connect
The landscape with the quiet of the sky.
The day is come when I again repose
Here, under this dark sycamore, and view
These plots of cottage-ground, these orchard-tufts,
Which at this season, with their unripe fruits,
Are clad in one green hue, and lose themselves
'Mid groves and copses. Once again I see

咏 怀

漫游中重访范水两岸，作于听屯寺上游数里处。

1798 年 7 月 13 日

〔1〕　五年过去了；五度炎夏，又加上
五遭悠远的隆冬！而我又听到
这些水流，从它们的山泉中滚滚
而来，鸣响着悦耳的内陆的潺湲。①
再一回我瞧见这些崇峻的巉岩，
对于这荒苍隐僻的景色，印记着
更加深沉的隐遁之思；而且将
这景色同长天的恬静连成一片。
这日子如今到来了，我又再一回
在这阴沉的大枫下边来安憩，
观赏这块块茅屋地，这些果树丛，
它们在这个季节，同未熟的果实，
披裹着一片青翠，消失在林木
和丛薮之中，跟荒苍的野景谐和
相一致。再一回我见到这些荆篱，

① 听屯寺上游若干里，河水不受涨潮影响。——原注

These hedge-rows, hardly hedge-rows, little lines
Of sportive wood run wild: these pastoral farms,
Green to the very door; and wreaths of smoke
Sent up, in silence, from among the trees!
With some uncertain notice, as might seem
Of vagrant dwellers in the houseless woods,
Or of some Hermit's cave, where by his fire
The Hermit sits alone.

〔2〕 These beauteous forms,
Through a long absence, have not been to me
As is a landscape to a blind man's eye:
But oft, in lonely rooms, and 'mid the din
Of towns and cities, I have owed to them
In hours of weariness, sensations sweet,
Felt in the blood, and felt along the heart;
And passing even into my purer mind,
With tranquil restoration: — feelings too
Of unremembered pleasure: such, perhaps,
As have no slight or trivial influence
On that best portion of a good man's life,
His little, nameless, unremembered, acts
Of kindness and of love. Nor less, I trust,
To them I may have owed another gift,
Of aspect more sublime; that blessed mood,
In which the burthen of the mystery,
In which the heavy and the weary weight

简直不像是篱列，而是一行行
嬉戏的小树行列在恣意跳踊：
这些垄苗直绿到田舍屋门前；
还有缕缕炊烟，寂静里自林间
升起！仿佛表示出，似乎在这个
没有住屋的林中，有浮浪的居民
趋止，或者有隐士的岩窟，那隐士
在炉旁独坐。

〔2〕　　　　　　这些至美的形象，
经过了长期告别，对于我却不曾
一片风景对一个盲人的眼睛：
但时时，在寂寞空房之内，在城镇
和都市的喧闹声中，于疲困之余，
我幸赖有它们给我甘醇的感觉，
在血脉里头，也沿着心腔感受到；
且沁入、渗透到我的神魂深处，
恢复我性灵的安和：遗忘的欢愉
感受：对一个恂良的人的一生
最好的部分，他的小小的、无名的、
不被记忆起来的慈和及仁爱
行为，它们说不定多少有细小
或轻微的影响。来自它们，我信，
我还许生受另一桩恩赐，那情状
要崇高得多；那个神圣的心境，

Of all this unintelligible world,
Is lightened: — that serene and blessed mood,
In which the affections gently lead us on, —
Until, the breath of this corporeal frame
And even the motion of our human blood
Almost suspended, we are laid asleep
In body, and become a living soul:
While with an eye made quiet by the power
Of harmony, and the deep power of joy,
We see into the life of things.

〔3〕 If this
Be but a vain belief, yet, oh! how oft —
In darkness and amid the many shapes
Of joyless daylight; when the fretful stir
Unprofitable, and the fever of the world,
Have hung upon the beatings of my heart —
How oft, in spirit, have I turned to thee,
O sylvan Wye! thou wanderer thro' the woods,
How often has my spirit turned to thee!

〔4〕 And now, with gleams of half-extinguished thought,
With many recognitions dim and faint,
And somewhat of a sad perplexity,
The picture of the mind revives again:
While here I stand, not only with the sense

在其中这整个无法理解的尘寰
俗世的、困人的重负被涣然消释：——
那高朗澄明的圣景，在其中至情
引我们前进，——直到这肉体的呼吸，
而甚至我们血流脉搏的行动，
也都几乎告停止，我们的肉体
投入了沉睡之中，我们变成个
活生生的灵魂：当时由于和谐
产生了力能，我们的眼睛显静光，
心头的欢快射发出深沉的能量，
我们便能洞察到事物的生命
里边去。
〔3〕 假使这只是虚幻的妄想，
可是，哎也！多么频仍啊，我在
暗夜里，无欢的日光之下众像中；
每当无益而恼人的扰攘和世间
风靡的癫狂笼罩在我的心搏上，
多么频繁地，我将心神转向你，
啊，葱茏的范水！在林木蓊菱里，
你这穿行的浪游者，多么频仍啊，
我将神魂转向你，求得到安慰！
〔4〕 而如今，怀着半寂灭的思想微光，
以及许多朦胧和幽玄的辨认，
再加上多少是一腔愁伤的困窘，
我往昔心神的图景重复苏醒了：
当我在这里站着，不仅感受到

Of present pleasure, but with pleasing thoughts
That in this moment there is life and food
For future years. And so I dare to hope,
Though changed, no doubt, from what I was when first
I came among these hills;when like a roe
I bounded o'er the mountains, by the sides
Of the deep rivers, and the lonely streams,
Wherever nature led: more like a man
Flying from something that he dreads, than one
Who sought the thing he loved. For nature then
(The coarser pleasures of my boyish days,
And their glad animal movements all gone by)
To me was all in all. — I cannot paint
What then I was. The sounding cataract
Haunted me like a passion: the tall rock,
The mountain, and the deep and gloomy wood,
Their colours and their forms, were then to me
An appetite; a feeling and a love,
That had no need of a remoter charm,
By thought supplied, nor any interest
Unborrowed from the eye. — That time is past,
And all its aching joys are now no more,
And all its dizzy raptures. Not for this
Faint I, nor mourn nor murmur; other gifts
Have followed; for such loss, I would believe,
Abundant recompence. For I have learned

眼前的欢快，而是欣然想念起
此时此刻正在为将来多少年
储存生命与粮食。我敢于如此
希望，虽然我无疑从我初来到
这些山中时，已有了变易；那时候，
像一头獐鹿，我在山崖上、沧江
深水旁、幽静的浅水滩前跳跃，
随着自然引我所到处：在阵阵
欢欣的兴奋中，与其像一个追寻
他所爱的东西的人那样，倒更像
一个逃避他所害怕的东西的人。
因为自然那时候（我童年时日
粗野的快感，它们那欢乐的动物
行动，都已经消逝）对于我是万有。——
我不能描摹我当时是什么情况。
那訇鸣的瀑布萦绕我像阵激情：
那块崇宏的巨石，那座山，那黑林
幽深而黝暗，它们的颜色和形状，
当时对于我是一桩嗜好；一泓
至情和滔天的恋爱，不需有思想
资助的较远的魔力，不用凭借于
非视觉的兴趣。——那时期已经过去，
还有它一切殷殷作痛的欢快，
和使人眩晕的狂喜，都已经没有。
我并不为此而沮丧，不悲也不怨；
有另外的天赐，对这些损失，我信

To look on nature, not as in the hour
Of thoughtless youth; but hearing oftentimes
The still, sad music of humanity,
Nor harsh nor grating, though of ample power
To chasten and subdue. And I have felt
A presence that disturbs me with the joy
Of elevated thoughts; a sense sublime
Of something far more deeply interfused,
Whose dwelling is the light of setting suns,
And the round ocean and the living air,
And the blue sky, and in the mind of man:
A motion and a spirit, that impels
All thinking things, all objects of all thought,
And rolls through all things. Therefore am I still
A lover of the meadows and the woods,
And mountains; and of all that we behold
Form this green earth;of all the mighty world
Of eye, and ear, — both what they half create,
And what perceive; well pleased to recognise
In nature and the language of the sense,
The anchor of my purest thoughts, the nurse,
The guide, the guardian of my heart, and soul
Of all my moral being.

〔5〕 Nor perchance,
If I were not thus taught, should I the more
Suffer my genial spirits to decay:

能提供充分的补偿。因为我已经
学到了对于自然的精真的照鉴，
不像在没有深思的青年时那样；
而是往往能听到人道的静谧
且哀怜的音乐，不严酷，也不轧轹，
可是有充分的力量来涤净缓和。
我且又感到有一座宏灵打动我
生高华情思的欢快：深深混融成
那么个崇高之感，它的所在是
落日的霞辉，圆周冥渺的大海洋，
和活跃的大气，蓝蓝荡荡，还有
在人的心灵神府之中：是一阵
运行和一宗精魂，它激动一切
能思想的群生，一切思想的群像，
贯通万有的心腔。故而我仍然是
青芜、丛林和山丘的衷心爱好者；
我爱这青青土地上能见的一切：
这眼睛、耳朵所见所闻的浩浩
世界，它们既然是觉察到，一半也
加以创造；我乐于在自然境界里
和感官语言之中，认识到我纯洁
情思的船锚，我这心灵的保姆、
向导、保护人，和我道根上的灵机。

〔5〕 假使我不是这样受自然的熏陶，
我也不会容我的温良的性灵
去颓唐堕毁；因为你同我在一起，

For thou art with me here upon the banks
Of this fair river; thou my dearest Friend,
My dear, dear Friend;and in thy voice I catch
The language of my former heart, and read
My former pleasures in the shooting lights
Of thy wild eyes. Oh! yet a little while
May I behold in thee what I was once,
My dear, dear Sister! and this prayer I make,
Knowing that Nature never did betray
The heart that loved her; 'tis her privilege,
Through all the years of this our life, to lead
From joy to joy: for she can so inform
The mind that is within us, so impress
With quietness and beauty, and so feed
With lofty thoughts, that neither evil tongues,
Rash judgments, nor the sneers of selfish men,
Nor greetings where no kindness is, nor all
The dreary intercourse of daily life,
Shall e'er prevail against us, or disturb
Our cheerful faith, that all which we behold
Is full of blessings. Therefore let the moon
Shine on thee in thy solitary walk;
And let the misty mountain-winds be free
To blow against thee: and, in after years,
When these wild ecstasies shall be matured
Into a sober pleasure; when thy mind

在这里，在这条芳川的岸边；你啊，
我的至爱的好友，我的亲爱的、
亲爱的好友，在你这声音里边，
我重新听到我往昔心中的言语，
在你这野逸的眼睛射光里我又
见到我过去的欢快。啊！稍一会
我在你身上见到我过去的自己，
我的亲爱的、亲爱的妹子！我发出
这祷辞，深知自然从不会背弃
爱她的那颗心；这乃是她的殊恩
经由我们生命的一切年代里，
引领我们从欢乐到欢乐：因为
她能这么对我们的内心施教，
这么以安静和美丽印记在我们
心上，使我们的神志充满峨思
伟想，乃至既没有恶意的唇舌，
鲁莽的判断，也没有自私之辈
所发的讥诮，也没有冷漠的敬礼，
也没有日常生活中一应的惨淡
交往，将胜过我们，或扰乱我们
欢愉的信仰，它确认我们一切
所见是充满了天恩。故而让月亮
在你孤独行走时照临你身上；
让夹雾的山风阵阵吹拂你：而且在
日后年代里，当这些如狂的欣喜
将会成熟为沉着的欢愉，你的心

Shall be a mansion for all lovely forms,
Thy memory be as a dwelling-place
For all sweet sounds and harmonies; oh! then,
If solitude, or fear, or pain, or grief,
Should be thy portion, with what healing thoughts
Of tender joy wilt thou remember me,
And these my exhortations! Nor, perchance —
If I should be where I no more can hear
Thy voice, nor catch from thy wild eyes these gleams
Of past existence — wilt thou then forget
That on the banks of this delightful stream
We stood together; and that I, so long
A worshipper of Nature, hither came
Unwearied in that service; rather say
With warmer love — oh! with far deeper zeal
Of holier love. Nor wilt thou then forget,
That after many wanderings, many years
Of absence, these steep woods and lofty cliffs,
And this green pastoral landscape, were to me
More dear, both for themselves and for thy sake!

会变作容纳众美好形象的殿堂，
你的记忆将是荟萃了众悦耳
声音与和谐的总汇；啊！那时节，
假使孤独，或恐惧，或痛苦，或悲哀，
将是你的份，你将比起我以及我
这些勤勉，以深情的欢快的多么
安慰的情思！也许，假使我将会
在那里听不到你的声音，也不能
从你野逸的眼中瞥见到这些
过去生涯的闪光，那时节你也
不会忘记我们曾一同在这条
可喜的河流旁站着；而我，一直是
自然的崇拜者，来到这里依然是
心香一瓣，虔诚不稍减：应当说，
有更加温存的宝爱，啊，更有其
神圣宝爱的更深的赤诚。你且也
不会忘记掉，经过了多次的漫游，
告别了好多年，这些峭拔的林木，
崇峻的巉岩以及这葱茏的田园
景色，对于我是显得更加亲爱，
为它们自己，也为了你的缘故！

1979 年 12 月 22 日

冬至夜（阴历己未年十一月初四）译竟。

Strange Fits of Passion Have I Known[①]

〔1〕 Strange fits of passion have I known:
And I will dare to tell,
But in the Lover's ear alone,
What once to me befell.

〔2〕 When she I loved looked every day
Fresh as a rose in June,
I to her cottage bent my way,
Beneath an evening moon.

〔3〕 Upon the moon I fixed my eye,
All over the wide lea;
With quickening pace my horse drew nigh
Those paths so dear to me.

① This and the four following pieces are often grouped by editors as the "Lucy poems". —Editor

我有过奇异的激情心境①

〔1〕　　我有过奇异的激情心境；
　　我敢于将它来诉说，
但只能讲给过来人聆听，
　　我受过怎样的摧挫。

〔2〕　　当我所爱的她一天天显得像
　　六月里一朵玫瑰，
我向她的小屋，迎对着月亮
　　前去，在马上揽辔。

〔3〕　　我眼睛注视着西天的月轮，
　　前面是一片青草地；
我的马加快了步蹄去行近
　　小径道，那对我很亲昵。

① 这首诗和以下四首常被人编在一起，冠以“露珊”，作为标题。——编者

〔4〕 And now we reached the orchard-plot;
And, as we climbed the hill,
The sinking moon to Lucy's cot
Came near, and nearer still.

〔5〕 In one of those sweet dreams I slept,
Kind Nature's gentlest boon!
And all the while my eyes I kept
On the descending moon.

〔6〕 My horse moved on; hoof after hoof
He raised, and never stopped:
When down behind the cottage roof,
At once, the bright moon dropped.

〔7〕 What fond and wayward thoughts will slide
Into a Lover's head!
"O mercy!" to myself I cried,
"If Lucy should be dead!"

〔4〕　现在我们已到了果园地；
　　当我们爬过小山脊，
西沉的月亮越来越降低
　　到露珊小屋的西顶壁。

〔5〕　我正在一场好梦里沉睡，
　　慈祥的造化赐深恩！
那整段时间里我凝眸面对
　　那明月，她正在西沉。

〔6〕　我的马在行进，一蹄又一蹄
　　跨着步，时刻不曾停；
这时节，落入她小屋顶后壁，
　　顷刻间，月亮忽消暝。

〔7〕　多么不经和痴爱的想法
　　会进入情人的头脑！
“天啊！”我对自己发惊诧，
　　“露珊若是已死掉！”

1980.4.18 译

She Dwelt Among the Untrodden Ways

〔1〕 She dwelt among the untrodden ways
Beside the springs of Dove,
A Maid whom there were none to praise
And very few to love:

〔2〕 A violet by a mossy stone
Half hidden from the eye!
— Fair as a star, when only one
Is shining in the sky.

〔3〕 She lived unknown,and few could know
When Lucy ceased to be;
But she is in her grave, and, oh,
The difference to me!

她住在人迹不到的所在

〔1〕　她住在人迹不到的所在，
　　在鸽子清泉近旁；
一个小姑娘，很少人疼爱，
　　没有人将她夸奖。

〔2〕　如青苔石边一棵紫罗兰，
　　给遮得一半瞧不见！
——美得像颗星，正当它闪闪
　　在天上独自显现。

〔3〕　她活在世上无人知，去后
　　很少人知道已殒逝；
但她已成了墓中人，唉啾！
　　对我是多大的丧失！

Three Years She Grew in Sun and Shower

〔1〕 Three years she grew in sun and shower,
Then Nature said, "A lovelier flower
On earth was never sown;
This Child I to myself will take;
She shall be mine, and I will make
A Lady of my own.

〔2〕 "Myself will to my darling be
Both law and impulse: and with me
The Girl, in rock and plain,
In earth and heaven, in glade and bower,
Shall feel an overseeing power
To kindle or restrain.

〔3〕 "She shall be sportive as the fawn
That wild with glee across the lawn
Or up the mountain springs;
And hers shall be the breathing balm,
And hers the silence and the calm
Of mute insensate things.

在阳光、淋雨中，三年她成长

〔1〕 在阳光、淋雨中，三年她成长；
于是造化说："从来这地上
未栽过更好的一株花；
这孩子要归我自己所占有；
她将是我的儿，我要把她收，
抚养她做我的小娇娃。

〔2〕 "我自己对我这爱女将既是
法令又冲劲：这姑娘，我一直
对于她在野外、山中，
在人间、天上，荫蔽、空旷处，
都会发一阵阵督促的力量，
去加以发挥或遥控。

〔3〕 "她将会像那小鹿般好戏耍，
蹦过草坪，把欢乐的野来撒，
或则是跳踊着上山坡；
她又将如涂了温馨的香油，
或则跟无知的木石相侔，
悄静得冥无声，尽默默。

〔4〕 “The floating clouds their state shall lend
To her; for her the willow bend;
Nor shall she fail to see
Even in the motions of the Storm
Grace that shall mould the Maiden’s form
By silent sympathy.

〔5〕 “The stars of midnight shall be dear
To her; and she shall lean her ear
In many a secret place
Where rivulets dance their wayward round,
And beauty born of murmuring sound
Shall pass into her face.

〔6〕 “And vital feelings of delight
Shall rear her form to stately height,
Her virgin bosom swell;
Such thoughts to Lucy I will give
While she and I together live
Here in this happy dell.”

〔7〕 Thus Nature spake — the work was done —
How soon my Lucy’s race was run!
She died, and left to me
This heath, this calm, and quiet scene;
The memory of what has been,
And never more will be.

〔4〕 “浮云将会把它们的悠悠
赋与她；为她弯腰有垂柳；
她也不会不感受到
在风云变幻中就寓有行动，
那优美能塑成处女的形容，
经由无声的同感交。

〔5〕 “午夜的星辰将会对她呈
珍异；而她将倾耳去谛听
在许多幽僻的场所，
溪流们不经地琤瑽起舞，
而盈盈流水把清音轻吐，
那秀美会进入她眼波。[①]

〔6〕 “且欢快之情的极度感应，
会将她培育得挺秀婷婷，
使她的胸脯丰满；
我将叫露珊怀这样的思想，
当她随同我一起在成长，
在这幽谷里边。”

〔7〕 造化这般说，就这般做到——
多么快露珊的行程已跑好！
她死了，留给我这片
荒地，这平静这宁谧的景色：
回忆起这段往事的故辙，
我永远不会得重见。

---

① 眼波，原文为“面部”。

A Slumber Did My Spirit Seal

〔1〕 A slumber did my spirit seal;
I had no human fears:
She Seemed a thing that could not feel
The touch of earthly years.

〔2〕 No motion has she now, no force;
She neither hears nor sees;
Rolled round in earth's diurnal course,
With rocks, and stones, and trees.

一阵安眠封闭我的神魂

〔1〕　一阵安眠封闭我的神魂；
　　我不复有人间的惊恐：
她像是一件灵物，不再能
　　感觉到岁月的来去。

〔2〕　她如今没有了行动和力气；
　　她不再能耳闻和目见；
在大地的周时轮转间，跟岩壁
　　石块和林木同滚旋！

1980.4.15 译毕

I Travelled Among Unknown Men

〔1〕 I traveled among unknown men,
In lands beyond the sea;
Nor, England! did I know till then
What love I bore to thee.

〔2〕 'Tis past, that melancholy dream!
Nor will I quit thy shore
A second time; for still I seem
To love thee more and more.

〔3〕 Among thy mountains did I feel
The joy of my desire;
And she I cherished turned her wheel
Beside an English fire.

〔4〕 Thy mornings showed, thy nights concealed
The bowers where Lucy played;
And thine too is the last green field
That Lucy's eyes surveyed.

我在海外的异邦、陌生人
中间旅游着作客

〔1〕 我在海外的异邦、陌生人
　　中间旅游着作客；
英伦！我到了那时才认真
　　感觉爱你爱得多深刻。

〔2〕 那个忧郁的魂梦已过去！
　　我再也不会二次
离开你，因为我幽深的衷曲
　　日益对于你情驰。

〔3〕 在你的山岳河川间我感眷
　　我衷心所愿的欢乐；
我所珍爱的意中人在旋转
　　她的纺轮于炉火侧。

〔4〕 你的晨昏显焕和掩隐着
　　露珊戏耍过的闺房；
你的绿油油田苗曾获得
　　露珊的秀眼施春光。

The Rainbow

My heart leaps up when I behold
A rainbow in the sky:
So was it when my life began;
So is it now I am a man;
So be it when I shall grow old,
    Or let me die!
The child is father of the Man;
And I could with my days to be
Bound each to each with natural piety.

虹

我的心顿时会欢腾跳跃，
当我见天边挂一条彩虹：
在过去我生之初是这样；
如今我成长壮盛也这样；
将来活到老，我还得这样，
　　否则不如让我死！
孩提是生育成人的父亲；
而我但愿我毕生的日子，
自然地虔诚，始终相缘因。

By the Sea

It is a beauteous evening, calm and free;
The holy time is quiet as a nun
Breathless with adoration; the broad sun
Is sinking down in its tranquillity;

The gentleness of heaven is on the Sea:
Listen! the mighty being is awake,
And doth with his eternal motion make
A sound like thunder — everlastingly.

卡来海滩上的晚照中[①]

这是个绚美的傍晚，宁静而高旷，
这神圣的时分怡谧得像个尼姑
屏息着在礼赞崇奉，闳浑的金朱
落日在一片绥和中沉沉地下降；

天宇的温存覆盖在苍茫的大海上：
听啊！这清醒的运载万物的神灵，
以他这永恒不息的行动在轰鸣，
声声如雷震——万世不绝的喧响。

① 这首商乃诗蕴蓄着浓郁的宗教情思；“亲爱的孩子！（亲爱的）小姑娘！”是对诗人的小女喀式琳（Catherine）的称谓。阜兹活斯的思想把基督教的上帝与泛神论（Pantheism）的神灵合而为一：世间一切大自然景物都是他的自然神的表现，一切大自然景物是 nature，自然神是 Nature，他主宰他们。而这个自然神又与他的基督教的上帝切合无间，化而为一。根据基督教的教义，童稚的幼儿、小女天真烂漫，不受世间习俗、社会计谋的污染，其灵魂与上帝的圣灵相通；诗人的自然神神灵亦与幼儿、小女的灵魂相通，这神灵对于善良的成人的灵明亦起到教育、提高、纯化的作用。这首商乃诗作于 1802 年，在卡来海滩上；十年后的 6 月 4 日他这小女辞世而去，他另有一首商乃诗悼念她。卡来海滩濒临英吉利海峡（the English channel），隔海隐约可望多弗（Dover）港迤北的白垩岩，相距 20 英里。亚伯拉罕（Abraham）为希伯来（Hebrew）民族的神圣始祖，见《圣经 · 创世记》第 11 至 25 章；传说他的裔孙子民徙居各地，遂有各地不同的民族。

Dear child! dear girl! that walkest with me here,
If thou appear untouch'd by solemn thought
Thy narture is not therefore less divine.

Thou liest in Abraham's bosom all the year,
And worshipp'st at the Temple's inner shrine,
God being with thee when we know it not.

亲爱的孩子！姑娘！你和我在这里
走着，你若是未曾被崇敬的神思
所影响，你这份天性并不欠神圣：

你终年在亚伯拉罕的怀中偎依；
你是在庙宇最深的殿堂上承命，
上帝正和你在一起，我们却不知。

1980.9.25 译

I Wandered Lonely As a Cloud

〔1〕 I wandered lonely as a cloud
That floats on high o'er vales and hills,
When all at once I saw a crowd,
A host, of golden daffodils;
Beside the lake, beneath the trees,
Fluttering and dancing in the breeze.

〔2〕 Continuous as the stars that shine
And twinkle on the milky way,
They stretched in never-ending line
Along the margin of a bay:
Ten thousand saw I at a glance,
Tossing their heads in sprightly dance.

水 仙

〔1〕 我独自漫步，像一朵白云
高高飘浮在山巅和谷上，
突然我望见好多的一群，
一大丛水仙，闪闪发金光，
在湖水附近，在疏树下面，
摇摆在风中，晃舞姿跹跹。

〔2〕 连绵不绝地光耀，像众星
在天河里头不断地闪烁，
它们一大片伸展得无尽
又无穷，沿着港湾的平坡：
我一眼望去，总有上万株
摇动它们的花梢在曼舞。

〔3〕 The waves beside them danced; but they
Out-did the sparkling waves in glee:
A poet could not but be gay,
In such a jocund company:
I gazed — and gazed — but little thought
what wealth the show to me had brought:

〔4〕 For oft, when on my couch I lie
In vacant or in pensive mood,
They flash upon that inward eye
Which is the bliss of solitude;
And then my heart with pleasure fills,
And dances with the daffodils.

〔3〕　它们近旁的湖波在舞蹈，
但它们比闪闪澄波更上劲：
一位诗人跟这丛欢伴逍遥
在一起，不能不感到欢欣！
我凝视——复凝视，不曾想到
这奇观带给我几多财宝；

〔4〕　因往往，当我偃卧在床头，
无忧无虑或默默沉思时，
它们跃上我内心的灵眸，
那真是幽静之中的福祉；
那时我的心便充满欢忭，
跟这片水仙共起舞联翩。

1980.4.10 译

Ode

Intimations of Immortality
from Recollections of Early Childhood

1

There was a time when meadow, grove and stream,
The earth, and every common sight,
    To me did seem
  Apparelled in celestial light,
The glory and the freshness of a dream.
It is not now as it hath been of yore; —
  Turn wheresoe'er I may,
    By night or day,
The things which I have seen I now can see no more.

颂赞

孩提时代早期回忆中的永生之暗示

1

曾经有一时，青芜、疏林和流水，
　　大地及任何寻常的景物，
　　　　对于我简直会
　　焕耀出上界的辉煌彩色，
　　有如梦幻般的鲜妍而宏亮。
现在可不是那样了，不再如往常：——
　　不论我转向哪一方，
　　　　向暗夜，对天光，
我往昔见到的东西，如今已不复在望。

2

The Rainbow comes and goes,
And lovely is the Rose,
The Moon doth with delight
Look round her when the heavens are bare,
Waters on a starry night
Are beautiful and fair;
The sunshine is a glorious birth;
But yet I know, where'er l go,
That there hath past away a glory from the earth.

2

彩虹来过了又消逝；

玫瑰开放得嫣红姹紫；

月亮欢欣地向四周环顾，

碧天宇空清澄净；

繁星闪烁的夜幕

覆罩着水波，清冥里透露着幽明；

朝阳是个显赫的新生；

可是我知道，不论到何方，

大地上我不再能见到光华灿烂的文章。

3

Now, while the birds thus sing a joyous song,
And while the young lambs bound
As to the tabor's sound,
To me alone there came a thought of grief:
A timely utterance gave that thought relief,
And I again am strong:
The cataracts blow their trumpets from the steep;
No more shall grief of mine the season wrong;
I hear the Echoes through the mountains throng,
The Winds come to me from the fields of sleep,
And all the earth is gay;
Land and sea
Give themselves up to jollity,
And with the heart of May
Doth every Beast keep holiday; —
Thou Child of Joy,
Shout round me, let me hear thy shouts, thou happy
Shepherd-boy!

3

如今，当鸟儿这么样欢声唱着歌，
　　当小羊儿们频频跳跃着，
　　像在对声声的小鼓相应和，
　　忽然有一阵忧思来袭我：
　　及时地宣泄我将它排遣掉，
　　我心头恢复了坚强和爽朗：
瀑布在高岩顶上欢啸着长鸣；
莫让我的哀情晦损这良辰美景；
我听到回响一阵阵穿过这群峦；
　　　　和风从休眠的田间
　　　　　　吹来施抚慰；
　　　　整个大地在嘻笑；
　　　　　　平陆和大海，
　　　　一片的采烈兴高；
　　　　　　每一个生灵
　　跟着五月天的心
　　　　尽情乐陶陶；——
你啊，欢乐的孩儿，你在我周围欢啸，
让我听你叫喊吧，快乐的牧羊年少！

4

Ye blessed Creatures, I have heard the call
    Ye to each other make; I see
The heavens laugh with you in your jubilee;
    My heart is at your festival,
        My head hath its coronal,
The fulness of your bliss, I feel — I feel it all.
        Oh evil day! if I were sullen
        While Earth herself is adorning,
            This sweet May-morning,
        And the Children are culling
            On every side,
        In a thousand valleys far and wide,
        Fresh flowers; while the sun shines warm,
And the Babe leaps up on his Mother's arm: —
        I hear, I hear, with joy I hear!
        — But there's a Tree, of many, one,
A single Field which I have looked upon,
Both of them speak of something that is gone:
    The Pansy at my feet
    Doth the same tale repeat:
Whither is fled the visionary gleam?
Where is it now, the glory and the dream?

4

受上天福佑的生灵们，我听见你们
彼此间的欢声呼唤；
我瞧见青天在你们喜庆中
和你们一同哗笑；
我的心和你们在一道；
我头顶戴着花冠；
你们的极乐我感觉——完全感觉到。
啊，那样才可恨！
倘使我衷心乖戾而忧愁，
当大地本身在装点
这可爱的清晨五月天，
当无数三三两两的孩子们
在这青嶂翠谷间，
左右前后，
到处采撷着鲜艳的花朵；
当阳光普照得暖融融，
那婴儿在他母亲臂腕上腾踊：
——但那儿有棵树，
许多棵中间有一棵，
我见过，还有那么一块田，
这二者都告我，
有什么东西已翳湮：
我这脚旁的三色堇
也将同样的消息来透露，
那一抹梦幻的闪光已消亡到哪里？
那荣华，那幻梦，如今到了哪里去？

5

Our birth is but a sleep and a forgetting:
The Soul that rises with us, our life's Star,
    Hath had elsewhere its setting,
        And cometh from afar:
    Not in entire forgetfulness,
    And not in utter nakedness,
But trailing clouds of glory do we come
    From God, who is our home:
Heaven lies about us in our infancy!
Shades of the prison-house begin to close
    Upon the growing Boy,
But He beholds the light, and whence it flows,
    He sees it in his joy;
The Youth, who daily farther from the east
    Must travel, still is Nature's Priest,
    And by the vision splendid
    Is on his way attended;
At length the Man perceives it die away,
And fade into the light of common day.

5

我们的诞生只是阵睡眠，只是阵遗忘，
跟我们同升的灵魂，我们生命的星辰，
原来在别处有它的背景，
它的来处，杳远得很：
既不是完全遗忘掉，
也并非精赤条条，
而是脚踩着辉煌的云彩，
我们从上帝那儿来——
他乃是我们的老家：
当婴稚时期，天堂在我们周遭！
囚牢的阴影开始笼罩
那渐渐长大的孩子，
可是他还见到那神光，它从何处来，
他在欢乐中见到它；
那青年，一天天要远离东方
向西行，依旧是自然的牧师，
在他途程上
有那闪耀的异像相随护；
最后那成人眼见它散失消亡，
化成日常生活中平淡的天光。

6

Earth fills her lap with pleasures of her own;
Yearnings she hath in her own natural kind,
And, even with something of a Mother's mind,
    And no unworthy aim,
    The homely Nurse doth all she can
To make her Foster-child, her Inmate Man,
    Forget the glories he hath known,
And that imperial palace whence he came.

6

大地在她怀抱中充盈着她本身的乐事；
她有她独特的自然景慕和神态，
　　　　存在个慈母的胸怀，
　　　　目的也无可非议；
　　这亲爱的保姆竭尽她所能，
使她的养子，她的寄居者，我们人，
　　忘却他所知道的那光灿，
以及他那所从来的崇弘的宫殿。

7

Behold the Child among his new-born blisses,
A six years' Darling of a pigmy size!
See, where 'mid work of his own hand he lies,
Fretted by sallies of his mother's kisses,
With light upon him from his father's eyes!
See, at his feet, some little plan or chart,
Some fragment from his dream of human life,
Shaped by himself with newly-learned art;
        A wedding or a festival,
        A mourning or a funeral;
                And this hath now his heart,
        And unto this he frames his song:
                Then will he fit his tongue
To dialogues of business, love, or strife;
        But it will not be long
        Ere this be thrown aside,
        And with new joy and pride,
The little Actor cons another part;
Filling from time to time his "humorous stage"
With all the Persons, down to palsied Age,
That Life brings with her in her equipage;
        As if his whole vocation
        Were endless imitation.

7

瞧这个孩子，在他这新生的盛福中，
一个六岁的宝贝，玲珑可爱的小家伙！
瞧吧，处在他自己手创的事业中，
时刻被他母亲的亲吻所打扰，
他父亲祥和的目光对他频映照！
瞧吧，他脚旁有个什么小计划或草图，
从他对于人生的梦里所得来的片段，
是由他所形成，经由他新学来的技巧；
　　　　一个庆典或婚礼，
　　　　一场哀悼或葬仪；
　　一会儿这件事在他心上，
　　他当即对此把歌儿来唱：
　　然后他将口齿适应好，
怎样做买卖，谈爱情，假装在争吵；
　　　　可是不会太久长，
　　这些个也会给扔在一旁，
　　　　用新生的欢乐和骄傲，
　　我们这小角色又来另一套；
　　时刻给搬上他“滑稽的舞台”，
　　有各个时期的人物，从少小
　　　　　　一直到衰老——
包含着人生所带来的整个卤簿；
　　　　仿佛他全部的任务
　　　　乃是没穷尽的仿效。

8

Thou, whose exterior semblance doth belie
    Thy soul's immensity;
Thou best Philosopher, who yet dost keep
Thy heritage, thou Eye among the blind,
That, deaf and silent, read'st the eternal deep,
Haunted for ever by the eternal mind, —
    Mighty Prophet ! Seer blest!
    On whom those truths do rest,
Which we are toiling all our lives to find,
In darkness lost, the darkness of the grave;
Thou, over whom thy Immortality.
Broods like the Day, a Master o'er a Slave,
A Presence which is not to be put by;
Thou little Child, yet glorious in the might
Of heaven-born freedom on thy being's height,
Why with such earnest pains dost thou provoke

8

你啊，你娇小的外形
跟你灵魂的深宏不相称；
你是最明智的英哲，你精魂深处
保持着上天赋予你的灵爽，
你是群盲之中的慧眼人，
耳聋而沉默，但洞察无穷的深奥，
永远被那无穷的神智所萦绕——
大力的先知！天佑的睿哲！
你一身承领了洪钧与大块的真实。
我们毕生劳瘁着去追寻探索，
而终于在坟墓的憧憧黑影里迷惘
而不知其所在；
你啊，你的永生
覆蔽着你的天性，
如白日之君临世界，如领主之君临奴婢，
——那是个推移不掉的存在；
坟墓对于你
只是张寂寞的眠床，
那儿，觉不到、看不见白日和天光，
那儿，我们稽迟着，在思念，在等待；
你啊，稚幼的儿孩，
当你的天赋自由正值红日丽中天，
煌煌然赫奕无边，
这时节，你为何费尽了心机，

The years to bring the inevitable yoke,
Thus blindly with thy blessedness at strife?
Full soon thy Soul shall have her earthly freight,
And custom lie upon thee with a weight,
Heavy as frost, and deep almost as life!

促使奄忽的年华速速地带来
那终于将无可避免的羁绊束缚，
这么样跟你的天赐福泽相抵触？
倏忽间你那灵魂将驮上它尘世的负荷，
习俗将压上你肩头一副重担，
风霜一般的沉重，人生似的艰难困苦！

9

O joy! that in our embers
Is something that doth live,
That nature yet remembers
What was so fugitive!
The thought of our past years in me doth breed
Perpetual benediction: not indeed
For that which is most worthy to be blest;
Delight and liberty, the simple creed
Of Childhood, whether busy or at rest,
With new-fledged hope still fluttering in his breast: —
Not for these I raise
The song of thanks and praise;
But for those obstinate questionings
Of sense and outward things,
Fallings from us, vanishings;
Blank misgivings of a Creature
Moving about in worlds not realised,
High instincts before which our mortal Nature
Did tremble like a guilty Thing surprised:

9

啊，真可喜！在我们的余烬里，
还留得有一些不灭的生机，
我们的天性还依稀未忘记
过去的、那么会消逝的东西！
回忆起我们既往的岁月时，我心中
当即产生了对天恩的感祷无穷：
倒不是为那些最该祝颂的种种——
欢欣和自由，孩提期单纯的信条，
不论在忙时或在安静之中，
以及新生的希望在他胸中展翅：——
        不是为这些，
    我高唱这感谢和赞美的歌诗，
    而是为那些执拗的、对感觉
    和外界事物所兴起的疑问，
    我们的〔意识和知觉的〕陨越，
〔耳闻、目睹及感受的〕消亡晦湮，
    在〔飘飘遐想〕世界中〔溟涬
    消遥〕的一个人的惘然的疑虑，
高华的天性（在它们之前，我们
凡俗的习性便像个罪恶的东西
    受了惊那样战栗频频）：

But for those first affections,
Those shadowy recollections,
Which, be they what they may,
Are yet the fountain light of all our day,
Are yet a master light of all our seeing;
Uphold us, cherish, and have power to make
Our noisy years seem moments in the being
Of the eternal Silence: truths that wake,
To perish never;
Which neither listlessness, nor mad endeavour,
Nor Man nor Boy,
Not all that is at enmity with joy,
Can utterly abolish or destroy!
Hence in a season of calm weather
Though inland far we be,
Our Souls have sight of that immortal sea
Which brought us hither,
Can in a moment travel thither,
And see the Children sport upon the shore,
And hear the mighty waters rolling evermore.

而是为那些最初的感情，
　　那些朦胧的回忆，它们
　　不管怎么样［迷离惝悦］，
毕竟是我们一生中光明的泉源，
毕竟是我们洞照一切的主光，
　　它们支撑、珍惜、爱抚我们，
而且力能使我们喧嚷的岁月
变得像那无穷的静谧中的时刻：
　　　它们是苏醒的真实，
　　　永远不会再亡失：
它们既不会被无精打采，
　　　也不会被疯狂的努力，
　　　更不会给成人或童孩，
以及跟欢乐相敌对的一切，
所完全废除或毁灭！
　　所以，当一个风和日丽的良辰，
　　我们虽已深入到内地，
我们的灵魂可还望得见将我们
　　载送到这里来的永生之海，
　　顷刻间我们便能向这大海趱行，
而瞧见孩子们在海滨游戏，
听碧海訇訇，看洪涛滚滚。

10

Then sing, ye Birds, sing, sing a joyous song!
　　And let the young Lambs bound
　　As to the tabor's sound!
We in thought will join your throng,
　　Ye that pipe and ye that play,
　　Ye that through your hearts to-day
　　Feel the gladness of the May!
What though the radiance which was once so bright
Be now for ever taken from my sight,
　　Though nothing can bring back the hour
Of splendour in the grass,of glory in the flower;
　　We will grieve not, rather find
　　Strength in what remains behind;
　　In the primal sympathy
　　Which having been must ever be;
　　In the soothing thoughts that spring
　　Out of human suffering;
　　In the faith that looks through death,
In years that bring the philosophic mind.

10

那么，唱啊，鸟儿，唱吧，唱一支欢乐之歌！
　　让小羊儿们跳跃着，
　　像在应和一声声的小鼓！
我们将在思想上加入你们成一伙，
　　你们鸣奏歌吹，跳踉戏耍的群生，
　　你们衷心感受到如今
　　这艳阳五月天的喜悦欢欣！
一度曾经是那么灿烂的光芒，
对于我，如今已永远不复在望；
　　我再也不能重见到好时光，
〔目睹儿时的〕芳草萋萋照眼明，
　　　鲜花灼灼吐辉煌：
〔不过，〕那〔虽已无可奈何，但〕又有何妨？
　　我们将不去叹逝而伤痛悲愁，
　　却要在留存的情事中去寻求
　　　支撑的力量；
　　去寻求那些既然已经有、
　　而将永远不会消失的人与人之间的同情；
　　去寻求那些对于人生的苦难
　　所起的哀怜恻隐；
　　去寻求那望穿死亡的信念——
　　坚信多年〔地受自然的鞠育，〕
终于会到达澄明莹澈的睿智。

11

And O, ye Fountains, Meadows, Hills, and Groves,
Forebode not any severing of our loves!
Yet in my heart of hearts I feel your might;
I only have relinquished one delight
To live beneath your more habitual sway.
I love the Brooks which down their channels fret,
Even more than when I tripped lightly as they;
The innocent brightness of a new-born Day
    Is lovely yet;
The Clouds that gather round the setting sun
Do take a sober colouring from an eye
That hath kept watch o'er man's mortality;
Another race hath been, and other palms are won.
Thanks to the human heart by which we live,
Thanks to its tenderness, its joys, and fears,
To me the meanest flower that blows can give
Thoughts that do often lie too deep for tears.

11

啊，流泉、青芜、林薄和丘山，
请莫预示你们和我的情好将中断！
我依旧深感到你们对我的吸引；
　　我只是捐弃了〔稚年的〕欢喜，
　　〔来自你们寄托我的疑惘，〕
冀求能〔从而〕获得你们的荫蔽。
　　我如今爱那〔淙淙的〕溪涧
　　　　跳踃踹踊下山脊，
　　　　比我在童年时和它们
　　　　同样地小跳轻蹀躞，
　　　　还更增几分怜惜；
新生的旭照辉耀出天真的光彩，
　　　　还是极可爱；
　　环绕着西沉红日的彤云
　　这时候抹上了深深一层
注目于人性的我这眼色的沉着；
　　日轮又一天的行程已度过，
　　　　另外的胜利已赢得。
感谢我们所借以生活的人心，
感谢它的温柔恺悌，欢乐和恐惧，
　　　　对于我，最微末的花朵，
　　　　只要它吐艳含英，
　　便能引出远远超过
　　涕泪所能唤起的思虑。

1978.8.1–18 译

The Solitary Reaper

〔1〕 Behold her, single in the field,
Yon solitary Highland Lass!
Reaping and singing by herself;
Stop here, or gently pass!
Alone she cuts and binds the grain,
And sings a melancholy strain;
O listen! for the Vale profound
Is overflowing with the sound.

〔2〕 No Nightingale did ever chaunt
More welcome notes to weary bands
Of travellers in some shady haunt,
Among Arabian sands:
A voice so thrilling ne'er was heard
In spring-time from the Cuckoo-bird,
Breaking the silence of the seas
Among the farthest Hebrides.

孤独的刈禾姑娘

〔1〕 你瞧她，单身来往在田中，
那边那孤独的高原小姑娘！
刈割着麦秆，又敞开喉咙，
停停又走走，她轻盈嘹亮！
她独自在收割，又绑着麦捆，
高唱起一支忧郁的声腔；
听啊！听那个山谷好深深，
泛滥着她的歌声应谷响。

〔2〕 没有夜莺呀，曾经歌唱过
更受欢迎的曲调，对旅游
疲劳的人群，在荫蔽的场所，
在杳遥阿剌伯的远处沙洲：
鸣声这般激动人从没有
听到过，来自春天的鸬鸠，
啼破大海的沉寂，在那里
远远的小岛群叫赫布里底。

〔3〕 Will no one tell me what she sings? —
Perhaps the plaintive numbers flow
For old, unhappy, far-off things,
And battles long ago:
Or is it some more humble lay,
Familiar matter of to-day?
Some natural sorrow, loss, or pain,
That has been, and may be again?

〔4〕 Whate'er the theme, the Maiden sang
As if her song could have no ending;
I saw her singing at her work,
And o'er the sickle bending; —
I listened, motionless and still;
And, as I mounted up the hill,
The music in my heart I bore,
Long after it was heard no more.

〔3〕 她歌唱什么，可没人告诉我？——
也许那悲伤的歌音流注
是为古时不幸的遥远事，
和古老沙场上开启的战祸：
或则是什么朴质的歌辞，
事情乃是在现今这当世？
自然的悲哀、丧亡或痛苦，
已经发生过，将来会再度？

〔4〕 不管唱什么，这姑娘高讴，
仿佛她唱得没完也没了；
我见她刈禾时歌唱过不休，
伛倒了身体还是不停口；——
我听着听着，停下步，静听；
当我跨步去爬上山边道，
我心中还满怀这阵歌声，
听不到她那讴唱已许久。

1979.12.24 夜译

Upon Westminster Bridge

Earth has not anything to show more fair:
    Dull would he be of soul who could pass by
    A sight so touching in its majesty:
This City now doth, like a garment, wear
The beauty of the morning; silent, bare,
    Ships, towers, domes, theatres and temples lie
    Open unto the fields, and to the sky;
All bright and glittering in the smokeless air.
Never did sun more beautifully steep
    In his first splendour, valley, rock, or hill;
Ne'er saw I, never felt, a calm so deep!
    The river glideth at his own sweet will:
Dear God! the very houses seem asleep;
    And all that mighty heart is lying still!

韦施敏斯忒桥头即景

大地再没有光景比这更峨巍：
　　谁倘使漠然不见这景色炜荧
　　瑰丽得动人，他当是灵智昏蒙：
这都城如今披着灿烂的朝晖，
像穿上一袭华衮；宁谧而宏恢，
　　有堡垒、穹窿、剧院、庙堂和舸艨，
　　坦然迎对着天光和一片田塍，
在无烟的碧空下面闪闪含徽。
太阳从没有将它初放的旭照
　　更美地浸渍溪谷、岩石或山丘；
我从未见过、感到恁深的静悄！
　　河水顺着它的意向悠然安流：
天哪！这列列房栊都似已睡着；
　　那整个豪迈的心腔正在眠休！

1979.6.3 译

The World

〔1〕 The World is too much with us; late and soon,
Getting and spending, we lay waste our powers:
Little we see in Nature that is ours;
We have given our hearts away, a sordid boon!

〔2〕 This Sea that bares her bosom to the moon;
The winds that will be howling at all hours
And are up-gather'd now like sleeping flowers,
For this, for everything, we are out of tune;

〔3〕 It moves us not. — Great God! I'd rather be
A Pagan suckled in a creed outworn, —
So might I, standing on this pleasant lea,

〔4〕 Have glimpses that would make me less forlorn;
Have sight of Proteus rising from the sea;
Or hear old Triton blow his wreathéd horn.

这世界

〔1〕 这世界对我们真够受的了；早晚
只营求和消耗，我们将精力荒废：
我们在自然中很少能见到嘉惠；
白白把心神抛掷掉，鄙残的奋勉！

〔2〕 海水的轻波仰对着月明呈裸袒；
　　那飑风时时刻刻呼啸着像轰雷，
如今却恬静得有如半展的花蕾；
对此，对一切，我们都不协调，乖舛；

〔3〕 我们却无所谓。——天哪！我衷心但愿
　　是个信某一过时的信条的异教徒；
那么，我能驻足于这愉快的草原，

〔4〕 见闻些使我心情少凄茫的事物；
　　能见到海里的多变神冒出波澜；
或听到幺龙王吹响他的弯号角。

1980.9.25 译

• 乔治 · 戈登 · 拜伦 •

George Gordon Byron

（1788—1824）

The Isles of Greece

1

The isles of Greece, the isles of Greece!
　　Where burning Sappho loved and sung,
Where grew the arts of war and peace,
　　Where Delos rose, and Phoebus sprung!
Eternal summer gilds them yet,
But all, except the sun, is set.

希腊列岛

1

希腊列岛哟！列岛缔同盟，
　那里多情的莎馥①曾歌唱
和恋爱武功和文治所芃生，
第洛斯小岛②兴，斐勃斯③放光芒！
永恒的夏天将它们镀上金，
但除了太阳外，一切已沉湮。

---

① 莎馥（Sappho, fl.600 B.C.），古希腊女抒情诗人，生于 Lesbos 岛上。她的作品都是爱情的篇什，现存不多，而且大多是片段。

② 第洛斯（Delos）是昔克拉第群岛中的一座，希腊神话里太阳神阿波罗（Apollo）在此诞生。公元前 477 年，希腊沿海各城邦，以雅典为首，在岛上缔结第洛斯同盟，并以此为海陆武备根据地，以抵御波斯人入寇。

③ 太阳神阿波罗又名斐勃斯（Phoebus）。他是天王宙斯（Zeus）和他的情妇理妲（Leto，又名 Latona）的儿子，年青，体貌优美，是音乐、诗歌、预言、医疗等事的神灵。他的妹子是清贞的月神与狩猎神阿忒密斯（Artemis）。

2

The Scian and the Teian muse,
    The hero's harp, the lover's lute,
Have found the fame your shores refuse,
    Their place of birth alone is mute
To sounds which echo further west
Than your sires' "Islands of the Blest".

2

赛里岛[①]连同替奥岛[②]的诗魂，

　英雄的竖琴，情人的琵琶[③]

已找到你们所摈拒的令闻：

唯独在他们所生身的胯下

听不到他们的名声在阛阓，

却回响过你们祖先的“蓬岛”。[④]

---

① 赛里岛的诗魂（Scian muse）：系指 Simonides of Ceos（公元前约 556—前 468），和 Bacchylides of Ceos（公元前约 500—?），他们都是抒情诗人。Scio 即 Ceos，Chios，或作 Keos，希腊名为 Khio。

② 替奥岛的诗魂（Teian muse）：系指阿那克里盎（Anacreon，公元前约 563—前 478，Teos 岛人），抒情诗人。

③ 英雄的竖琴，情人的琵琶（The hero’s harp，the lover’s lute）：竖琴形制很大，三角形，竖立在地上，有数十弦，弹者坐在旁边用手指拨动，发展成西欧 16 至 18 世纪的大键琴（harpsichord），再发展为 19 世纪的大钢琴（Pianoforte），更进而为现在的（大）钢琴（Piano），应仍保持三角形，故竖琴（harp）当是文艺复兴早期 14—15 世纪时由古希腊轻便的手抱竖琴（lyre，有七根弦，它在太阳神阿波罗手里代表诗歌与音乐）发展繁复起来的形式；至于鲁特琴（lute）则是 14—17 世纪时的西欧弦乐器，其形制酷似我们的曲颈琵琶。拜伦在这里提起这两件乐器是出于联想（数十弦的大竖琴伴奏英雄战阵的乐曲，六弦的鲁特琴则伴奏抒情和恋爱的小曲）以及押“lute”与“mute”二字的韵而已。

④ “蓬岛”（Islands of the Blessed，或可作“仙岛”），假想在西溟（Western Ocean）中，为天神所垂爱的凡人在死后灵魂住在这里，永享快乐。这一节大意是说 [Sappho,] Simonides，Bacchylides，Anacreon 等诗人在他们的故国后人中，因被敌寇所占领而奴役，已湮没而不彰，没有人知道，反而在你们祖先的“蓬岛”之西，即如今的西欧诸国，因受文艺复兴的教化，他们倒颇为人们所珍视，声名藉藉。

3

The mountains look on Marathon —
    And Marathon looks on the sea;
And musing there an hour alone,
    I dream'd that Greece might still be free;
For standing on the Persians' grave,
I could not deem myself a slave.

3

连绵的山岭目注着马拉商[①]——
　马拉商目注着淼淼的大海；
我独自在那里萦思而凝望，
　梦见到希腊有一天会奏凯
而自由[②]，因站在波斯人墓上，
我不能自认是奴性的窝囊。

---

① 马拉商（Marathon）今译马拉松，依山凭海之战（公元前490），入寇的波斯人大败，希腊大捷，这场战事记录在西方最早的史家海罗铎德斯（Herodotus，约公元前484—前425）的史乘第7卷中。马拉松大捷既成，希腊军派信使斐迪匹第斯（Pheidippides）送捷报到雅典，奔驰26英里余，喜讯送到。力竭而死。1896年希腊开奥林匹克运动会，有马拉松长跑项目，距离为29英里385码。

② 这首“希腊列岛”是拜伦插在他的长诗《唐璜》（*Don Juan*）第3章里的短歌。当时希腊还在土耳其人的铁骑占领之下，人民被奴役。拜伦后来在参加希腊独立战争时在密梭朗其（Missolonghi）军次得病而殁，时在1824年，方36岁。

4

A king sate on the rocky brow
    Which looks o'er sea-born Salamis;
And ships, by thousands, lay below,
    And men in nations; — all were his!
He counted them at break of day —
And when the sun set, where were they?

5

And where are they? and where art thou,
    My country? on thy voiceless shore
The heroic lay is tuneless now —
    The heroic bosom beats no more!
And must thy lyre, so long divine,
Degenerate into hands like mine?

4

一位君王高踞在石壁上，
　石壁俯瞰着海生的萨拉密[①]，
成千条战船息桨在下方，
　城邦的战卒在脚下麇集！
他计数着他们，恰时当清早——
待红日西沉时，都哪里去了？

5

他们在哪里？你又在哪里，
　我的宗邦哟？你沉寂的岸上，
英勇的歌词如今渺声息——
　英勇的壮怀如今不震荡！
而你的七弦竖琴，本奕奕
显神灵，竟堕入我手中，没出息？

① 萨拉密（Salamis）又名库卢里（Kouloure），是伊杰那（Ægina）海湾中一个岛屿，在它周遭于公元前 480 年发生波斯与希腊的海军大战，希腊战船大败入侵的波斯船队。

6

’Tis something in the dearth of fame,
    Though link’d among a fetter’d race,
To feel at least a patriot’s shame,
    Even as I sing, suffuse my face;
For what is left the poet here?
For Greeks a blush — for Greece a tear.

7

Must we but weep o’er days more blest?
    Must we but blush? — Our fathers bled.
Earth! render back from out thy breast
    A remnant of our Spartan dead!
Of the three hundred grant but three,
To make a new Thermopylae!

6

在荣名缺乏的时刻至少是，
　虽跟被奴役的国族在一起，
能感到个爱国志士的羞耻，
　当我歌唱着，红晕了脸皮；
一介诗人啊，有什么答对？
为希腊人脸红——为希腊流泪。

7

仅仅为荣幸的往日而哀恸？
　仅仅把脸羞红？——我们的先人们
却流血。大地！从你的胸怀中
　还我们斯巴达先烈的残剩！
那三百英烈里只给还三名，
我们来再造塞冒泼里[①]的雷鸣！

---

① 塞冒泼里（Thermopylæ）之役的神勇鏖战，在物质上是个败迹，在精神上则是一场英名赫赫的凯旋，令人感泣奋发。在这场与波斯人的战役中，希腊主将荔昂聂达斯见败局已不可挽回之际，下令全军撤退，只留下他自己的三百名斯巴达勇士拼死扼守，决不动摇，终于全部壮烈牺牲。

8

What, silent still? and silent all?
    Ah! no; — the voices of the dead
Sound like a distant torrent's fall,
    And answer, "Let one living head,
But one arise, — we come, we come!"
'Tis but the living who are dumb.

9

In vain — in vain: strike other chords;
    Fill high the cup with Samian wine!
Leave battles to the Turkish hordes,
    And shed the blood of Scio's vine!
Hark! rising to the ignoble call —
How answers each bold Bacchanal!

8

什么，还悄静？全没有声息？
　哎哟！非也；——死者的喧噪声
呜响着像一阵远处的退汐，
　回答道：“让一个活着的群生，
只一个，起来，——我们来，我们来！”
恨只恨活着的群生太噤呆。

9

不中用——不中用；奏别的曲调；
　樽盏里斟满萨摩岛的酒浆！
把战阵付与土耳其的蛮豪，
　大觚中倾注赛奥岛的红酿！
听啊！响应这不光彩的叫唤，
每一个酒狂喧嚷得多果敢！

10

You have the Pyrrhic dances yet;

Where is the Pyrrhic phalanx gone?

Of two such lessons, why forget

    The nobler and the manlier one?

You have letters Cadmus gave —

Think ye he meant them for a slave?

11

Fill high the bowl with Samian wine!

    We will not think of themes like these!

It made Anacreon's song divine:

    He served — but served Polycrates —

A tyrant; but our masters then

Were still, at least, our countrymen.

10

你们还有那匹力克的战舞[①]；
　但哪里还有那匹力克的方阵[②]？
有两个这样的明教，何以故
　把高贵、勇武的忘掉，使销隐？
你们继承着凯特默[③]的字母，
难道他留传给一族遗奴？

11

将巨觥斟满萨摩岛的酒浆！
　我们不去想这样的题旨！
这使人念阿那克里盎而神往；
　他侍奉——只侍奉鲍拉克拉底斯[④]——
一尊君[⑤]；但我们的主子们当时
至少还只是宗邦的人氏。

---

① 古希腊军中气势雄壮的武舞。

② 古希腊四千战士各执长枪所紧密列成的方阵。

③ Cadmus：传说他由腓尼基亚（Phoenicia，为一古航海贸易国族）传 16 个字母至古希腊，后希腊人增添了 8 个，成 24 个。

④ Polycrates：他是公元前 6 世纪上半叶统治 Samos 岛的恶君。

⑤ 此尊君系指赢得马拉松大捷的米太雅第。

12

The tyrant of the Chersonese
　　Was freedom's best and bravest friend;
That tyrant was Miltiades!
　　Oh! that the present hour would lend
Another despot of the kind!
Such chains as his were sure to bind.

13

Fill high the bowl with Samian wine!
　　On Suli's rock, and Parga's shore,
Exists the remnant of a line
　　Such as the Doric mothers bore;
And there, perhaps, some seed is sown,
The Heracleidan blood might own.

12

这希腊半岛的赫赫尊君
　是自由的最好最英勇的友人；
那尊君是米太雅第将军！
　但愿如今这风雨的晦辰
能再有一位这般的君长！
他锻铸的锁链使邦国雄强。

13

将巨觥斟满萨摩岛的酒浆！
　在塞利石壁上，派茄岸滩头，
还遗存茕茕的裔族于梓邦，
　陶列斯[①]的后人那里还留得有；
在那里，也许有神勇的种子，
大力神海拉克里斯寄后嗣。

---

① 陶列亚人（Dorians），古希腊主要种族之一，其特性为尚武、刚毅、单纯而尚美。相传本居住在帕那萨斯（Parnassus）山麓陶列斯（Doris）地区，为大力神海拉克里斯（Heracles）的后裔；后来移居伯罗奔尼撒（Peloponnesus）半岛，在考林斯（Corinth）湾之南，及以斯巴达（Sparta）为主各岛屿上，成立斯巴达王国，拜伦在这几行里缅怀的是荔昂聂达斯在塞昌泼里战役中率领三百斯巴达勇士壮烈就义的浩气，希望再有这样一位英豪起来，挥戈举义，驱逐土虏。

14

Trust not for freedom to the Franks,
    They have a king who buys and sells.
In native swords and native ranks,
    The only hope of courage dwells:
But Turkish force and Latin fraud
Would break your shield, however broad.

15

Fill high the bowl with Samian wine!
    Our virgins dance beneath the shade —
I see their glorious black eyes shine;
    But gazing on each glowing maid,
My own the burning tear-drop laves,
To think such breasts must suckle slaves.

14

莫把自由信托给法兰克人——
　他们有一个做买卖的君王；
英武的唯一希望须依存
　于本土的人群、本地的武装：
土耳其的暴力和拉丁的奸诈，
会破你们的盾牌，不论多广大。

15

将巨觥斟满萨摩岛的酒浆！
　我们的处女舞蹈在荫影下——
她们光耀的黑眼珠在闪亮；
　但凝视每一个耀眼的鬟丫，
热泪噙满了我灼热的眼眶，
当想起她们将乳哺小奴郎。

16

Place me on Sunium's marbled steep,
    Where nothing, save the waves and I,
May hear our mutual murmurs sweep;
    There, swan-like, let me sing and die:
A land of slaves shall ne'er be mine —
Dash down yon cup of Samian wine!

16

放我在塞涅磨大理石的岩端，
　那里只有我和汹涌的海涛，
能听到我们的呻唔声在交感；
　那里，天鹅般让我亡命去啸遨：
遍地奴隶的决非我的宗邦——
泼掉那巨觥里萨摩岛的酒浆！

1980.7.7 译毕

She Walks in Beauty

〔1〕 She walks in beauty, like the night
Of cloudless climes and starry skies;
And all that's best of dark and bright
Meet in her aspect and her eyes:
Thus mellowed to that tender light
Which heaven to gaudy day denies.

〔2〕 One shade the more, one ray the less,
Had half impaired the nameless grace
Which waves in every raven tress,
Or softly lightens o'er her face;
Where thoughts serenely sweet express
How pure, how dear their dwelling place.

〔3〕 And on that cheek, and o'er that brow,
So soft, so calm, yet eloquent,
The smiles that win, the tints that glow,
But tell of days in goodness spent,
A mind at peace with all below,
A heart whose love is innocent!

她在俏丽中行走

〔1〕 她在俏丽中行走，像良宵
　　云彩全无和满天的星斗；
光天和暗夜里所有最好
　　最美的都在她眼角眉头：
这般糅和成温存的情调，
　　天公不叫炫耀的白昼有。

〔2〕 增一分阴影，减一分光线，
　　会损害无名的风韵一半，
那在每一绺乌发里回旋，
　　或在她脸上轻轻地映焕，
那里宁静的神思在表现
　　它们的居处多高洁醇甘。

〔3〕 在那双颊上，在那秀额际，
　　恁温柔、恁宁静、澄明畅亮，
可爱的微笑、生辉的肌理，
　　只显示情操的高洁馨香，
意念与人交和谐而亲密，
　　一颗心它的爱天真安详。

——1980 年 5 月 24 日译

When We Two Parted

〔1〕 When we two parted
In silence and tears,
Half broken-hearted
To sever for years,
Pale grew thy cheek and cold,
Colder thy kiss;
Truly that hour foretold
Sorrow to this!

〔2〕 The dew of the morning
Sunk chill on my brow;
It felt like the warning
Of what I feel now.
Thy vows are all broken,
And light is thy fame:
I hear thy name spoken
And share in its shame.

我们俩分手时

〔1〕 我们俩分手时，
沉默中流着泪，
心印心，满悲思，
得长年各分飞，
你的脸苍白且冰冷，
更冰寒，你的吻；
果真，那时刻已告警
如今这热泪涔！

〔2〕 那早晨降冷露，
滴落上我额角，
它像是在预诉
我此刻的感觉。
你发的信誓全打破，
你声名太浮薄，
听你的名字一数说，
我就觉荣誉抛。

〔3〕 They name thee before me,
A knell to mine ear;
A shudder comes o'er me —
Why wert thou so dear?
They know not I knew thee
Who knew thee too well:
Long, long shall I rue thee
Too deeply to tell.

〔4〕 In secret we met:
In silence I grieve
That thy heart could forget,
Thy spirit deceive.
If I should meet thee
After long years,
How should I greet thee? —
With silence and tears.

〔3〕 当我面，提到你，
对我是敲丧钟；
我一阵发惴栗——
为什么恁情重？
他们不知我认识你，
我认得太真切：
我要久久地悔恨你，
悔恨得永不绝。

〔4〕 私下里，两相见：
默默地我衔悲，
你灵明，能欺骗，
你的心，如死灰。
我若是还会碰到你，
在好多年以后，
我将会怎样迎对你？——
沉默中，苦流泪。

——1980 年 4 月 24 日译

So We'll Go No More A-Roving

〔1〕 So we'll go no more a-roving
So late into the night,
Though the heart be still as loving,
And the moon be still as bright.

〔2〕 For the sword outwears its sheath,
And the soul wears out the breast,
And the heart must pause to breathe,
And Love itself have rest.

〔3〕 Though the night was made for loving,
And the day returns too soon,
Yet we'll go no more a-roving
By the light of the moon.

我们将不再去漫游

〔1〕 所以，我们将不再去漫游
这么晚直到夜未央，
虽则两心还如此地绸缪，
月色还总是这样亮。

〔2〕 因为剑刃比剑鞘要耐久，
灵魂比胸膛要坚实，
心儿得歇下来呼吸夷犹，
爱情本身要栖迟。

〔3〕 虽然这夜晚正宜于钟情，
白昼回来得太匆匆，
可是我们将不再去宵行，
在这良夜的月明中。

1980.5.20 译

Stanzas for Music

There Be None of Beauty' s Daughters

〔1〕 There be none of Beauty's daughters
With a magic like thee;
And like music on the waters
Is thy sweet voice to me:
When, as if its sound were causing
The charméd ocean's pausing,
The waves lie still and gleaming,
And the lulled winds seem dreaming;

〔2〕 And the midnight moon is weaving
Her bright chain o'er the deep;
Whose breast is gently heaving,
As an infant's asleep:
So the spirit bows before thee,
To listen and adore thee;
With a full but soft emotion,
Like the swell of summer's ocean.

配 乐

没有个姣丽的化身能美得你这般神奇

〔1〕 没有个姣丽的化身
能美得你这般神奇；
对于我，你呖呖莺声
像水上妙乐奏丽靡：
这娇音，仿佛在促使
海浪入了神而静止，
叫微波停漾兴闪烁，
习习的轻飔梦无奈：
〔2〕 午夜的月明在沧溟
泓洄上编织着银链；
浩淼的胸膛在轻盈
起伏，像婴儿正睡眠：
我灵明对着你低头
倾听你，崇拜你，无侔；
用丰满、温柔的感情，
像夏日海洋的潮汛。

1980.5.22 译

· 波西 · 比希 · 雪莱 ·

Percy Bysshe Shelley

（1792—1822）

Ozymandias

I met a traveller from an antique land,
Who said — "Two vast and trunkless legs of stone
Stand in the desart ... Near them, on the sand,
Half sunk a shattered visage lies, whose frown,
And wrinkled lip, and sneer of cold command,
Tell that its sculptor well those passions read
Which yet survive, stamped on these lifeless things,
The hand that mocked them, and the heart that fed;
And on the pedestal, these words appear:
My name is Ozymandias, King of Kings,
Look on my Works, ye Mighty, and despair!
Nothing beside remains. Round the decay
Of that colossal Wreck, boundless and bare
The lone and level sands stretch far away."

奥捷曼狄亚斯

我遇见一个远来自古邦的旅客，
他说道："两根巨大、没躯干的石腿
站在沙漠中。相近，在沙上，半埋着
一具破毁了的容颜，它那阵颦眉，
撇嘴，[①]冷酷的命令的嘲诮和蹙额，
表示石像的雕刻人是深深领会
这些激情的，如今还留在相貌上
活现着；他的手仿效，他的心嘲诙。
在那台座上，刻得有这两行字迹——
'我名叫奥捷曼狄亚斯，王中之王；
你们众英豪，瞧我的功勋，去悲戚！'
再没有别的留下来。在那座残存
巨像的周围，无边无际的大沙碛，
荒凉而冥漠，向渺茫的天际延伸。"

1980.6.12 译

① 原文"wrinkled lip"直译为"皱唇"，但在译文里似作"撇嘴"（偏斜嘴唇，表示轻蔑）为适切。同一动作在中英两种语文里说法不同，但涵意一样。

Stanzas Written in Dejection — December 1818, near Naples

〔1〕 The Sun is warm, the sky is clear,
The waves are dancing fast and bright,
Blue isles and snowy mountains wear
The purple noon's transparent might,
The breath of the moist earth is light
Around its unexpanded buds;
Like many a voice of one delight
The winds, the birds, the Ocean-floods;
The City's voice itself is soft, like Solitude's.

〔2〕 I see the Deep's untrampled floor
With green and purple seaweeds strown;
I see the waves upon the shore
Like light dissolved in star-showers, thrown;
I sit upon the sands alone;
The lightning of the noontide Ocean
Is flashing round me, and a tone
Arises from its measured motion,
How sweet! did any heart now share in my emotion.

伤 怀

1818 年 12 月赋于拿坡里

〔1〕 阳光照得暖，穹苍清灿烂，
波浪跳踊得急速又明亮，
青青的小岛和雪盖的群山
披着紫艳的晌午间的明爽；
潮湿的气流簇微风跌宕
在没有吐放的芽苞四周；
像一阵愉快的协和音响——
风声、鸟鸣和海浪的嗖嗖——
这城市的微哗本身便如同宁静的悠悠。

〔2〕 我眼望海底无踪印的海床，
交互散布着青紫的海藻；
我望见岸上一排排海浪
像湮灭的光波消散成星潮，
我独自在沙滩上踞坐逍遥；
正午时海洋的闪电般光华
在我的四周照彻，从滔滔
白浪的行动中起着轻哗——
多可爱！深情这时候开放了我的心花。

〔3〕 Alas, I have nor hope nor health
Nor peace within nor calm around,
Nor that content surpassing wealth
The sage in meditation found,
And walked with inward glory crowned;
Nor fame nor power nor love nor leisure —
Others I see whom these surround,
Smiling they live and call life pleasure:
To me that cup has been dealt in another measure.

〔4〕 Yet now despair itself is mild,
Even as the winds and waters are;
I could lie down like a tired child
And weep away the life of care
Which I have borne and yet must bear
Till Death like Sleep might steal on me,
And I might feel in the warm air
My cheek grow cold, and hear the Sea
Breathe o'er my dying brain its last monotony.

〔3〕 嗳呀！我没有希望和健康，
内里欠安详，四周无宁静，
缺少那超财富的衷心弥望，
圣者在沉思里所得的充盈，
行步时冠戴着内在的光荣——
没名声、权势，没爱情、闲适；
我眼见旁人被这些所牵萦——
他们乐此生，含着笑度时日：
对于我，人生的酒卮注的是酸涩的苦汁。

〔4〕 可现在失望显得还温和，
正如我周遭的海风和浪涛；
我能躺下来像一个［饥饿
又］疲困的孩童，把所负的烦恼，
已负上而不能不负，全哭掉，
待到死亡将如同睡眠般
袭上我心头，而我将感觉到
在和暖的风中脸颊转阴寒，
听海浪以单调的低喧催我的脑子去长眠。

1980.4.29 译

〔原诗尚有一节，译者未译。〕——编者

Ode to the West Wind

1

O wild West Wind, thou breath of Autumn's being,
Thou, form whose unseen presence the leaves dead
Are driven, like ghosts from an enchanter fleeing,

Yellow, and black, and pale, and hectic red,
Pestilence-stricken multitudes: O Thou,
Who chariotest to their dark wintry bed

The winged seeds, where they lie cold and low,
Each like a corpse within its grave, until
Thine azure sister of the Spring shall blow

Her clarion o'er the dreaming earth, and fill
(Driving sweet buds like flocks to feed in air)
With living hues and odours plain and hill:

Wild Spirit, which art moving everywhere;
Destroyer and Preserver; hear, O hear!

西风颂

1

啊，猛烈的西风，你深秋的嘘气，
从你这无形的所在处，这阵落叶
被驱除，像鬼魂从妖巫身旁逃避，

枯黄、乌黑、苍白和肺痨的赤黝，
染上了恶疠的群众啊：嗳，你哟，
你把有翅膀的种子吹送到阴郁、

冬寒的床上，它们全躺倒在那里
冷而低，粒粒像一具尸体在墓中，
要等你蔚蓝的青春小妹来吹起

她嘹亮的号角，唤醒做梦的原坐
(赶着鲜嫩的幼芽像羊群饲阳和)，
将原野和山丘布满色彩和香浓：

猛烈的神灵，你到处去漫游作客；
毁灭者，又是保存者；听我这浩歌！

2

Thou on whose stream, 'mid the steep sky's commotion,
Loose clouds like earth's decaying leaves are shed,
Shook from the tangled boughs of Heaven and Ocean,

Angels of rain and lightning: there are spread
On the blue surface of thine aery surge,
Like the bright hair uplifted from the head

Of some fierce Mænad, even from the dim verge
Of the horizon to the zenith's height,
The locks of the approaching storm. Thou Dirge

Of the dying year, to which this closing night
Will be the dome of a vast sepulchre,
Vaulted with all thy congregated might

Of vapours, from whose solid atmosphere
Black rain, and fire, and hail will burst: O, hear!

2

在你那湍流上，陡峭高天的骚扰中，
乱云像地上的败叶一般给洒落，
洒散自海天交互缠结的杈丫丛，

雨阵和闪电的神使群：在你那空廓
巨涛的蔚蓝海面上，披散着，有如
什么暴戾的妖婆头上的亮髻螺，

从隐约的地平边际到天顶最高处，
这阵迫近的风暴的漫天蓬乱发。
你这垂死残年的哀婉曲，这夜幕

将是个广大墓茔的穹窿顶，你挥发
郁蒸的湿气，将这座高坟拱撑起，
从它稠密的氤氲里，雨点黑压压，

还有火焰和冰雹阵，都将会一齐
迸发出：请听我这支浩歌，务请你！

3

Thou who didst waken from his summer dreams
The blue Mediterranean, where he lay,
Lulled by the coil of his chrystalline streams,

Beside a pumice isle in Baiæ's bay,
And saw in sleep old palaces and towers
Quivering within the wave's intenser day,

All overgrown with azure moss and flowers
So sweet, the sense faints picturing them! Thou
For whose path the Atlantic's level powers

Cleave themselves into chasms, while far below
The sea-blooms and the oozy woods which wear
The sapless foliage of the ocean, know

Thy voice, and suddenly grow gray with fear,
And tremble and despoil themselves: O, hear!

3

你曾将碧澄的地中海之灵从朦胧
夏梦里唤醒，他躺在那边被水晶
浪卷所催眠而睡去，在巴伊湾中

一个浮石的小岛旁，梦里他分明
瞥见到古时的宫阙堡邸荣盛时，
都已生满了碧苔和香花，那芳馨

叫人嗅到了神昏迷！为你的飞驰，
大西洋平稳的水波慌让路，巨浪
壁立成危崖，洋下方海花和干枝

泥滑的海林扶苏茂，听到你踉跄
阔步的轰鸣阵阵喧，原先本没精
打采无声息，一听你高吭发喧响，
忽地里脸色变灰败，都战栗频仍
乱摇落，枝柯纷脱叶：啊，请你听！

4

If I were a dead leaf thou mightest bear;
If I were a swift cloud to fly with thee;
A wave to pant beneath thy power, and share

The impulse of thy strength, only less free
Than thou, O Uncontrollable! If even
I were as in my boyhood, and could be

The comrade of thy wanderings over Heaven,
As then, when to outstrip thy skiey speed
Scarce seem'd a vision; I would ne'er have striven

As thus with thee in prayer in my sore need.
Oh, lift me as a wave, a leaf, a cloud!
I fall upon the thorns of life! I bleed!

A heavy weight of hours has chained and bowed
One too like thee: tameless, and swift, and proud.

4

但愿我是你卷起的一片焦叶；
能和你一起奋飞的一朵急疾云，
当一个浪头，在你的威力下激切，

能和你同受威棱的冲击，只因
我不如你自由，无法控驭的神灵！
只要我能和童年时那样，能紧跟

在你身后边，当你的游天小崽生，
那时候，要超越你的飞空高速度，
不像是一个幻想；那我就决不应

在无可奈何中，如此祷求你苦苦。
举起我，像是一片叶，一朵云，一个浪！
我掉在人生的荆刺上！血流如注！

时光的重负加给我锁链铁锒铛，
我和你太相像：太粗豪，疾速，轻狂。

5

Make me thy lyre, even as the forest is:
What if my leaves are falling like its own!
The tumult of thy mighty harmonies

Will take from both a deep, autumnal tone,
Sweet though in sadness. Be thou, Spirit fierce,
My spirit! Be thou me, impetuous one!

Drive my dead thoughts over the universe
Like withered leaves to quicken a new birth!
And, by the incantation of this verse,

Scatter, as from an unextinguished hearth
Ashes and sparks, my words among mankind!
Be through my lips to unawakened Earth

The trumpet of a prophecy! O Wind,
If Winter comes, can Spring be far behind?

5

将我当你的瑶竖琴，像这森林般，
我的黄叶正如它纷纷坠，那何妨！
你雄劲的和谐声声哗啸应天喧，

从落木和我身上摄得的深秋腔，
虽悲怆，却显得甜美。凌厉的神灵，
峻急的浩魄，请赋予我你那精爽！

将我这没生命的沉思赶去周行
全宇宙，有如枯叶般，去加快活跃
那新生，且凭咒诵这颂辞的歌声，

像从一个还未曾熄灭的炉窟穴，
散发出灰烬和火星，向人间传报
我这些言辞！对沉睡的尘寰世界，

经我的唇舌，作预言的号筒！凉飙，
寒冬既已至，阳春怎么能长迢遥？

1980.1.17 译完

The Indian Girl's Song
[The Indian Serenade]

〔1〕 I arise from dreams of thee
In the first sleep of night —
The winds are breathing low
And the stars are burning bright.
I arise from dreams of thee —
And a spirit in my feet
Has borne me — Who knows how?
To thy chamber window, sweet! —

〔2〕 The wandering airs they faint
On the dark silent stream —
The champak odours fail
Like sweet thounghts in a dream;
The nightingale's complaint —
It dies upon her heart —
As I must die on thine
O beloved as thou art!

印度小夜曲

〔1〕 从初夏开始的酣睡中，
我梦里见到你睡醒来；
当微风轻轻地吹拂着，
看星斗满天宇，我徘徊：
我醒来自睡梦蒙眬中，
两足里像有个小精灵
在引领——谁知道怎么着，
到了你房栊前，好亲亲！

〔2〕 浮游着的轻飔湮没在
幽暗、悄静的气流里——
金香木的芳馨消失得
像柔思隐晦在魂梦里；
夜莺的悲啼声再再
泯灭在她自己的心头，
让我在你心头来摧折，
我爱你，我这么向你求！

〔3〕 O lift me from the grass!
I die, I faint, I fail!
Let thy love in kisses rain
On my lips and eyelids pale.
My cheek is cold and white, alas!
My heart beats loud and fast.
Oh press it close to thine again
Where it will break at last.

〔3〕 将我从草地上扶起来！

我晕眩，我昏厥，我魂断！

让你的哀怜用亲吻

落上我的嘴唇和眼睑。

我的脸冰冷且灰白，

我的心跳动得响又急；

把它啊！贴紧着你的心，

在那里它终于会破裂。

1980.4.22 译

Love's Philosophy

〔1〕 The fountains mingle with — the river,
　　And the rivers with the ocean;
The winds of Heaven mix for ever
　　With a sweet emotion;
Nothing in the world is single;
　　All things by a law divine
In one another's being mingle —
　　Why not I with thine?

〔2〕 See the mountains kiss high Heaven,
　　And the waves clasp one another;
No sister flower would be forgiven
　　If it disdained its brother;
And the sunlight clasps the earth,
　　And the moonbeams kiss the sea:
What are all these kissings worth,
　　If thou kiss not me?

爱的哲学

〔1〕 泉水同江河混和着流注，
江河跟大海汇集成沧溟，
天上的清风永远相欢呼，
吹拥到一起彼此都钟情；
这世上没东西独处孤零，
一切都依据着那神律
交互相融合，联结缔成亲——
我为何不跟你成佳侣？

〔2〕 望远处崇山亲吻着高天，
海浪和河波各各相拥抱；
没有姐妹花会受到恕原，
假如她藐忽她的兄弟曹：
阳光总是在搂抚着大地，
月照在亲吻碧海——
这一切亲吻有什么意义，
若是你对我不爱？

1980.4.24 译

The Cloud

〔1〕 I bring fresh showers for the thirsting flowers,
　　From the seas and streams;
I bear light shade for the leaves when laid
　　In their noon-day dreams.
From my wings are shaken the dews that waken
　　The sweet buds every one,
When rocked to rest on their mother's breast,
　　As she dances about the Sun.
I wield the flail of the lashing hail,
　　And whiten the green plains under,
And then again I dissolve it in rain,
　　And laugh as I pass in thunder.

云

〔1〕 我为干渴的百花送新鲜的雨阵，
　　从海里，以及从河川当中；
花木上绿叶纷披，午梦着在打盹，
　　我替它们将荫影轻笼。
从我翅膀上抖落了晶莹的露珠，
　　去唤醒每一颗芽苞和蓓蕾，
当它们在慈母怀里给催眠安抚，
　　她则在阳光下摇曳而含辉。
我先把撒落冰雹的连枷去挥舞，
　　使下界青绿的大地变银白，
接着我又将融冰的雨水来洒布，
　　哗笑出隆隆的雷震以倾泼。

〔2〕 I sift the snow on the mountains below,
And their great pines groan aghast;
And all the night' tis my pillow white,
While I sleep in the arms of the blast.
Sublime on the towers of my skiey bowers,
Lightning my pilot sits;
In a cavern under is fettered the thunder,
It struggles and howls at fits;
Over Earth and Ocean, with gentle motion,
This pilot is guiding me,
Lured by the love of the genii that move
In the depths of the purple sea;
Over the rills, and the crags, and the hills,
Over the lakes and the plains,
Wherever he dream, under mountain or stream,
The Spirit he loves remains;
And I all the while bask in Heaven's blue smile,
Whilst he is dissolving in rains.

〔2〕　我筛散雪花到下方的山岭上面，
　　它们的松林发骇怪的呻吟；
整夜里是我的枕片在凌空招展，
　　当我睡在巨风臂抱中行云。
峨峨耸踞着幽玄寥廓处的层垒，
　　我的导航人闪电兀坐着；
在下边洞窟里锁禁了赫赫宏雷——
　　它阵阵地挣扎，频频在咆哮；
飞过平陆和汪洋，以温存的行动，
　　我这导航人将我来指引，
潜泳在紫海深处的神灵爱之宗，
　　他遥遥在驾驭，加以挥运；
越溪涧，跨巉岩峭壁，迈岗峦山丘，
　　过大小湖泊和荡荡平原，
不拘在哪里梦寐着：在山下，沿水流，
　　他所奉的神灵总在那盘桓；
而我则常在苍穹的蓝笑中沐温柔，
　　正当他消融成霖雨的潺湲。

〔3〕 The sanguine Sunrise, with his meteor eyes,
And his burning plumes outspread,
Leaps on the back of my sailing rack,
When the morning star shines dead;
As on the jag of a mountain crag,
Which an earthquake rocks and swings,
An eagle alit one moment may sit
In the light of its golden wings.
And when Sunset may breathe, from the lit Sea beneath,
Its ardours of rest and of love,
And the crimson pall of eve may fall
From the depth of Heaven above,
With wings folded I rest, on mine aëry nest,
As still as a brooding dove.

〔3〕 鲜红的黎明睁大流星般的眼睛，
蓬松着他那如焚的羽毛，
跳上我扬着帆篷的飞云的背翎，
正当启明星暗淡而冥邈；
如在山崖岩壁上有一块巨石，
逢到地震时突然地摇晃，
一尾大苍鹰倏忽间停飞，正敛翅
而栖止，它两翼放射出金光。
而当日暮从它下方的霞海中
摄取了安息和喜爱的深情，
晚照的深红的外套将会从高空
苍茫的深处下降到人间，
那时我便在空灵的高巢上息躬，
宁静得像一尾驯鸽在孵卵。

〔4〕 That orbed maiden with white fire laden
Whom mortals call the Moon,
Glides glimmering o'er my fleece-like floor,
By the midnight breezes strewn;
And wherever the beat of her unseen feet,
Which only the angels hear,
May have broken the woof, of my tent's thin roof,
The stars peep behind her, and peer;
And I laugh to see them whirl and flee,
Like a swarm of golden bees,
When I widen the rent in my wind-built tent,
Till the calm rivers, lakes, and seas,
Like strips of the sky fallen through me on high,
Are each paved with the moon and these.

〔4〕 那球形的处女披着白花花银焰，
　　尘世人都管她叫作月亮，
闪耀着溜过我铺羊毛般的地板，
　　那披离被午夜的轻风所飐；
而不管哪里，她无形的脚步所至
　　(那只有天使们才听得分明)，
请稍稍踩破了我这帐篷的织丝，
　　众星辰便都来窥睇个不停；
欢笑着，我望见它们回旋而飞腾，
　　像一窠金蜂，闪耀着光芒，
我当即扩大这风制帐篷的裂缝，
　　直到沉静的江湖同海洋，
就像一片片高天都经我而沉降，
　　各各铺满了明月和繁星。

〔5〕 I bind the Sun's throne with a burning zone
    And the Moon's with a girdle of pearl;
The volcanos are dim and the stars reel and swim
    When the whirlwinds my banner unfurl.
From cape to cape, with a bridge-like shape,
    Over a torrent sea,
Sunbeam-proof, I hang like a roof—
    The mountains its columns be!
The triumphal arch, through which I march
    With hurricane, fire, and snow,
When the Powers of the Air, are chained to my chair,
    Is the million-coloured Bow;
The sphere-fire above its soft colours wove
    While the moist Earth was laughing below.

〔5〕 我扣着月亮座，使一根珍珠链圈，
用火环把太阳的宝座拴住；
火山暗沉沉，星星们震颤而晕眩，
在旋风将我的旗帜吹开处。
从海角伸展到海角，像一座高桥，
我横跨浪涛湍急的海面，
阳光照不透，有山峰把我来擎高，
我空悬在天半如房顶一片。
在我灵舆上镇锁着弥空的力能，
我麾同烈焰、大雪和飘风，
引领浩荡的行列通过的凯旋门，
便是那纷呈万彩的长虹；
顶上有天光吐放出柔和的霁氛，
大地在下方欢笑对长空。

〔6〕 I am the daughter of Earth and Water,

And the nursling of the Sky;

I pass through the pores, of the ocean and shores;

I change, but I cannot die —

For after the rain, when with never a stain

The pavilion of Heaven is bare,

And the winds and sunbeams, with their convex gleams,

Build up the blue dome of Air —

I silently laugh at my own cenotaph,

And out of the caverns of rain,

Like a child from the womb, like a ghost from the tomb,

I arise and unbuild it again. —

〔6〕 我乃是地母和水波的生身小女，
　　又是青天保姆的婴孩，
我穿透海洋和平陆，经无数萦纡；
　　变幻无穷尽，但不死也不坏。
因经过雨打后，空中被洗净涤荡，
　　天宇的穹苍显空旷无垠，
晴飏同阳明和它的鼓凸的光芒，
　　构筑起空气的碧琉璃高旻，
我默不作声，对我的丰碑嬉笑，
　　而从已止的雨脚洞穴里，
像孩子从母亲胎内，鬼魂从墓窖，
　　我起来把它再一度毁弃。

1980.4.6 深夜译竟

To a Sky-Lark

〔1〕 Hail to thee, blithe spirit!
Bird thou never wert —
That from Heaven, or near it,
Pourest thy full heart
In profuse strains of unpremeditated art.

〔2〕 Higher still and higher
From the earth thou springest
Like a cloud of fire;
The blue deep thou wingest,
And singing still dost soar, and soaring ever singest.

〔3〕 In the golden lightning
Of the sunken Sun —
O'er which clouds are brightning,
Thou dost float and run;
Like an unbodied joy whose race is just begun.

云雀[①]歌

〔1〕 欢呼你，欢乐的精灵！
　　你也许决不是只鸟，
从天上，或是近天庭，
　　倾吐你满腔的高妙，
使不经思虑的美技，用无比充沛的曲调。

〔2〕 一程又一程向苍旻，
　　从地上你朝高处飞，
像一朵腾空的火云，
　　你展翅捷掠登清辉，
一边儿升登又鸣唱，一边儿鸣唱又超翚。

〔3〕 在落日西沉的时候，
　　金光像闪电耀西天，
那上方云霞全亮透，
　　你如浮如奔疾无前；
像一团没形体的欢乐，它的翻腾方开展。

① 云雀，也叫百灵，又名叫天子，凌晨向高空一边疾飞，一边鸣唱。

〔4〕 The pale purple even
Melts around thy flight,
Like a star of Heaven
In the broad day-light
Thou art unseen, — but yet I hear thy shrill delight,

〔5〕 Keen as are the arrows
Of that silver sphere,
Whose intense lamp narrows
In the white dawn clear
Until we hardly see — we feel that it is there.

〔6〕 All the earth and air
With thy voice is loud,
As when Night is bare
From one lonely cloud
The moon rains out her beams — and Heaven is overflowed.

〔4〕 淡淡的紫霭这薄暮，
　　围着你的飞扬在融化；
像天上没颗星儿露，
　　在白日晴天笼罩下，
遥望不见你，我却听到你欢忭的高哗，

〔5〕 尖锐似银白的光轮
　　射出白闪闪的银针，
它那盏炽烈的明灯
　　在茫茫晓光中消隐，
直到我们几乎不见它——只觉它化了形。

〔6〕 整个大地和长空
　　被你的鸣声所响彻，
好比深夜里苍穹
　　只有一片云，皓月射
云端，倾泻出光明，满天宇泛滥着月色。

〔7〕 What thou art we know not;
What is most like thee?
From rainbow clouds there flow not
Drops so bright to see
As from thy presence showers a rain of melody.

〔8〕 Like a poet hidden
In the light of thought,
Singing hymns unbidden,
Till the world is wrought
To sympathy with hopes and fears it heeded not:

〔9〕 Like a high-born maiden
In a palace-tower,
Soothing her love-laden
Soul in secret hour,
With music sweet as love — which overflows her bower:

〔7〕 我们不知你是什么；

什么才和你最相像？

挂虹的霁云间，不放射

灿烂的水珠有这样

澄明，如从你口中流泻出恁美妙的新腔。

〔8〕 像一位诗人消隐在

诗思霭霭的光辉里，

吟哦着赞歌抒幽怀，

直到这世界被激起

它不介的冀希和恐惧，化作同情和和熙：

〔9〕 像一位名门贵娟秀，

在高塔楼头居璇闺，

调脉脉柔情的弹奏

对她的芳心施温慰，

在悠悠独处中，乐声盈溢她幽居的绣帏。

〔10〕 Like a glow-worm golden
In a dell of dew,
Scattering unbeholden
Its aerial hue
Among the flowers and grass which screen it from the view:
〔11〕 Like a rose embowered
In its own green leaves —
By warm winds deflowered —
Till the scent it gives
Makes faint with too much sweet those heavy-winged thieves:
〔12〕 Sound of vernal showers
On the twinkling grass,
Rain-awakened flowers,
All that ever was
Joyous, and clear and fresh, thy music doth surpass.

〔10〕 似飞萤一点闪金光

于蒙蒙雾重的空谷中，

在花草蓬茸间它散放

它的光芒不矜功，

花荣叶茂将它遮，掩蔽得冥晉渺无踪。

〔11〕 似一朵玫瑰吐红芳，

绿叶在四周相掩护，

熏风鼓翅膀来偷香

等到她吐放的香雾

使那些载满了重负的偷儿香浓醉迷糊。

〔12〕 潺潺的春雨连珠洒，

淋在闪烁的芳草上，

雨打得花梦醒来浹，

欢乐加清新的景象

千百种，全都不敌你清越的脆歌嗓。

〔13〕 Teach us, Sprite or Bird,
What sweet thoughts are thine;
I have never heard
Praise of love or wine
The panted forth a flood of rapture so divine:

〔14〕 Chorus Hymeneal
Or triumphal chaunt
Matched with thine would be all
But an empty vaunt,
A thing wherein we feel there is some hidden want.

〔15〕 What objects are the fountains
Of thy happy strain?
What fields or waves or mountains?
What shapes of sky or plain?
What love of thine own kind? what ignorance of pain?

〔13〕 教我们，精灵或是鸟，
　　你那高华的好思想：
我从未听到过称道
　　情爱或美酒的赞扬，
倾注出这般狂喜的欢潮如此超凡响。

〔14〕 燕尔新婚的合唱曲，
　　或是祝捷的赞美歌，
跟你的鸣声比夸诩，
　　都将成虚骄的莫奈何，
而你的鸣啼，激曜而清厉，我们全喜乐。

〔15〕 你高唱入云的因缘
　　是为怎样的俊目标？
怎样的田畴或丘山
　　或水流？怎样的青霄
或平野好景色？怎样爱自族？怎样的不知忉？

〔16〕 With thy clear keen joyance
Languor cannot be —
Shadow of annoyance
Never came near thee;
Thou lovest — but ne'er knew love's sad satiety.

〔17〕 Waking or asleep,
Thou of death must deem
Things more true and deep
Than we mortals dream,
Or how could thy notes flow in such a chrystal stream?

〔18〕 We look before and after,
And pine for what is not —
Our sincerest laughter
With some pain is fraught —
Our sweetest songs are those that tell of saddest thought.

〔16〕 困倦决不能跟你

清厉的欢乐在一块：

烦恼的阴影也决计

不能靠近你身边来：

你恋爱——但从不感到餍足了情爱的难熬挨。

〔17〕 清醒时或者睡梦里，

你一准看待亡故

比我们尘世人梦寐

所见的要真切和深固，

否则你嘹亮的嘤鸣怎能晶莹地恁流注？

〔18〕 我们向前瞻，向后顾，

为不如意事兴叹息，

我们最真诚的欢呼

都不免含几分悲戚，

我们最甜蜜的歌辞总讴唱最悲伤的心迹。

〔19〕 Yet if we could scorn

Hate and pride and fear;

If we were things born

Not to shed a tear,

I know not how thy joy we ever should come near.

〔20〕 Better than all measures

Of delightful sound —

Better than all treasures

That in books are found —

Thy skill to poet were, thou Scorner of the ground!

〔21〕 Teach me half the gladness

That thy brain must know,

Such harmonious madness

From my lips would flow

The world should listen then — as I am listening now.

〔19〕 可我们若是能蔑视

仇恨与骄矜与恐惧，

我们若是能入世

不逢到哀哭的遭遇，

我真不知道我们将多挨近你欢腾的心曲。

〔20〕 你这副绝艺对诗人

比可喜的声音的一切

度量还要好，比万本

书卷中所含的一切

宝藏还要妙，你这鄙视尘俗的英杰！

〔21〕 教给我一半你衷心

定必知道的欢快，

那怎样和谐的隆情

从我的口头会敞开，

这世界将会谛听着，有如我现在正在。

1980.2.7 译

I Fear Thy Kisses

〔1〕 I fear thy kisses, gentle maiden;
Thou needest not fear mine;
My spirit is too deeply laden
Ever to burthen thine

〔2〕 I fear thy mien, thy tones, thy motion;
Thou needest not fear mine;
Innocent is the heart's devotion
With which I worship thine.

我怕你的亲吻

〔1〕 我怕你的亲吻，温柔的姑娘；
你不用为我的过虑；
负载得深重的是我的精爽，
它不该使你生疑惧。

〔2〕 我怕你的神态、声调和行动；
你不用为我的过虑；
我一心对你的无限钟情，
天真崇敬得无可惧。

1980.6.14 译

Hymn of Pan

〔1〕 From the forests and highlands
We come, we come;
From the river-girt islands,
Where loud waves are dumb
Listening my sweet pipings.
The wind in the reeds and the rushes,
The bees on the bells of thyme,
The birds on the myrtle bushes,
The cicalas above in the lime,
And the lizards below in the grass,
Were as silent as ever old Tmolus was,
Listening my sweet pipings.

潘灵[①]的圣歌

〔1〕　从高地上头，从森林里边，
　　我们来，我们来；
从河流萦绕的小岛跟前，
　　那里的涛声嘈，
正在听我吹甜蜜的排箫。
　芦苇中、蒲草里的轻风，
　百里香花铃上的青蜂，
　　桃金娘花丛上的歌鸟，
　　宜母子树枝头的知了，
和下面草窝里的蜥蜴，
都悄静如老神忒莫栗，
正在听我吹甜蜜的排箫。

① 古希腊神话中阿凯狄亚（Arcadia）山里的树林与牧羊神潘（Pan），上身人样，下体是山羊，喜欢音乐，吹奏排箫（Pandean pipe）。

〔2〕 Liquid penëus was flowing,

And all dark Tempe lay

In Pelion's shadow, outgrowing

The light of the dying day,

Speeded by my sweet pipings.

The Sileni, and Sylvans, and Fauns,

And the Nymphs of the woods and the waves,

To the edge of the moist river-lawns,

And the brink of the dewy caves,

And all that did then attend and follow,

Were silent with love, as you now, Apollo,

With envy of my sweet pipings.

〔2〕 澄明的盼虞斯[①]在流动，

谭比谷[②]呈一片美景，

琵荔翁雄峙它那高峰，

送落日的斜晖西暝，

我催快着河流，吹甜蜜的排箫。

田野一带的醉仙翁，[③]

以及林神跟护畜神，

和山林水泽的美女仙，

连同江畔的草莽地

和露滋的山缘峒谷边

一切追随我、跟着的，

都因爱而沉默，正如你，

阿波罗，可是你因妒忌，

忌妒我吹奏这甜蜜的排箫。[④]

---

① Peneus 是古希腊一条河流，在希腊半岛东北部古 Thessaly 地区，现在叫萨兰勃利亚（Salambria），河两岸花木葱茏，风景优美，有 5 300 英尺的琵荔翁（Pelion）高山山脉俯瞰着它。

② Tempe 谷就是它的流域。

③ Silenus 本为神，是个秃顶、多髭髯、扁鼻子的矮老头，好酗酒，上身人样，下体为马或山羊，传说中系神使 Hermes 之子，又为酒神 Bacchus 的义父及伴侣。这里 Sileni 是 Silenus 一词的复数形式，通指这样的半人半神形象。

④ 第二节多出一行，第三节多出三行，无法避免此缺失。

〔3〕 I sang of the dancing stars,

I sang of the daedal Earth,

And of Heaven — and the giant wars,

And Love, and Death, and Birth, —

And then I changed my pipings, —

Singing how down the vale of Maenalus

I pursued a maiden and clasped a reed:

Gods and men, we are all deluded thus!

It breaks in our bosom and now would,

If envy or age had not frozen your blood,

At the sorrow of my sweet pipings.

〔3〕 我奏鸣飞舞的星辰，

　　我歌吹奇妙神灵的大地，

奏苍穹一片——和滔天的战事，

　　和爱情和死亡和新生；——

我接着改变了鸣奏的曲子，

　　歌吹我怎样进弥那勒山谷，

追一个少女，搂住了支芦荻，

　　神和人，我们都这样受欺！

它在我们的胸头破裂，

　　于是我们都流血，大家哭，

　　我想你们都会这么样

　　如果忌妒和老衰

还未把你们的血冻结，

　　为了我这甜蜜的歌吹

所招引起来的满腔悲伤。

1980.3.15 译

The Question

〔1〕 I DREAMED that, as I wandered by the way,
    Bare winter suddenly was changed to spring,
And gentle odours led my steps astray,
    Mixed with a sound of waters murmuring,
Along a shelving bank of turf which lay
    Under a copse — and hardly dared to fling
Its green arms round the bosom of the stream,
But kissed it and then fled — as thou mightest in dream.

〔2〕 There grew pied wind-flowers and violets,
    Daisies, those pearled Arcturi of the earth —
That constellated flower that never sets;
    Faint oxlips, — tender blue bells, at whose birth
The sod scarce heared, and that tall flower that wets —
    Like a child, half in tenderness and mirth —
Its mother's face with Heaven's collected tears,
When the low wind, its playmate's voice, it hears.

问语

〔1〕我梦见，当我在路上随意漫游时，

　　赤裸裸的寒冬忽然变成了新春；

温馨的花香引得我步履都迷失，

　　又加上一阵阵汩没的流水声音，

沿着一湾矮树丛的泥草地涯涘

　　在鸣唱，它不怎么敢挥它那绿嫩

翠肥的两臂去拥抱流水的酥胸，

只吻它一下而逃走，像你在梦中。

〔2〕那里长着斑驳的白头翁、紫罗兰；

　　雏菊，人间的珍珠般牧夫座大星，

它这星座似的繁花从来不凋残；

　　淡黄的报春；初生时，娇嫩的蓝铃，

草泥还没有给涨松；还有那华冠

　　玉立的高花——像孩子，娇柔，发稚兴，

当它听到它玩伴轻风的声音时，

便用水晶珠将母亲的脸去露滋。

〔3〕 And in the warm hedge grew lush eglantine,
Green cow-bind and the moonlight-coloured May,
And cherry blossoms, and white cups whose wine
Was the bright dew yet drained not by the day;
And wild roses, and ivy serpentine,
With its dark buds and leaves, wandering astray;
And flowers azure, black, and streaked with gold,
Fairer than any wakened eyes behold.

〔4〕 And nearer to the river's trembling edge
There grew broad flag-flowers, purple prankt with white,
And starry river buds among the sedge,
And floating water-lilies broad and bright,
Which lit the oak that overhung the hedge
With moonlight beams of their own watery light;
And bulrushes and reeds, of such deep green
As soothed the dazzled eye with sober sheen.

〔3〕 温郁的树篱间长满茂盛的玫瑰，
　　绿的白南瓜和月白色的山楂花，
樱花，和清露斟进洁白的小酒杯，
　　还未被晴明的昼天所挹干晾乏；
又有缭绕的长春藤，以及野蔷薇，
　　藤蔓上黝暗的芽苞和叶子在扒；
更有些花儿呀，天蓝、乌黑、起舍线，
比什么清醒的眼睛见到的鲜妍。

〔4〕 而靠近河水晃漾着的边缘所在，
　　那里开放着菖蒲花，紫色饰上白，
还有菅茅里杂生着星星的江苔，
　　和浮在水上的睡莲，花明而叶阔，
它们用自己盈盈的水月般光彩
　　照亮悬垂在树篱上的橡峨嵯；
还有香蒲和这样碧深深的芦苇，
安抚昏眩的眼睛，以沉着的清辉。

〔5〕 Methought that of these visionary flowers

I made a nosegay, bound in such a way

That the same hues which in their natural bowers

Were mingled or opposed — the like array

Kept these imprisoned children of the Hours

Within my hand ... and then elate and gay

I hastened to the spot whence I had come,

That I might there present it! — oh! to whom?

〔5〕　我以为，我把这些幻象中的鲜花
　　做成了一个花束，捆扎得这么样，
同一颜色在自然生长的情况下
　　混合或对衬着，我也按照那情况，
把那些时光所羁绊的孩儿盈把
　　握在我手掌中；——然后，兴高而气扬，
赶往我开始所从来的那处通逵，
以便在那里把花束献赠给——啊，谁？

1980.6.10 译

To the Moon

〔1〕 And like a dying lady, lean and pale,
Who totters forth, wrapt in a gauzy veil,
From her dim chamber, led by the insane
And feeble wanderings of her fading brain,
The moon arose up on the murky earth,
A white and shapeless mass.

〔2〕 Art thou pale for weariness
Of climbing heaven, and gazing on the earth,
Wandering companionless
Among the stars that have a different birth, —
And ever-changing, like a joyless eye
That finds no object worth its constancy?

月 亮

〔1〕 像个垂死的大娘，消瘦又苍白，
笼一条轻纱面罩，从房里踩着
碎步踉跄跨出来，神志迷惘中
瞑瞀且似梦似疾，不分辨西东，
月亮从黝暗的东方冉冉上升，
一片白糊涂，灰败而无形。

〔2〕 你是否因为攀援着上天
又俯瞰大地而疲累所以苍白，
浪游中没有伴侣，形单
影只，跟不是族类的群星同出没，
故不断盈亏变换，像一只眼睛
落落寡欢，没东西值得它钟情？

To Night

〔1〕 Swiftly walk over the western Wave,
Spirit of Night!
Out of the misty eastern cave
Where all the long and lone daylight,
Thou wovest dreams of joy and fear,
Which make thee terrible and dear, —
Swift be thy flight!

〔2〕 Wrap thy form in a mantle grey
Star-inwrought!
Blind with thine hair the eyes of Day,
Kiss her until she be wearied out,
Then wander o'er city, and sea, and land,
Touching all with thine opiate wand —
Come, long-sought!

〔3〕 When I arose and saw the dawn,
I sighed for thee;
When light rode high, and the dew was gone,
And noon lay heavy on flower and tree,
And the weary Day turned to his rest,
Lingering like an unloved guest,
I sighed for thee.

致 夜

〔1〕 速速跨上了西海的波涛，
　　暗夜的精灵！
步出雾蒙蒙的东方山坳，
那儿，整长天寂寂的光阴，
你织着欢乐和恐惧的梦，
这使你显得可怕又可亲，——
　　要飞得捷敏！

〔2〕 将你的形体裹在灰氅中，
　　包进了星星！
披发使白日的眼睛变瞽矇，
吻着她，直等她精疲力尽，
然后过城市、海洋和平陆，
都用你催眠的魔杖去一触——
　　来，我久久将你寻！

〔3〕 当我起身见到了黎明，
　　我为你叹息，
看晨晖高升，朝露全化尽，
亭午迟重得使花树昏迷，
疲惫的长日留久了晷刻，
不走，像个不欢迎的来客，
　　我为你嘘唏。

〔4〕 Thy brother Death came, and cried,
Wouldst thou me?
Thy sweet child Sleep, the filmy-eyed,
Murmured like a noon-tide bee,
Shall I nestle near thy side?
Wouldst thou me? — And I replied,
No, ... not thee!

〔5〕 Death will come when thou art dead,
Soon, too soon —
Sleep will come when thou art fled;
Of neither would I ask the boon
I ask of thee, beloved Night —
Swift be thine approaching flight,
Come soon, soon!

〔4〕 你的弟兄死亡来，他问我：

“你要我不要？”

你喜爱的孩儿睡眠，眼翳膜，

嗡嗡哼响着像午刻蜜蜂叫：

“可要我偎依在你的身旁边？

你要我不要？”——我当即回言：

“不要你，不要！”

〔5〕 你死后，死亡将会要到来，

快快地，火速——

你若飞逝后，睡眠将会来；

我不会对它们央求我所作

对你的央求，至爱的暗夜——

请你的飞临要来个腾越，

快快来，火速！

1980.4.18 深夜译

To —
[Music, When Soft Voices Die]

〔1〕 Music, when soft voices die,
Vibrates in the memory —
Odours, when sweet violets sicken,
Live within the sense they quicken.

〔2〕 Rose leaves, when the rose is dead,
Are heap'd for the beloved's bed;
And so thy thoughts, when Thou art gone,
Love itself shall slumber on.

音乐声，当轻歌曼唱已沉寂

〔1〕 音乐声，当轻歌曼唱已沉寂，
依然在记忆里震颤不息；
芳馨，当馥郁的紫罗兰已凋敝，
还活跃在花香引起的感觉里。
〔2〕 玫瑰的花瓣，当玫瑰已死亡，
被铺叠起来，作情侣的眠床；
所以，萦念你的思想，你虽去，
眷恋将寤寐反侧地去凝聚。

1980.5.17 译

Invocation

〔1〕 Rarely, rarely, comest thou,
Spirit of Delight!
Wherefore hast thou left me now
Many a day and night?
Many a weary night and day
'Tis since thou art fled away.

〔2〕 How shall ever one like me
Win thee back again?
With the joyous and the free
Thou wilt scoff at pain.
Spirit false! thou hast forgot
All but those who need thee not.

〔3〕 As a lizard with the shade
Of a trembling leaf,
Thou with sorrow art dismay'd;
Even the sighs of grief
Reproach thee, that thou art not near,
And reproach thou wilt not hear.

召 唤

〔1〕 绝少有，绝少有，你光降
　　欢快的精灵！
你为何离开我这茫茫
　　好许多夜和明？
这么多劳累的日和夜，
自从你逃跑走，和我别？

〔2〕 我这样的人儿怎么能
　　赢得你肯再来？
如欢乐和自由的人们，
　　你鄙弃苦熬挨。
虚假的精灵！你忘却，
只除不要你的，那一切。

〔3〕 像一条蜥蜴怕风动
　　一张树叶影，
你对于悲伤总惊恐；
　　愁苦的叹息声
也骂你总不在它身边，
有呵斥，你便听不见。

〔4〕 Let me set my mournful ditty
To a merry measure; —
Thou wilt never come for pity,
Thou wilt come for pleasure; —
Pity then will cut away
Those cruel wings, and thou wilt stay.

〔5〕 I love all that thou lovest,
Spirit of Delight!
The fresh Earth in new leaves drest
And the starry night;
Autumn evening, and the morn
When the golden mists are born.

〔6〕 I love snow and all the forms
Of the radiant frost;
I love waves, and winds, and storms,
Everything almost
Which is Nature's, and may be
Untainted by man's misery.

〔7〕 I love tranquil solitude,
And such society
As is quiet, wise, and good;
Between thee and me
What difference? but thou dost possess
The things I seek, not love them less.

〔4〕 让我唱我的悲来吟，
　　用欢乐的曲调；——
你决不会来，为怜悯，
　　你会来，为喜好；——
怜悯会把你的翅膀裁，
你那时也就会耽下来。

〔5〕 你爱的一切我都爱，
　　欢快的精灵！
新装的大地碧油彩，
　　长空闪繁星；
秋日的黄昏，和凌晨，
当金黄的朝雾方新生。

〔6〕 我爱白雪，爱严霜，
　　和它的一切形象，
爱暴风骤雨和波浪，
　　爱几乎每一样
自然的景物，那大多
未曾遭人间的疾苦。

〔7〕 我喜爱宁静的孤单，
　　和凡是悠然，
聪敏和恂良的友伴；
　　在你我之间
有什么区别？你奄有
这种种，且骀荡优游。

〔8〕 I love Love — though he has wings,
　　And like light can flee,
But above all other things
　　Spirit, I love thee —
Thou art love and life! O come!
Make once more my heart thy home!

〔8〕 我也爱情爱——他展翼

能到处飞临，

但胜如其他的一切，

我爱你，精灵——

你是爱和生命！来呀！

再将我的心，作你的家！

1980.4.28 译

A Lament

1

O World! O life! O time!
On whose last steps I climb,
    Trembling at that where I had stood before;
When will return the glory of your prime?
    No more — Oh, never more!

2

Out of the day and night
A joy has taken flight:
    Fresh spring, and summer, and winter hoar,
Move my faint heart with grief, but with delight
    No more — Oh, never more!

浩叹

1

世界！嗳呀！时间！嗳呀！人生！
我在它们末了的踏级上攀升，
　　目对着刚才站过的梯阶发抖；
何时能重见你们辉煌的荣盛？
　　不会——啊，永远不会有！

2

明来，夜去，明来，夜去，又明朝，
一场欢乐已经长此逃跑掉，
　　灿烂的新春、夏天和冬日皑皑
以悲怆震动我的心，但采烈兴高
　　不再会——决不会再来！

1980.4.10 深夜译

One Word Is Too Often Profaned

1

One word is too often profaned
For me to profane it,
One feeling too falsely disdain'd
For thee to disdain it;
One hope is too like despair
For prudence to smother,
And pity from thee more dear
Than that from another.

一个字亵渎得过于见惯了

1

一个字亵渎得过于见惯了，
　　毋须我再来亵渎它，
一注感情太被人轻慢了，
　　毋须你再来屈辱它。
一线冀希太过于像绝望，
　　不该由审慎去窒息，
怜悯出自你，非别的姑娘，
　　才带来春风般的快意。

2

I can give not what men call love:
    But wilt thou accept not
The worship the heart lifts above
    And the heavens reject not,
The desire of the moth for the star,
    Of the night for the morrow,
The devotion to something afar
    from the sphere of our sorrow?

2

我不能轻抛俗人的所谓爱。
　　但难道你吝于接受
至忱所高举的倾慕和拥戴，
　　苍天也不拒的情窦；
飞蛾对星光所怀的向往，
　　暗夜向晨曦的企盼，
从我们这悲哀、昏懵的世上，
　　神魂飞翚向云山？

1980.4.25 译

Chorus from *Hellas*

〔1〕 The world's great age begins anew,
　　The golden years return,
The earth doth like a snake renew
　　Her winter weeds outworn;
Heaven smiles, and faiths and empires gleam
Like wrecks of a dissolving dream.

希 腊[①]

〔1〕 世界的伟大时代重新起，
　　黄金的华年已再度到来，
大地像条蛇已睡过冬眠期，
　　更新了它那越冬的穿戴：
天在笑，宗教和帝邦在闪耀，
像消融的梦境里的残漂。

① 这是雪莱的抒情戏剧诗《希腊》（*Hellas*）剧终时的一首合唱曲（Chorus），诗中叨念古希腊的一些往事，憧憬未来的希腊能荡涤历史疮痍而得到真正自由的新生。这首政治戏剧诗作于1821年秋天，在意大利的比萨（Pisa）。早在那年的春天之前，西班牙革命引起了意大利的一些城市和地区如拿坡里（Napoli）、佩蒙德（Piemonte）、杰诺伐（Genova）、喀拉拉（Carrara）等纷纷响应，革命党人卡蓬拿利（Garbonari）风起云涌，推翻异族征服与封建统治，缔造共和。雪莱本来对古希腊的文化艺术深深钦佩。在当年四月一日，他听到君士坦丁堡的一位希腊爱国人士亚历山大·马扶洛考达笃亲王（Prince Alexander Mavrocordato）向他报喜，说他表兄亿泼锡朗蒂亲王（Prince Ipsilanti）已在希腊宣布推翻了土耳其征服者的统治，他的故国将从此得到自由和新生。雪莱对于希腊的前途，当然欣喜若狂，而且存有厚望，但不无几分含有忧虑的恐惧。故这首合唱曲的最后一行说，如果最后能得到休安最好，否则，若要重复过去的种种苦难，不如让它完结了也罢。

〔2〕 A brighter Hellas rears its mountains
From waves serener far,
A new Peneus rolls his fountains
Against the morning-star,
Where fairer Tempes bloom, there sleep
Young Cyclads on a sunnier deep.

〔2〕　　一个更灿烂的希腊从远处

　　澄明的浪涛里掀举出山峰；

又一条盼虞斯在翻滚波涛，

　　直对着启明星滚滚前冲；

更美的谭比谷开花处，那里

年轻的昔克拉群岛[①]在斜倚。

① Cyclands 群岛在它的东南方爱琴海（Ægean Sea）中，包括 Andros，Naxos，Santorin，Paras，Syra，Delos 等岛屿。

〔3〕 A loftier Argo cleaves the main,
Fraught with a later prize;
Another Orpheus sings again,
And loves, and weeps, and dies;
A new Ulysses leaves once more
Calypso for his native shore.

〔3〕 更峨观的阿告神舟[①]在航行，

　　装载着一束后世的金羊毛；

另一个奥菲斯[②]又复在歌吟，

　　以及恋爱，和哭泣，和早夭；

一名新生的攸力赛[③]再一回

离开凯律梭[④]向故国来归。

① 伊琛（Æson）的儿子，Iolcus 国王 Pelias 的侄子，名叫杰生（Jason）。Pelias 因抢夺了他的王位，故叫他去做一件不可能做到的事，去觅取 Colchis 国王 Æetes 所宝藏的金羊毛［Golden fleece，牡羊名 Chrysomallus 身上的金毛，杰生一伙 54 人，其中有个名叫 Argonaut 的，乘着大船阿告（Argo）帮他去设法觅取］，企图置他于死地。而 Æetes 则要他驾驭两头喷火的魔牛去播种毒龙的牙齿。但他依靠 Æetes 王的女儿妖姑 Medea 的帮助，克服了种种困难，终于同手下人乘着阿告大船将金羊毛取回。

② 奥菲斯（Orpheus）是古希腊神话中一位惊人的青年诗人与音乐家，是音乐的始祖；他吟咏起抒情诗来，伴奏着七弦琴（lyre），能使禽兽木石感动共鸣而舞蹈。他的恋人优律笛西（Euridice）早夭，进入地府；他以他悲怆的哀吟和竖琴上凄楚奏鸣，使冥王动情，开启地府之门，放她出来。不过有一条件，她只能在他背后跟着他的奏鸣步出地府；在返回人世之前，他可不准回顾她一眼。不幸他正在走出地府时，情不自禁，忘记了那条禁律，竟回顾一下；于是立即得而复失，她又被摄回了阴曹。他因而终于哀愁死去。

③ 攸力赛（Ulysses）是古罗马人称呼他的名字，在古希腊荷马（Homer）的史诗《奥特赛》（*Odyssey*）中他本来名叫奥特修斯（Odysseus）；他是伊萨格（Ithaca）国王，在希腊对特洛伊（Troy）的七年战争里他是希腊的领袖之一，以机智闻名。他在返回伊萨格途中十年的漫游经历，就是这首史诗的叙事端末。

④ 凯律梭（Calypso）是史诗《奥特赛》中 Ogygia 岛上的女海神，奥特修斯在岛上遭破船之厄，是她收留了他七年并缔结燕好。不幸七年后他遗弃了她返回故国。

〔4〕 O, write no more the tale of Troy,
    If earth Death's scroll must be!
Nor mix with Laian rage the joy
    Which dawns upon the free;
Although a subtler Sphinx renew
Riddles of death Thebes never knew.

〔4〕 这世界若定要成死亡的卷轴，

再莫写特洛伊的七年战争[①]——

也莫将刚获得自由者的欢呼

和弑父娶母的悲剧[②]相淆混，

纵或有更诡谲的狮身女首怪

再抛出死亡谜，底皮斯难悬揣。

---

① 古希腊荷马所作史诗《伊列亚特》（*Iliad*）叙述雅典（Athens）城邦与特洛伊（Troy）岛之间的七年战争，双方损兵折将，死亡酷烈，造成两败俱伤的惨剧。

② 原文 Laian rage 系指底皮斯（Thebes）国王 Laius 及其王后 Jocasta 之子伊狄浦斯（Œdipus）。他出生时，有一神使预言国王将来会被这孩子所弑；他们当即将此婴儿抛弃在荒野里，让他自灭。但机缘凑巧，伊狄浦斯被 Corinth 国王所收养，等到长大成人，听一神使说他要弑父婚母，遂惊恐而逃走。但在浮游中正巧遇到他的生父 Laius，而且发生了争执，当即把他杀死。随后又遇到狮身人面女怪，她盘据在底皮斯国门口，提出一个难于猜测的哑谜（起初四只脚，接着两只脚，最后三只脚是什么？），迫使过路人猜测，猜不中的都被她扑杀。伊狄浦斯一下子猜中了（是人），此怪即投海而死。伊狄浦斯以此殊功，被底皮斯国人拥为君王，当即与寡孀王后成婚。但一登王位，天地变异不断，疫疬流行；向神灵问卜，乃知犯了滔天大祸。王后随即自杀而死，伊狄浦斯则弄瞎了自己的眼睛而外出流浪忏悔，最后死在雅典，成为它的守护神。这传说故事被古希腊诗人索福格里斯（Sophocles，公元前 496?—前 406）写成悲剧诗《伊狄浦斯王》（*Œdipus Tyrannus*）传世。

〔5〕 Another Athens shall arise,
And to remoter time
Bequeath, like sunset to the skies,
The splendour of its prime,
And leave, if nought so bright may live,
All earth can take or Heaven can give.

〔6〕 Saturn and Love their long repose
Shall burst, more bright and good
Than all who fell, than One who rose,
Than many unsubdued;
Not gold, not blood their altar dowers
But votive tears and symbol flowers.

〔5〕 另一个雅典将会升起来，

对于遥远的将来会给予

像落日对于暮天的云彩，

它全盛时期的光华炳煜；

如没有这样亮的东西能存留，

要遗下天所能给予的，地所能受。

〔6〕 农神和爱神将破除了休息，

比一切倒下的，一个上升的，

比还有许多没有被克服的，①

更显得容光焕发而仁慈：

不是黄金和碧血去美化

他们的圣坛，是许愿泪，象征花。

① 原文“an who fell”（一切倒下的）据雪莱自己在一条注释里说，是指希腊、亚洲和埃及的所有偶像神祇，“One who rose”（一个上升的）则指耶稣。雪莱是个无神论者，他不信基督教。在1811年春天的报喜节（Lady Day，三月二十五日），当时他在牛津大学读书，距他满19足岁还相差十天，因他写了一篇震惊社会习俗的文章《无神论的需要》（*The Necessity of Atheism*）并印成小册子而被大学当局开除学籍。雪莱对耶稣却绝无反感，但基督教作为一门宗教他是反对的。原文“Than many unsubdued”（比还有许多没有被克服的），雪莱说是指中国、印度、南冰洋上一些岛屿和美洲土人的偶像崇拜。他认为稼穑和泛爱是人间两桩最好的事，农神（Saturn）与爱神（Love）便代表了它们，它们也就是天真与快乐的现实与想象境界。

〔7〕 O cease! must hate and death return?

Cease! must men kill and die?
Cease! drain not to its dregs the urn
Of bitter prophecy.
The world is weary of the past,
O might it die or rest at last!

〔7〕 停止哟！仇恨和死亡一定要

回来吗？停止！人定得杀和死？

停止！莫喝干苦涩的预告

之瓮，〔使旧时的悲苦再开始，〕

这世界对疲累的过去已厌倦，

但愿它死亡或最后得休安！

1980.6.1 译

A Widow Bird

〔1〕 A widow bird sate mourning for her Love
Upon a wintry bough;
The frozen wind crept on above,
The freezing stream below.

〔2〕 There was no leaf upon the forest bare,
No flower upon the ground,
And little motion in the air
Except the mill-wheel's sound.

孤 禽

〔1〕 一只丧偶的孤禽栖在冬枝上，
为她的爱侣哀悼；
寒风爬行在她的上方，
冻流在下边缓潮。
〔2〕 光赤的林柯上没有一张树叶，
地上没有一朵花，
空中很少有响动些些，
只除磨轮的沉哗。

1980.6.13 译

Lines

1

When the lamp is shattered,
The light in the dust lies dead —
When the cloud is scattered,
The rainbow's glory is shed.
When the lute is broken,
Sweet tones are remembered not;
When the lips have spoken,
Loved accents are soon forgot.

2

As music and splendour
Survive not the lamp and the lute,
The heart's echoes render
No song when the spirit is mute: —
No song but sad dirges,
Like the wind through a ruined cell,
Or the mournful surges
That ring the dead seaman's knell.

诗 行

1

当明灯破成碎片时，
　　灯光在尘埃里熄灭；
当霁云刮得四散时，
　　彩虹的光华便完结：
当琵琶打得残破时，
　　悠扬的乐声被忘却；
当唇舌将话说过时，
　　眷爱的语调便响绝。

2

正如弦奏声和灯光
　　残留不住灯和琵琶，
心灵的放歌唱不响，
　　当神明的灵爽已喑哑——
不能唱，只除掉挽曲
　　像悲风在洞窟里呜啸，
或者像哀呻的海浪
　　为淹死的水手丧钟敲。

3

When hearts have once mingled,
Love first leaves the well-built nest;
The weak one is singled
To endure what it once possesst.
O, Love! who bewailest
The frailty of all things here,
Why choose you the frailest
For your cradle, your home, and your bier?

4

Its passions will rock thee,
As the storms rock the ravens on high:
Bright reason will mock thee,
Like the sun from a wintry sky.
From thy nest every rafter
Will rot and thine eagle home
Leave thee naked to laughter,
When leaves fall and cold winds come.

3

当两心一经相团圞，
　　爱情便先行离香巢；
柔弱的一方独可怜，
　　去消受失恋的苦恼。
爱情啊，你为了人间的
　　万事太脆弱而唏嘘，
却为何挑选最脆弱的
　　当摇篮、家庭和灵车？

4

心儿的激情会震荡你，
　　如高飙会震渡乌：
光耀的理智会嘲诮你，
　　像冬日高空的阳乌。
你窠上每一根椽桷
会朽烂，而你的云阁[①]
　　将会把你暴露给嬉笑，
　　当落叶纷飞寒天到。

1980.5.15 译

① 原文直译为“鹰居”，即极高或最理想的居处。

To Jane. The Invitation

〔1〕 Best and brightest, come away —
Fairer far than this fair day
Which like thee to those in sorrow
Comes to bid a sweet good-morrow
To the rough year just awake
In its cradle on the brake. —
The brightest hour of unborn spring
Through the winter wandering
Found, it seems, this halcyon morn
To hoar February born;
Bending from Heaven in azure mirth
It kissed the forehead of the earth
And smiled upon the silent sea,
And bade the frozen streams be free
And waked to music all their fountains,

致絜恩——邀请[①]

〔1〕 最美好，也最明媚的，起去来！
你远比这晴阳天气要光彩；
这朗照，好比你对于伤心人，
前来把甜蜜的早安道一声，
向这个风雪飘飖的新岁首，
它在灌木丛摇篮里刚抬头。
这未诞新春的最亮的时辰，
宛转地浪游得经历隆冬尽，
似乎找到了这宁静的清早
在霜皤的二月寒天来光照。
从天上俯首，喜乐得碧澄澄，
它在大地的前额上接过吻，
向沉默的海水盈盈含着笑，
使冰冻的百川雪化也冰消，
唤醒了它们的水流使含欢，

---

① 雪莱的朋友威廉斯（Edward Williams）在他二月二日（1821）的日记里记述这一短游如后："温暖的晴日。絜恩陪同玛丽和雪莱经俱乐部（the Cascine）到海边去。他们约于三点钟时回来。"絜恩是威廉斯的妻子，玛丽为雪莱的妻子。此诗初次发表于雪莱夫人（Mary Godwin）的1824年的《雪莱遗诗集》中，措辞稍有不同；现在的形式（译笔即据此）是根据她1839年所出的《雪莱全集》本。

And breathed upon the frozen mountains,
And like a prophetess of May
Strewed flowers upon the barren way,
Making the wintry world appear
Like one on whom thou smilest, dear.

〔2〕 Away, away from men and towns
To the wild wood and the downs,
To the silent wilderness
Where the soul need not repress
Its music lest it should not find
An echo in another's mind,
While the touch of Nature's art
Harmonizes heart to heart. —
I leave this notice on my door
For each accustomed visitor —
"I am gone into the fields
To take what this sweet hour yields.
Reflexion, you may come tomorrow,
Sit by the fireside with Sorrow —
You, with the unpaid bill, Despair,
You, tiresome verse-reciter Care,
I will pay you in the grave,
Death will listen to your stave —

嘘暖气又融化凝冻的群山；
且像个初夏五月的女先知，
在荒芜的道上遍插百花枝，
使寒凝的世界忽地里变成
像是你对它在微笑呀，絜恩。[①]

〔2〕 去来啊，去来，别人群和城镇，
到荒林野地里去栖息安身——
去到那默默无声的大荒中，
在那里你灵魂毋须去箝控
它自己的清音，只为了生怕
在旁人心里头得不到回喳，
而造化的仁灵施展它的妙，
却能在心和心之间起谐调。
我在我寓所的门首要留示
给每个来访者这样的通知：——
“我已经出得门去到了田间，
去消受这甜蜜的良时所献。
‘思考’，你可以等待到明天来；
就坐在炉火旁，陪伴着‘悲哀’。
你来送未清付的账单，‘怅惘’，——
你这个讨厌的诵诗者，‘凄惶’，——
我要在坟墓里还你们的账，——
将会听你们乐曲的是‘死亡’。

① 这里原文是“亲爱的”。

Expectation too, be off!
To-day is for itself enough —
Hope, in pity mock not woe
With smiles, nor follow where I go;
Long having lived on thy sweet food,
At length I find one moment's good
After long pain — with all your love
This you never told me of."

〔3〕 Radiant Sister of the day,
Awake, arise and come away
To the wild woods and the plains
And the pools where winter-rains
Image all their roof of leaves,
Where the pine its garland weaves
Of sapless green and ivy dun
Round stems that never kiss the Sun —
Where the lawns and pastures be
And the sandhills of the sea —
Where the melting hoar-frost wets
The daisy-star that never sets,
And wind-flowers, and violets
Which yet join not scent to hue
Crown the pale year weak and new,
When the night is left behind
In the deep east dun and blind
And the blue noon is over us,

此外是‘期待’，也没有你的份！
今天已足够了，光是它本身。
‘希望’啊，请垂怜，别使用微笑
去嘲弄‘悲痛’，也不要跟我跑；
我久久依仗你赐予我恩德，
最后在长期痛苦后，我能得
顷刻的安顿：尽管你深爱我，
你对此可从未向我说起过。”

〔3〕 灿烂的晴天的辉煌的小妹，
振奋啊！起身！和我们去来喂！
去到野林中和漠漠的平荒；
还有那冬雨积成的小水塘，
映照着漫天的绿叶和青枝；
那一带茂密的乔松到处是，
有干碧的藓苔、棕色常春藤，
在阳光不照的树干上爬行；
那里有成片的草场和牧地，
及海滨沙丘群，累累又迤迤；
在开始融化的严霜滋润下，
长命的雏菊正初开不谢花，
还有那白头翁和紫花地丁
(它吐放异彩，春未到，不含馨)，
华装这苍白的岁首弱而新；
当昨宵的暗夜深深遗留在
东方隈，颜色玄黄而灰败，
而蔚蓝的午分高高在上空，

And the multitudinous
Billows murmur at our feet
Where the earth and ocean meet,
And all things seem only one
In the universal Sun. —

沧海的澄波则无尽又无穷，
在我们脚下边哦哦相应和，
那里是，大地和海洋两交错，
而宇宙的万汇显得像一体，
在普照大千的熠熠阳光里。

1980.5.12 译

• 约翰·济慈 •

John Keats

（1795—1821）

La Belle Dame Sans Merci

〔1〕 O what can ail thee, Knight at arms,
Alone and palely loitering?
The sedge has withered from the Lake
And no birds sing!

〔2〕 O what can all thee, Knight at arms,
So haggard, and so woe-begone?
The squirrel's granary is full
And the harvest's done.

〔3〕 I see a lily on thy brow
With anguish moist and fever dew,
And on thy cheeks a fading rose
Fast withereth too.

〔4〕 "I met a Lady in the meads.
Full beautiful, a faery's child,
Her hair was long, her foot was light
And her eyes were wild.

〔5〕 "I made a garland for her head,
And bracelets too, and fragrant zone;
She looked at me as she did love
And made sweet moan.

〔6〕 "I set her on my pacing steed
And nothing else saw all day long,

残忍的姣娘

〔1〕 嗳嗳，骑士啊，为什么苦恼，
独自徘徊着，苍白又迷惘？
湖中的芦苇都已经枯萎，
没鸟儿在啼唱。

〔2〕 嗳嗳，骑士啊，为什么悲苦，
脸色恁憔悴，愁眉不展翘？
松鼠的窠藏都已经装满，
收割已完成好。

〔3〕 你额上我瞧见一朵百合花，
苦痛得汗湿，发烧沁珠露，
你脸上红潮像玫瑰已褪色，
快凋残委泥土。

〔4〕 “我在草原上见一位姣娘，
一位绝色天生的女仙姬，
她鬘发修长，她脚步轻盈，
她秀眼野而奇。

〔5〕 “我替她头上编一顶花冠，
腕上双花镯，颈里香花环；
她对我凝睇，像显示恩情，
呻吟里含爱怜。

〔6〕 “我扶她跨上我缓步的青玉骢，
整天价眼不见地来也不见天，

For sidelong would she bend and sing
A faery's song.

〔7〕 "She found me roots of relish sweet,
And honey wild, and manna dew,
And sure in language strange she said
'I love thee true.'

〔8〕 "She took me to her elfin grot
And there she wept and sighed full sore,
And there I shut her wild wild eyes
With kisses four.

〔9〕 "And there she lulled me asleep,
And there I dreamed, Ah! Woe betide!
The latest dream I ever dreamt
On the cold hill side.

〔10〕 "I saw pale kings, and princes too,
Pale warriors, death-pale were they all;
They cried, 'La belle dame sans merci
Thee hath in thrall!'

〔11〕 "I saw their starved lips in the gloam
With horrid warning gaped wide,
And I awoke, and found me here
On the cold hill's side.

〔12〕 "And this is why I sojourn here,
Alone and palely loitering;
Though the sedge is withered from the lake
And no birds sing."

有她斜倚在我胸头声声唱
　　一曲小飞仙。
〔7〕　“她为我采觅得鲜美的嫩根芽，
　　还有野蜂蜜和天粮甘玉露，
她当真用奇特的语言对我说，
　　‘我对你真爱慕！’
〔8〕　“她带我去到她仙家的小洞窟，
　　在那里她泣叹得使我动哀矜；
在那里我吻闭她一双野眼睛，
　　用轻轻四个吻。
〔9〕　“在那里她抚慰得使我入睡去，
　　在那里我梦见——啊也！灾殃到！
在那里我梦见的最后那个梦，
　　是在那寒山坳。
〔10〕　“我眼见苍白的君王和士子们，
　　苍白的军伍士，他们都死灰白；
大伙儿齐声叫——‘那残忍的姣娘
　　摄得你丧魂魄！’
〔11〕　“我看到他们的饥唇在阴影中，
　　发可怕的警告，口张得大大地，
惊恐中我醒来，发现我在此地，
　　在这里寒山阿。
〔12〕　“这便是为什么我耽留在这里，
　　独自徘徊着，苍白又迷惘，
虽然这湖中的芦苇已枯萎，
　　没鸟儿在啼唱。”

1981.3.16 译

Ode to a Nightingale

〔1〕 My heart aches, and a drowsy numbness pains
My sense, as though of hemlock I had drunk,
Or emptied some dull opiate to the drains
One minute past, and Lethe-wards had sunk:
'Tis not through envy of thy happy lot,
But being too happy in thine happiness, —
That thou, light-wingèd Dryad of the trees,
In some melodious plot
Of beechen green, and shadows numberless,
Singest of summer in full throated ease.

〔2〕 O, for a draught of vintage! that hath been
Cool'd a long age in the deep-delved earth,
Tasting of Flora and the country green,
Dance, and Provençal song, and sunburnt mirth!
O for a beaker full of the warm South,
Full of the true, the blushful Hippocrene,

夜莺颂

〔1〕 我的心在作痛，一阵欲睡的昏沉
殷殷摧楚我的感觉，仿佛顷刻前
我饮过一服毒参液，堕入了迷魂阵，
或喝干一杯鸦片剂，化进奈何天：
这不是为了妒忌你欢乐的幸福，
而是因沉醉于你的陶陶福泽中，——
你哟，幽林里轻翼的瑶仙小神灵，
凭楠柏的青春的聚簇，
那绿树的丛枝密叶和叠叠的荫浓，
以满腔舒畅唱夏夜的良辰美景。

〔2〕 啊也，但愿能满口饫葡萄的酒浆！
那曾经深埋的土地里，累月长年，
酒中含得有女花神，乡村的碧草场，
舞蹈，泼罗旺[①]的歌唱和日晒的欢颜！
啊也，但愿有一樽注满着南国春！
承足了满泛红晕的真正的飞马泉，[②]

---

① Provencal song：泼罗旺斯（Provence，法兰西东南部古州）的歌唱，那里的居民以喜好用他们的方言唱歌谣闻名。

② 希腊东部皮奥希亚（Boeotia）古邦海列根（Helicon）山有一泉山名喜卜克璃恩（Hippocrene），相传神话中的飞马（Pegasus）马蹄踢破山石，遂涌出这泉水，据说这泉水能激发诗人们的灵感。

With beaded bubbles winking at the brim,
And purple-stained mouth;
That I might drink, and leave the world unseen,
And with thee fade away into the forest dim:

〔3〕 Fade far away, dissolve, and quite forget
What thou among the leaves hast never known,
The weariness, the fever, and the fret
Here, where men sit and hear each other groan;
Where palsy shakes a few, sad, last gray hairs,
Where youth grows pale, and spectre-thin, and dies;
Where but to think is to be full of sorrow
And leaden-eyed despairs,
Where Beauty cannot keep her lustrous eyes,
Or new Love pine at them beyond to-morrow.

〔4〕 Away! away! for I will fly to thee,
Not charioted by Bacchus and his pards,
But on the viewless wings of Poesy,
Though the dull brain perplexes and retards:
Already with thee! tender is the night,
And haply the Queen-Moon is on her throne,
Cluster'd around by all her starry Fays;
But here there is no light,
Save what from heaven is with the breezes blown
Through verdurous glooms and winding mossy ways.

沿着樽盏边闪烁着滚珠的泡沫，
以及染紫艳的朱唇；
我便能醉饮，离开了这世间，杳然
跟同你消逝入暗林中，悠悠默默：

〔3〕 消逝得远去，融化掉，整整地忘记
你在浓荫的绿树芃丛中所从来
未曾知道的，这疲累，烦躁和奋厉，
在这里，人们危坐着，听彼此伤怀；
瘫痪在这里摇撼着最后的几根
灰头发，华年变灰白，鬼干瘪，死掉；
在这里只要一想起就勾引出哀愁
万种，绝望将病眼瞪；
在这里花容保不住她的明眸妙，
或是新生的眷恋相思到明朝后。

〔4〕 去来！去来！因为我只想飞向你，
不是驾驭酒神班格斯[①]的灵豹车，
而是驰驱着无形的诗思的玄妙机，
虽然这迟钝的脑筋困窘而阻拒：
已跟你在一起了！夜色无比地温存，
月亮女神也许已升登到宝座上，
四周环绕着是众星历历的群仙；
但这里还不见丛辰，
只除从天上被轻飔吹下的微亮，
经过碧澄澄的朦胧和苔滑的盘旋。

① 班格斯（Bacchus）：古希腊、罗马神话里的酒神，传说他驾驭一辆灵豹拖拽的神车。

〔5〕 I cannot see what flowers are at my feet,
Nor what soft incense hangs upon the boughs,
But, in embalmed darkness, guess each sweet
Wherewith the seasonable month endows
The grass, the thicket, and the fruit-tree wild;
White hawthorn, and the pastoral eglantine;
Fast-fading violets cover'd up in leaves;
And mid-May's eldest child,
The coming musk-rose, full of dewy wine,
The murmurous haunt of flies on summer eves.

〔6〕 Darkling I listen;and, for many a time
I have been half in love with easeful Death,
Call'd him soft names in many a mused rhyme,
To take into the air my quiet breath;
Now more than ever seems it rich to die,
To cease upon the midnight with no pain,
While thou art pouring forth thy soul abroad In such
an ecstasy!
Still wouldst thou sing, and I have ears in vain —
To thy high requiem become a sod.

〔5〕 看不见在我脚边是什么花在开，

也不辨挂在枝头哪种花吐幽香，

我却在温馨的暗中，不看也能猜

每一朵竞放的芳蕾当令正辉煌，

在草里，丛薄中，果树枝桠的枝上头；

白花山楂子，牧歌里边的野蔷薇，

易萎的紫罗兰，有树叶把它们遮掩，

和五月的大儿吐英秀，

那待放的麝香玫瑰，满含着香露酯，

夏日夜晚时萤火虫嘤嘤去聚攒。

〔6〕 黝暗中我倾耳在谛听；有好多回次

我曾跟舒和的寂灭几乎相爱上，

在沉思的诗句里用温存的名字

呼唤它，使我安静的呼吸告消亡；

此刻比任何往常时似乎要死得

更豪奢，午夜里殒逝得渺无痛苦，

正当你倾吐你的灵魂恢宏充沛，

泄泻出无比的欢乐！

你会要酣唱无休，而我将长瞑目——

对你的安魂曲变成了泥土一抔。

〔7〕 Thou wast not born for death, immortal Bird!
No hungry generations tread thee down;
The voice I hear this passing night was heard
In ancient days by emperor and clown:
Perhaps the self-same song that found a path
Through the sad heart of Ruth, when, sick for home,
She stood in tears amid the alien corn;
The same that oft-times hath
Charm'd magic casements, opening on the foam
Of perilous seas, in faery lands forlorn.

〔8〕 Forlorn! the very word is like a bell
To toll me back from thee to my sole self!
Adieu! the fancy cannot cheat so well
As she is famed to do, deceiving elf.
Adieu! adieu! thy plaintive anthem fades
Past the near meadows, over the still stream,
Up the hill-side;and now 'tis buried deep
In the next valley-glades:
Was it a vision, or a waking dream?
Fled is that music: — Do I wake or sleep?

〔7〕 你不是注定要死亡，永生的良禽！
没有饥饿的世代人会把你踩倒；
这消逝的夜里我所耳闻的清音
曾在古代被帝王和伧夫所听到：
也许同样的一支歌曾进入露斯
悲感的心中，当她在外地思乡邈，
流着泪站在异邦谷田里所闻听；
同一曲歌声也常时
吸引着入魔的窗棂，面对那惊涛
骇浪的大海，在渺茫的神仙奇境。

〔8〕 渺茫！正好是这句话像一声宏钟，
震得我从对你的倾倒里遄返灵明！
告别了！幻想不可能那样施欺蒙，
如闻名她会那么做，行骗的妖精。
再会了！再会！你这阵凄婉的放歌，
从近旁的草坪，越过静谧的溪流，
飞升上山阜；此刻已埋藏入深深
邻近山腰间的空壑：
这可是个梦境，还是阵空想浮游？
那歌声已逝：——我醒着，还是片梦魂？

1980.9.16 译

Ode on a Grecian Urn

〔1〕 Thou still unravish'd bride of quietness,
Thou foster-child of silence and slow time,
Sylvan historian, who canst thus express
A flowery tale more sweetly than our rhyme:
What leaf-fring'd legend haunts about thy shape
Of deities or mortals, or of both,
In Tempe or the dales of Arcady?
What men or gods are these? What maidens loth?
What mad pursuit? What struggle to escape?
What pipes and timbrels? What wild ecstasy?

〔2〕 Heard melodies are sweet, but those unheard
Are sweeter; therefore, ye soft pipes, play on;
Not to the sensual ear, but, more endear'd
Pipe to the spirit ditties of no tone:
Fair youth, beneath the trees, thou canst not leave
Thy song, nor ever can those trees be bare;
Bold Lover, never, never canst thou kiss,
Though winning near the goal — yet, do not grieve;
She cannot fade, though thou hast not thy bliss,
For ever wilt thou love, and she be fair!

希腊古瓮赞

〔1〕 你这位含苞未放的静谧的新娘，
　　沉寂和缓慢的时光的螟蛉小女，
山林的史家，你竟能这么样显彰
　　这如花的故事，胜如我们用韵语：
甚么有叶饰缘边的传奇出没在
　　有神仙或凡人，或仙、凡都有的这媚妩
　　形体间，在谭比或在阿凯狄峡谷中？
　　这些是什么仙、凡人？怎不愿的小姑？
是多么疯魔的追求？逃逸的姿态？
　　甚么箫管和铃鼓？多欢喜的轰动？
〔2〕 听到的曼歌妙曲很甜蜜，但那些
　　无声的更甘醇；故而，吹奏着，箫管们；
不是对有感的耳朵，而是，更欢谐，
　　要吹奏不发音响的乐曲，对神魂：
俊美的青年，在树下，你不能离开
　　你那支妙曲，那些树也不会光秃；
　　放纵的情郎，你终竟不能吻到她，
虽然快接触那樱唇——可是莫伤怀；
　　她不会消亡，虽然你吻不到那春华，
因你将永远热恋着，她永远如仙姝！

〔3〕 Ah, happy, happy boughs! that cannot shed
Your leaves, nor ever bid the Spring adieu;
And, happy melodist, unwearied,
For ever piping songs for ever new;
More happy love! more happy, happy love!
For ever warm and still to be enjoy'd,
For ever paning, and for ever young;
All breathing human passion far above,
That leaves a heart high-sorrowful and cloy'd,
A burning forehead, and a parching tongue.

〔4〕 Who are these coming to the sacrifice?
To what green altar, O mysterious priest,
Lead'st thou that heifer lowing at the skies,
And all her silken flanks with garlands drest?
What little town by river or sea shore,
Or mountain-built with peaceful citadel,
Is emptied of this folk, this pious morn?
And, little town, thy streets for evermore
Will silent be;and not a soul to tell
Why thou art desolate, can e'er return.

〔5〕 O Attic shape, fair attitude! with brede
Of marble men and maidens overwrought,
With forest branches and the trodden weed;
Thou, silent form! dost tease us out of thought
As doth eternity: Cold Pastoral!
When old age shall this generation waste,

〔3〕 啊也，幸福的枝桠！你们不可能
　　把叶片脱落，也不会跟春光告别；
还有，幸福的乐曲奏鸣人，你精英
　　健旺，永远吹奏着新歌调，不休歇；
多幸福的恩情！多幸福、幸福的热恋！
　　永远炽烈的、欢乐的脉脉浓情，
　　永远气嘘嘘，永远是青春而年少；
一切都远远超脱了激越的恩怨，
　　人们不相思病苦便腻烦而败兴，
　　额上如火焚，或者唇舌间起焦爆。
〔4〕 到来献祭的这些是什么人群？
　　到什么新绿的祭坛，神秘的祭司
你牵着那头小牡牛，它对天在啸吟，
　　它丝光的腰间披挂着花环串子？
是什么河流近旁或海滨的乡镇，
　　或筑在山肩上，建有护城的碉堡，
　　倾吐它的居民，在这虔敬的早上？
而小镇，你的街衢啊，将永远无人
　　行走，静悄悄；且不会有人能报道
　　为什么你门庭岑寂，为来此而空巷。
〔5〕 啊，雅典的形状哟！优美的神态！
　　整个装饰着大理石琢成的英俊
和姣娃的浮雕，琼枝飘和芳草被蹂躏；
　　你啊，玄默的形相！你逗得我们
神飞如天纵着奇思。出尘的牧歌！
　　当老衰将把这一代化成灰烬，

Thou shalt remain, in midst of other woe
Than ours, a friend to man, to whom thou say’st,
“Beauty is Truth, Truth Beauty,” — that is all
Ye know on earth, and all ye need to know.

你将留存着，在我们之外的悲苦中，
做个尘世人的朋友，你会告人们，
“美是真，真即美，”——这是你在世上洞察
所得，也是你必须知道的造化功。

1981.3.11 译

To Autumn

1

Season of mists and mellow fruitfulness,
    Close bosom-friend of the maturing sun;
Conspiring with him how to load and bless
    With fruit the vines that round the thatch-eves run;
To bend with apples the moss'd cottage-trees;
    And fill all fruit with ripeness to the core;
      To swell the gourd, and plump the hazel shells
    With a sweet kernel;to set budding more,
And still more, later flowers for the bees,
Until they think warm days will never cease,
    For summer has o'er-brimm'd their clammy cells.

秋日咏

1

雾蒙蒙、果实醇熟的三秋季节！
　　催熟果谷的骄阳的知心好友；
伙同他如何去计谋使檐边屋角
　　藤蔓上结满累累的葡萄紫秀；
使茅舍旁枝干苔绿的小树弯腰
　　挂足了熟到核心深处的香苹；
　　使葫芦饱胀，榛子的壳儿肥胖，
　　充盈着甘仁；使迟迟开放的花心
含苞缓缓地吐艳，为蜂儿呈娇，
使它们以为暖天永远过不掉，
　　因长夜已充溢它们潮而黏的窠房。

2

Who hath not seen thee oft amid thy store?
    Sometimes whoever seeks abroad may find
Thee sitting careless on a granary floor,
    Thy hair soft-lifted by the winnowing wind;
Or on a half-reap'd furrow sound asleep,
    Drows'd with the fume of poppies, while thy hook
      Spares the next swath and all its twined flowers:
And sometimes like a gleaner thou dost keep
    Steady thy laden head across a brook;
    Or by a cyder-press, with patient look,
      Thou watchest the last oozings hours by hours.

2

谁没看到你总守着你的蕴藏？
　　有时不论谁到外边去找，会见你
无忧无虑地坐在谷仓地板上，
　　你头发轻轻被簸谷的风儿扬起；
或在半收割的犁沟上沉沉熟睡，
　　给罂粟的浓薰所醉倒，当你的镰钩
　　来不及刈割到旁边去，那儿花更密；
有时像个拾穗者，保头顶的穗堆
　　不撒落，你将脑袋高昂着过溪流；
或挨着榨取苹果汁的压机在等候，
　　你耐守在那里看果汁缓流慢滴。

3

Where are the songs of spring? Ay, where are they?
    Think not of them, thou hast thy music too, —
While barred clouds bloom the soft-dying day,
    And touch the stubble-plains with rosy hue;
Then in a wailful choir the small gnats mourn
    Among the river sallows, borne aloft
      Or sinking as the light wind lives or dies;
And full-grown lambs loud bleat from hilly bourn;
    Hedge-crikets sing; and now with treble soft
    The red-breast whistles from a garden-croft,
      And gathering swallows twitter in the skies.

3

阳春的颂歌在哪儿？哦，在哪儿？

　　别想起它们，你有你自己的歌声，——

当如罗的秋云使迟暮像开放着花儿，

　　落霞纵横映红了满残梗的田塍；

那时丛飞的蠓蚋正含悲在合唱，

　　在水杨柳之间，一阵轻风徐徐来，

　　或是缓缓去，一会儿升高或降低；

成长的羊羔咩咩高叫自山丘旁；

　　篱旁蟋蟀鸣；一会儿知更鸟畅开

它的软高音，从小园一角发异彩；

　　飞集的燕子在天上作归窠的啾唧。

1981.2.24 译

• 罗伯特·白朗宁 •

Robert Browning

（1812—1889）

安特利亚·代尔·沙多

安特利亚·代尔·沙多（Andrea del Sarto）有“无疵的画家”之称，又名“无疵的安特利亚”（Andrea Senza Errori），为翡冷翠艺派中一大画家。他父亲是个缝衣匠：意大利人喜欢起绰号，所以称他作“缝衣匠的（儿子）安特利亚”（按意大利文缝衣匠一语为sarto，音“沙多”）。1487年他生于翡冷翠城（Florence）；真姓氏已湮没不传——有人说是梵奴奇（Vannuchi），但无确据。他最初学过冶金术；随后因性情不近，改在一个刻木师兼画师吉安·拔列尔（Gian Barill）处习艺；11岁时他转到彼罗·提·谷西摩（Piero di Cosimo）门下去专攻绘画，在那里他临习过达·芬奇（Leonardo da Vinci）与米珂朗琪罗（Michaelangelo）的画稿。自1509—1514年，他应了“圣母仆从会”（The Order of the Servi）的聘请，为他们在翡冷翠城里的“告生院”（The Church of the Annunziata）作壁画。据说他禀性闲散，耐贫贱，与世无争。他的画技术精熟，但欠缺深刻性与力量，弱于明暗的变幻或触觉的价值，很逼真，不超脱。他爱上了一个帽子匠人卡罗·累卡那底（Carlo Recanati）的女人，名叫露蔻嘉·代尔·费特（Lucrezia del Fede）：凑巧她丈夫死了，这裁缝的儿子便在1512年12月16日和她结了婚。她生得很美，安特利亚留下来的画里有好些圣母像是用她作蓝本的。曾在他手下当过艺徒的乔其·瓦沙利（Giorgio Vasari）说她对丈夫不贞，既悍且妒，对学徒们非常泼辣。1516年末他有一张《圣母承耶稣尸身图》（*Pieta*），随后又有张圣母像，送往法兰西宫廷上去。这两张画很得称赏；1518年以珍爱艺术闻名的法王弗郎西斯一世（Francis I）便召他去巴黎。他别了妻子北上，在那边备蒙礼遇，有生以来那是他第一次受到厚酬，但露蔻嘉要他回意大利。国王准了他，可是他得赶快回法，当即交给他一大注款子，托他回去买画。安特利亚敌不住这番诱惑，就用这笔钱在翡冷翠盖了一所屋子；这样他便失去了法王的宠幸，虽然并没有受到严惩。自1520年起他重复在翡冷翠依卖画为生；翡冷翠被围之役和过后的那阵大疫疠时他都没有离开他的本乡。他染了疫，未得他妻子的看护，于1531年正月22日去世，死时只43岁。又过了40年他的妻子才死。

此诗作者罗伯特·白朗宁（Robert Browning，1812—1889）的作品我十之八九都不喜欢，本篇乃为例外。他通常的弊病在于造句遣词突兀而粗糙，千篇一律，往往涵义肤浅而过作艰难晦涩之态。最糟糕不过的要算他那鸵鸟式的乐观主义：我信除了智能较差的人，传教师们，老姑姑，老婶母等以外，谁也受不了他诗里的那“傻瓜的天堂”。本篇我极心爱，描写一个软骨头的惨极了的艺人。真可说是尽了“缠绵悱恻，低徊咏叹”的能事。虽然诗中“灵魂”字样还嫌太多了些——这在白朗宁是几乎绝对不可免的，能避去的我已在译诗中设法避去。

此诗格式在英文诗里名为“戏剧的抒情诗”（Dramatic lyric），为白氏所擅长。此类诗我国似尚未见翻译过。原诗的格律则为英文诗里最精深博大的Blank Verse；译诗亦追随原来形式，每行以五音步为准则，而不押脚韵——至于抑扬一事则为我国文字所不许可，只得听它去。我的翻译有些地方很自由；又说不定有几处跟旁人的解法不尽相同，那只有读者包容了。

诗中有三处特别名词需要作注：

费梭里（Fiesole）为意大利一有名的小教城，在一座小山顶上，位于翡冷翠城西约三英里。冒兰罗（Morello）是阿魄奈大山脉（Apennines）里的一尊山。“那欧皮诺青年”指拉飞尔，因为他生在欧皮诺（Urbino）。

乔其·瓦沙利（Giorgio Vasari），画家，著有《意大利艺人集传》

（*Lives of the Most Excellent Italian Painters Sculptors and Architects*）一大部，白氏本诗的材料即从这部书上得来的。达·芬奇（Leonardo da Vinci，1452—1519），盎琪罗或米珂朗琪罗（Michaelangelo Buonarroti，1475—1564）及拉飞尔（Raffaello Sanzio，1483—1520）为意大利文艺复兴全盛期之艺坛三杰。芳丹卜罗（Fontainebleau）系城名，在巴黎城东南37英里，以宫殿富丽著称，法国革命前为历朝君主之别业。“前一幅你最好对着它低头作祈祷”，可是天主教徒通常并不在名画的耶稣像或圣母像前作祈祷仪式。

“耶鲁撒冷新城”等见《圣经·新约·启示录》（*Revelation*）21章。

1935年3月21日译者附识于北平

Andrea Del Sarteno[①]

〔1〕 But do not let us quarrel any more,
No, my Lucrezia; bear with me for once:
Sit down and all shall happen as you wish.
You turn your face, but does it bring your heart?
I'll work then for your friend's friend, never fear,
Treat his own subject after his own way,
Fix his own time, accept too his own price,
And shut the money into this small hand
When next it takes mine. Will it? tenderly?
Oh, I'll content him, — but tomorrow, Love!
I often am much wearier than you think,
This evening more than usual, and it seems
As if — forgive now — should you let me sit
Here by the window with your hand in mine
And look a half hour forth on Fiesole,
Both of one mind, as married people use,
Quietly, quietly the evening through,
I might get up tomorrow to my work
Cheerful and fresh as ever. Let us try,
Tomorrow, how you shall be glad for this!

---

① Andrea Del Sarto was also called "The Faultless Painter".

安特利亚·代尔·沙多

〔1〕 别那样，小妹露蔻嘉，别让我们
再又来争闹：请就容忍我一遭；
坐下来，一切都得依你的愿望。
你回过脸来，你的心可也跟着回？
别耽心，我准替你朋友的朋友工作，
听他的指点，画他指定的画材，
由他定交画的时间，也由他去估价，
等下回这柔荑似的手牵着我的手，
（会不会？轻轻的？）我把钱便搏进这掌心。
啊，等明天准叫他如愿，心肝！
你只道我乏了，那知我乏得多厉害，
但今晚要比素常时分外的疲惫，
看来是假使——请恕我——你要是让我
坐在这窗前，我的手握着你的手，
对窗外费梭里的山头凝望半小时，
同心一意的，像人家夫妇们一样，
静悄悄，静悄悄，凝望这暮光逝去，
我信我明天起身工作时，就许会
身心都爽健而欢愉。我们且试试。
明天你会说多亏依了我这句话！

〔2〕 Your soft hand is a woman of itself,
And mine the man's bared breast she curls inside.
Don't count the time lost, neither; you must serve
For each of the five pictures we require:
It saves a model. So! keep looking so —
My serpentining beauty, rounds on rounds!
— How could you ever prick those perfect ears,
Even to put the pearl there! oh, so sweet —
My face, my moon, my everybody's moon,
Which everybody looks on and calls his,
And, I suppose, is looked on by in turn,
While she looks — no one's: very dear, no less.
You smile? why, there's my picture ready made,
There's what we painters call our harmony!
〔3〕 A common grayness silvers everything —
All in a twilight, you and I alike
— You, at the point of your first pride in me
(That's gone, you know) — but I, at every point;
My youth, my hope, my art, being all toned down
To yonder sober pleasant Fiesole.
There's the bell clinking from the chapel-top;
That length of convent-wall across the way
Holds the trees safer, huddled more inside;
The last monk leaves the garden; days decrease,

〔2〕 这柔和的小手，它本身便是个女人，
拳在我掌中，在男子赤裸裸的胸头。
莫计数给耗掉的时分多少：你还得
为我要画的五张画一张张地坐彻——
省得看模型。别动！就这么望着——
一圈又一圈，金发袅袅的天仙！
啊，即使你为了要佩戴那珠环，
也怎忍用针尖穿透着这一双妙耳！
这脸庞，这明月，光照我也光照任何人，
我说是我的，任何人也都说是他的，
我想决无人对着它不悠然神往，
可是它无猜地顾盼天然——不属谁。
但并不因此失掉了它天生的可爱！
你笑吗？哦，那就是现成的一幅画。
这光景我们画家便叫做和谐！
〔3〕 一片银灰的雾縠轻笼着一切，——
你跟我，我们两人都在暮霭中
——你，正开初在矜贵有我的恩情
(那已然过去，你知道)，——可是我，随时
都把你当作自持骄矜的慰藉；
我一生的艺术，希望，和年轻，都跟那
费梭里晚色的迷离调和成一致。
晚祷钟已在那寺塔尖端响动；
那僧院的围墙，迤逦绵延，无非葆
墙内枝干相偎傍的丛树们的平安；
最末个寺僧离了园已进了寺里去；

And autumn grows, autumn in everything.
Eh? the whole seems to fall into a shape
As if I saw alike my work and self
And all that I was born to be and do,
〔4〕 A twilight-piece. Love, we are in God's hand,
How strange now looks the life he makes us lead;
So free we seem, so fettered fast we are!
I feel he laid the fetter: let it lie!
This chamber for example — turn your head —
All that's behind us! You don't understand
Nor care to understand about my art,
But you can hear at least when people speak:
And that cartoon, the second from the door
— It is the thing, Love! so such things should be —
〔5〕 Behold Madonna! — I am bold to say.
I can do with my pencil what I know,
What I see, what at bottom of my heart
I wish for, if I ever wish so deep —
Do easily, too — when I say, perfectly,
I do not boast, perhaps: yourself are judge
Who listened to the Legate's talk last week,
And just as much they used to say in France.
At any rate 'tis easy, all of it!
No sketches first, no studies, that's long past:
I do what many dream of all their lives.
— Dream! strive to do, and agonize to do,

日短了，秋在滋长，万物都含秋。
哎？这一切都仿如化成了一体，
我能想象到自己的艺事和生命，
所有终身的抱负和死前的成功，
整整化作了一幅衰秋晚景图。

〔4〕 心肝，我们逃不出上帝的手掌。
真奇怪，他叫我们度这样的身世！
看来像自由，实际却双双地系紧！
我觉到他下的这锁链：就让它锁着吧！
比如说，这屋子——别恼，回过头来——
那早已成了不相干的往事！你不懂，
也不想懂得关于我画艺的甚么事，
但人家说话时你至少该能听到；
那一张画稿，心肝，门旁第二张
——全没有半点差池，要这样才对——
我敢大胆向人说，瞧那张圣母像。

〔5〕 我能把我所知道的，见到的，我心坎
深处向往的，（只要我向往得那么深，）
运笔传神，不费几多气力——
我若说传神得微妙，许并非在夸口：
前礼拜你亲自听教皇的使臣那称赏，
那正同他们在法兰西赞颂我一样。
总之，这一切都容易，不需打草底，
起初稿，那些事都早已成了过去——
多少人毕生的梦想我全已达到
——梦想？殚精竭虑，心痛着去追求，

And fail in doing. I could count twenty such
On twice your fingers, and not leave this town,
Who strive — you don't know how the others strive
To paint a little thing like that you smeared
Carelessly passing with your robes afloat —
Yet do much less, so much less, Someone says
(I know his name, no matter) — so much less!
〔6〕 Well, less is more, Lucrezia: I am judged.
There burns a truer light of God in them,
In their vexed beating stuffed and stopped-up brain,
Heart, or whate'er else, than goes on to prompt
This low-pulsed forthright craftsman's hand of mine.
Their works drop groundward, but themselves, I know,
Reach many a time a heaven that's shut to me,
Enter and take their place there sure enough,
Though they come back and cannot tell the world.
My works are nearer heaven, but I sit here.
The sudden blood of these men! at a word —
Praise them, it boils, or blame them, it boils too.
I, painting from myself and to myself,
Know what I do, am unmoved by men's blame
Or their praise either. Somebody remarks
Morello's outline there is wrongly traced,
His hue mistaken; what of that? or else,
Rightly traced and well ordered; what of that?
Speak as they please, what does the mountain care?

但依然不能追到。就在这本城
你能用指头数他二十个人来，
挣扎着——你不知他们怎样的挣扎，
为要想画成你飘着长衣拂过时
无意中抹糊的那么一点点的小品，——
但他们成功得真少，真少，有人说，
(我知道这人的姓名，不用说）真少！
〔6〕 唉，真少就是多，露蔻嘉！我完了。
在他们那昏头涨脑里，闭塞的心中，
神思缭乱或凝冻的性灵间，可亮着
有一支上帝赐予的纯真的光焰；
我空有这一手画工的技巧算什么？
他们的作品往下掉，但他们自己，
我知道，常向我无缘的天上升超，
排天关，进阊阖殿，昂着头登堂入座，
虽然他们回来时说不清那极乐。
我的画近了天，我自己却困在这地下。
这班人，好嫩的皮肤！只轻轻一句——
赞一声，就眉飞；一声责难，就耳赤，
我，从自己开端到自己终止，
全都在自己心中，旁人的毁誉
搅不起分毫的喜怒。有人指摘
那画里冒罗兰的轮廓描绘得有错，
色彩也失误——有什么相干？要不然，
轮廓和构图全对了——那又怎么样？
随他们说吧，山岳哪会去计较？

〔7〕 Ah, but a man's reach should exceed his grasp,
Or what's a heaven for? All is silver-gray,
Placid and perfect with my art: the worse!
I know both what I want and what might gain;
And yet how profitless to know, to sigh
"Had I been two, another and myself,
Our head would have o'erlooked the world!" No doubt.
Yonder's a work now, of that famous youth
The Urbinate who died five years ago.
('Tis copied, George Vasari sent it me.)
Well, I can fancy how he did it all,
Pouring his soul, with kings and popes to see,
Reaching, that heaven might so replenish him,
Above and through his art — for it gives way;
〔8〕 That arm is wrongly put — and there again —
A fault to pardon in the drawing's lines,
Its body, so to speak: its soul is right,
He means right — that, a child may understand.
Still, what an arm! and I could alter it:
But all the play, the insight and the stretch —
Out of me, out of me! And wherefore out?
Had you enjoined them on me, given me soul,
We might have risen to Rafael, I and you!
Nay, Love, you did give all I asked, I think —

〔7〕 啊，一个人总该有时能超越
他寻常的把握，能升进非凡的奇境，
不然要天堂做什么？我的画总是
一片安详无疵的银灰——那才糟！
我明知自己的缺欠，又如何去弥补——
明知了可依然无用，还得喟叹：
“如果我是自己再加上另一人，
我们便不必对世人顾虑！”说得对。
那边是一张五年前去世的那欧皮诺
青年的油绘，他享的是多大的声名。
(那是张临本，乔其·瓦沙利送我的。)
哦，我能想象他画时的情景，
全神贯注着，预备给教主与王侯
去凝眸向往，卸下了艺术的羁绊，
脱去了形骸的桎梏，向那边终竟会
补报他的那无际的云天扶摇直上；
〔8〕 那一只胳膊可错了——还有那边——
画面下那线条的错误也需人原宥，
但那些都只是形骸：那精神却全对，
他用意原来对——任是孩童也懂得。
那胳膊，可毕竟太坏！我能改正它。
但是那明暗的变幻，那洞知，那力量，
我却全没有！全没有！为什么没有？
要是你替我添上，给了我灵魂，
我们便能和拉飞尔齐名，我跟你。
不对，心肝，你已给了我一切——

More than I merit, yes, by many times.
But had you — oh, with the same perfect brow,
And perfect eyes, and more than perfect mouth,
And the low voice my soul hears, as a bird
The fowler's pipe, and follows to the snare —
Had you, with these the same, but brought a mind!
〔9〕 Some women do so. Had the mouth there urged,
"God and the glory! never care for gain.
The present by the future, what is that?
Live for fame, side by side with Agnolo!
Rafael is waiting: up to God, all three!"
I might have done it for you. So it seems:
Perhaps not. All is a God overrules.
Beside, incentives come from the soul's self;
The rest avail not. Why do I need you?
What wife had Rafael, or has Agnolo?
In this world, who can do a thing, will not;
And who would do it, cannot, I perceive:
Yet the will's somewhat — somewhat, too, the power —
And thus we half-men struggle. At the end,
God, I conclude, compensates, punishes.
'Tis safer for me, if the award be strict,
That I am something underrated here.
Poor this long while, despised, to speak the truth,
I dared not, do you know, leave home all day,

给过我应享的，不错，已经好多倍。
不过假使你——唉，这无疵的眉宇，
这无疵的妙眼，这非止无疵的小口，
都依然如旧，还有那软语轻声，
一阵阵叫彻我灵魂，招致它直像只
小鸟中了捕鸟者那勾魂的小笛，
甘心投入樊笼——假使你，我说，
这种种都依旧，只另下加上个心灵！
〔9〕 确有这样的女人，果然你劝我：
“上帝和光荣！切莫去顾虑酬报。
现在跟未来打比，又算得什么？
要为了荣誉生存，比肩着盎琪罗——
拉飞尔在守候。你们三人同上天！”
为了你，我许会做到。看来是如此——
也许不。一切都得归上帝去命定。
又况动因本发自灵魂的内奥，
外来的没有用。为什么我不能少你？
拉飞尔有什么妻子，盎琪罗有吗？
这世上，能做的不要做，要做的又不能：
意志果然不可少，能力也重要——
我们不是全人的便这般挣扎。
最后来我信上帝会补偿，会惩罚。
要是惩赏严明，我如今这般
受一点委屈，穷苦了这许久时候，
说实话，还遭人鄙弃，我就安心些。
我整天，你知道没有，不敢离家，

For fear of chancing on the Paris lords.
〔10〕 The best is when they pass and look aside;
But they speak sometimes; I must bear it all.
Well may they speak! That Francis, that first time,
And that long festal year at Fontainebleau!
I surely then could sometimes leave the ground,
Put on the glory, Rafael's daily wear,
In that humane great monarch's golden look, —
One finger in his beard or twisted curl
Over his mouth's good mark that made the smile,
One arm about my shoulder, round my neck,
The jingle of his gold chain in my ear,
I painting proudly with his breath on me,
All his court round him, seeing with his eyes,
Such frank French eyes, and such a fire of souls
Profuse, my hand kept playing by those hearts, —
And, best of all, this, this, this face beyond,
This in the background, waiting on my work,
To crown the issue with a last reward!
〔11〕 A good time, was it not, my kingly days?
And had you not grown restless ... but I know —
'Tis done and past; 'twas right, my instinct said;
Too live the life grew, golden and not gray,
And I'm the weak-eyed bat no sun should tempt
Out of the grange whose four walls make his world.

生怕在街头遇到巴黎的贵卿们。
〔10〕最好是他们旁视着匆匆过去；
但有时却和我交谈；我唯有忍受。
也无怪他们！那位弗朗西，那初次
在芳丹卜罗的那酣歌曼舞的长年！
那里我有时确是升离了这地下，
戴上光华，拉飞尔日常的佩戴，
在那仁慈博大的君王青睐里——
他一手撚着须，或捻着腮边口角
那掩住一抹微笑的卷曲的髯髭，
一手围在我肩头，环在我颈上，
金链子在我耳旁零丁作响，
我身披这异宠，画得心花怒放，
满朝的文武随着他眼波上下，
一双双法兰西的眸子，有那般清明
坦白，放射出那般照人的灵光，
我这手在他们心头来回地弹拨——
还有，最妙不过，是这个，这一个，
这脸庞，在天边，背景里，只等我工作
完成，便会赐一个最后的褒奖！
〔11〕快乐，是不是，我那个扬眉的往日？
只要你当时躁急——不过我知道——
过去的过去了；没有错，我抚心自问：
那生涯太活跃，黄金的，没有一斑灰暗——
我生来原是只蝙蝠，目光很微弱，
谷仓的四壁乃是我份内的世界，
阳光本不该引诱我飞进那晴空。

How could it end in any other way?
You called me, and I came home to your heart.
The triumph was — to reach and stay there; since
I reach it ere the triumph, what is lost?
Let my hands frame your face in your hair's gold,
You beautiful Lucrezia that are mine!
"Rafael did this, Andrea painted that;
The Roman's is the better when you pray,
But still the other's Virgin was his wife" —
Men will excuse me. I am gald to judge
Both pictures in your presence; clearer grows
My better fortune, I resolve to think.
〔12〕 For, do you know, Lucrezia, as God lives,
Said one day Agnolo, his very self,
To Rafael ... I have known it all these years ...
(When the young man was flaming out his thoughts
Upon a palace-wall for Rome to see,
Too lifted up in heart because of it)
"Friend, there's a certain sorry little scrub
Goes up and down our Florence, none cares how,
Who, were he set to plan and execute
As you are, pricked on by your popes and kings,
Would bring the sweat into that brow of yours!"
To Rafael's! — And indeed the arm is wrong.
I hardly dare ... yet, only you to see,

我怎能有个和如今不相同的结局?
你叫我，我就回到你心里的家来。
我从此不复去高飞，这是我的胜利；
但假如我未经高飞远走，就回来
息翅在你身旁，那也是损失。
让我托着你这发上的黄金作画框，
配在你脸庞的周遭，我醉心的露蔻嘉!
“这幅是拉飞尔，那幅是安特利的手笔——
前一幅你最好对着它低头作祈祷，
后一幅那画里的圣母可原是他的妻——”
人家会对我原谅。我喜欢当着
你面前就把这两幅画来品评优劣，
这一比我信我分明是交的好运。

〔12〕 因为，知道吗，露蔻嘉，有一天盎琪罗
亲口向拉飞尔说过这样一句话……
我这些年前早知道，至今还记得……
(当时那少年正在那宫廷的墙上
驰骋着神思，使罗马全城惊异，
因此他的心不在这人间留驻。)
“朋友，我们翡冷翠的街头有一个
失志的画奴在徘徊，没有人理睬，
他若是也像你这样精构图，勤绘事，
也有你这班教主和王侯鞭策他，
便会叫你那额上涔涔地渗汗!”
对拉飞尔说这话!——那胳膊，固真不对。
我不敢冒昧——不过，只有你瞧见，

Give the chalk here — quick, thus the line should go!
Aye, but the soul! he's Rafael! I rub it out!
Still, all I care for, if he spoke the truth,
(What he? why, who but Michel Agnolo?
Do you forget already words like those?)
If really there was such a chance, so lost, —
Is, whether you're — not grateful — but more pleased.
〔13〕 Well, let me think so. And you smile indeed!
This hour has been an hour! Another smile?
If you would sit thus by me every night
I should work better, do you comprehend?
I mean that I should earn more, give you more.
See, it is settled dusk now; there's a star;
Morello's gone, the watch-lights show the wall,
The cue-owls speak the name we call them by.
Come from the window, Love, — come in, at last,
Inside the melancholy little house
We built to be so gay with. God is just.
King Francis may forgive me: oft at nights
When I look up from painting, eyes tired out,
The walls become illumined, brick by brick
Distinct, instead of mortar, fierce bright gold,
That gold of his I did cement them with!
Let us but love each other. Must you go?
That Cousin here again? he waits outside?

给我支粉笔——快，这线条该这样！
咳，可是那画里的灵魂，灵魂！
毕竟他是拉飞尔，这不成！快擦掉！
我关心的只是，如果他说的是实话，
（什么他？哦，除了米珂朗琪罗
还有谁？你莫非已忘掉那话不成？）
如果真有个这样的机会给失掉——
只是你是否——并非说感激——高兴些。
〔13〕好吧，就让我这么想。你果然笑了！
这点钟才真叫一点钟！再笑一下？
要是你每晚上都肯陪着我这样坐，
我便能工作得好些，你懂得没有？
我说是多得些画酬，都给你使用。
你看，暮色已静止；那边有颗星；
冒兰罗已隐去，守夜的灯光照着墙，
枭啼四起，一声声在交相应答。
从窗外探进头来，心肝——进来吧，
还是回进这愁人的小屋，造它时
我们原预备为寻乐。上帝最公正。
法王弗朗西也许会恕我。我夜晚
看完画，举起疲乏的眼睛，但见
四壁都发亮，墙砖一块块的分明，
砖缝里没有灰泥，却满是生光
刺眼的黄金，我用来砌墙的金子。
只要我们能互相爱好。你得去？
那表哥又来了？正在外边守候？

Must see you — you, and not with me? Those loans?
More gaming debts to pay? you smiled for that?
Well, let smiles buy me! have you more to spend?
While hand and eye and something of a heart
Are left me, work's my ware, and what's it worth?
I'll pay my fancy. Only let me sit
The gray remainder of the evening out,
〔14〕 Idle, you call it, and muse perfectly
How I could paint, were I but back in France,
One picture, just one more — the Virgin's face,
Not yours this time! I want you at my side
To hear them — that is, Michel Agnolo —
Judge all I do and tell you of its worth.
Will you? Tomorrow, satisfy your friend.
I take the subjects for his corridor,
Finish the portrait out of hand — there, there,
And throw him in another thing or two
If he demurs; the whole should prove enough
To pay for this same Cousin's freak. Beside,
What's better and what's all I care about,
Get you the thirteen scudi for the ruff!
Love, does that please you? Ah, but what does he,
The Cousin! what does he to please you more?

〔15〕 I am grown peaceful as old age tonight.
I regret little, I would change still less.
Since there my past life lies, why alter it?

得见你——你，不用我在旁？那些债？
还有点赌账要偿还？你觉得好笑？
好，就让笑买了我！你还得多花些？
只要我还有手和眼睛和小小一颗心，
工作是我的，多画几张算什么？
我愿意出足我嗜好的代价。只让我
静静坐彻这暮色苍灰的余意，
〔14〕 你说是无谓，让我沉思这片刻：
只要能回了法兰西，我便能怎样
再画一张，只一张——圣母的脸庞，
这回可不再是你的！我要你靠在
我身旁，听他们——米珂朗琪罗——评判
一切，告诉你我的画价值的高低。
你肯吗？明天，准叫你朋友如愿。
我答应用他那题材，画他那通廊，
又完成这手头的画像——好了，好了，
他还不应承，便另外再加他一两件；
这整数该尽够你表哥付他那笔账，
还有，更要紧，最叫我关心的，乃是为
设法十三元，买你那心爱的绉颈衣。
心肝，可喜欢？啊，他做了什么，
那表哥？他做的是什么，能使你更喜欢？
〔15〕 今晚上我变得和老了的一般平静。
我并不悔恨，更不愿有分毫的变动。
过去的生活已过去，为什么要更改？

The very wrong to Francis! — it is true
I took his coin, was tempted and complied,
And built this house and sinned, and all is said.
My father and my mother died of want.
Well, had I riches of my own? you see
How one gets rich! Let each one bear his lot.
They were born poor, lived poor, and poor they died:
And I have labored somewhat in my time
And not been paid profusely. Some good son
Paint my two hundred pictures — let him try!
No doubt, there's something strikes a balance. Yes,
You love me quite enough, it seems tonight,
This must suffice me here. What would one have?
In heaven, perhaps, new chances, one more chance —
Four great walls in the New Jerusalem,
Meted on each side by the angel's reed,
For Leonard, Rafael, Agnolo and me
To cover — the three first without a wife,
While I have mine! So — still they overcome
Because there's still Lucrezia, — as I choose.
Again the Cousin's whistle! Go, My Love.

Men and Women

就说对弗朗西的那番不义！不错，
我领了他的钱，遭了诱惑，禁不住
便造起屋子，造了孽，话都已说尽。
我父母都在贫寒里过世。我自己
可有钱？你瞧，一个人怎样发的财！
还是让各人担起他自己的命运。
他们生来穷，活着穷，死时仍是穷：
我呢，过来也总算劳苦了半世，
仍不曾得到丰裕的酬报。哪一个
好儿子且试试画我这二百张图画！
不用说，这便能均衡我所有的失败。
是的，今晚上看来，你爱我并不少。
你这爱就够我尽量在人间消受。
除了这一层，一个人还希求些什么？
在天上，也许，再得一次新机会——
那耶鲁撒冷新城四面的巨墙，
每一方都经天使的金苇给量定，
派给达芬奇，拉飞尔，盎琪罗和我
作壁画——前三人都没有妻子，我却有！
这是我本心所愿——他们还是
比我高，因为我仍有露蔻嘉在身边。
那表哥的哨子又响了！去吧，宝贝。

初载于《武汉日报·现代文艺》
第八期（1935.4.5）
第九期（1935.4.12）

· 瓦尔特·梅勒 ·

Walter de la Mare

（1873—1956）

The Listeners

〔1〕 "Is there anybody there?" said the Traveller,
    Knocking on the moonlit door;
And his horse in the silence champed the grasses
    Of the forest's ferny floor:
And a bird flew up out of the turret,
    Above the Traveller's head:
And he smote upon the door again a second time;
    "Is there anybody there?" he said.
But no one descended to the Traveller;
    No head from the leaf-fringed sill
Leaned over and looked into his grey eyes,
    Where he stood perplexed and still.
〔2〕 But only a host of phantom listeners
    That dwelt in the lone house then
Stood listening in the quiet of the moonlight
    To that voice from the world of men;
Stood thronging the faint moonbeams on the dark stair,
    That goes down to the empty hall
Hearkening in an air stirred and shaken
    By the lonely Traveller's call.
And he felt in his heart their strangeness,

林中无人

〔1〕 不知名的远客动问道："里边有人吗？"
　　他叩着一扇映满了月明的门；
万籁寂静里只听得那丛林深处
　　他的马啮着林下凤尾草的微声。
剥啄声惊起了塔楼上的一只睡鸟，
　　高高地飞过这叩门的远征人的头；
他重复叩门，这个远来的旅客，
　　他高声重问道："里边有人没有？"
但没有人下来应答这远客的叩关，
　　没有头探出那藤萝爬满的窗台，
来睇视这远征人一双灰色的眸子，
　　看他惶惑地静静地在门前等待。
〔2〕 那屋里只有一大群幽灵屏着息，
　　寂静的屋里只有那倾听的幽灵；
在寂静无声的月色中他们在倾耳
　　谛听这来自人间的远客的声音：
密集在黝暗的楼梯上，微明的月色中，
　　(楼梯直达到下边那寂静的空堂，)
在这征客的叩门声所惊动的氛围里，
　　幽灵们挤满了楼头月色的微芒。
这远征人的心中只觉得他们的可讶，

Their stillness answering his cry,

〔3〕 While his horse moved, cropping the dark turf,

'Neath the starred and leafy sky;

For he suddenly smote on the door, even

Louder, and lifted his head: —

"Tell them I came, and no one answered,

That I kept my word," he said.

Never the least stir made the listeners,

Though every word he spake

Fell echoing through the shadowiness of the still house

From the one man left awake:

Ay, they heard his foot upon the stirrup,

And the sound of iron on stone,

And how the silence surged softly backward.

When the plunging hoofs were gone.

为什么把寂静回答他叩关的喊叫；
〔3〕 这时候叶影掩映着星斗满天，
下面是他的马咀嚼着露淋的湿草。
忽然他重复在门上用劲一击，
提高了嗓音，抬头对着门扉：
“告他们一声我来了，可没有人应我，
告诉他们我没有把信誓失坠。”
虽然他的话字字穿进了里边，
响透寂静的空房里每一个屋角，
倾听的幽灵们对着这远征人却并无
半声的回响、一点点轻微的动作。
哎，他们听到他踏上了鞍蹬，
又听到蹄铁与路石声声相击撞，
听到拨水似的蹄声慢慢地远去，
又听到寂静的回来，像轻潮涌小浪。

初载于《人世间》第 15 期

1934.11.5

· 约翰·梅斯菲尔德 ·

John Masefield

（1878—1967）

Sea-Fever

〔1〕 I must down to the seas again, to the lonely sea and the sky,
And all I ask is a tall ship and a star to steer her by,
And the wheel's kick and the wind's song and the white sail's
shaking,
And a gray mist on the sea's face and a gray dawn breaking.

〔2〕 I must down to the seas again, for the call of the running tide
Is a wild call and a clear call that may not be denied;
And all I ask is a windy day with the white clouds flying,
And the flying spray and the blown spume, and the seagull's
crying,

〔3〕 I must down to the seas again to the vagrant gipsy life,
To the gull's way and the whale's way where the wind's like a
whetted knife;
And all I ask is a merry yarn from a laughing fellowrover,
And a quiet sleep and a sweet dream when the long trick's over.

海狂

〔1〕 我还得往海上去，去看脉脉的长天和大海洋，
我要一艘高桅的大舟和一座星斗去定向，
我只要机轮震撼海风歌，海风吹得白帆涨，
灰色的晓天蒙着灰色的早雾在慢慢地亮。

〔2〕 我还得往海上去，因为海上的风波在叫我，
又是豪放又清新，叫得我心旌动荡莫奈何；
我只要一个大风天气天上到处有白云飞，
白浪四溅白沤沸，白羽的海鸥在声声地唳。

〔3〕 我还得往海上去，那逍遥自在的生涯实在好，
海鸥的老家鲸鱼道，海风直像把磨快的刀；
我只要一个放浪的同伴说些往事大家笑，
忙过了这阵做他个好梦睡他个甜甜的觉。

初载于《大公报·文艺》
1934 年 8 月 25 日